SHOPPING CAN BE DEADLY

A DISCOUNT DETECTIVE MYSTERY

SHOPPING CAN BE DEADLY

A DISCOUNT DETECTIVE MYSTERY

CHARLOTTE STUART

Walrus Publishing | St. Louis, MO 63116

Shop till you drop.

CHAPTER 1
RUN! HIDE!

WHEN YOU WAKE UP in the morning, the only thing you know for sure is that you are still alive. You may *think* your day will be like any other—get up, get dressed, see your kids off to school, take the dog out for his morning constitutional, then go to work. But in an instant, something can happen that will turn your day and your world upside down. Intellectually I know this to be true. But when one familiar day follows another familiar day, it is easy to start feeling as though you can anticipate what will happen next.

One Friday morning in early spring, my routine had gone as usual, and I was on my way to work. My employer is Penny-wise Investigations, a detective agency located in a suburban shopping mall. Even though we deal mostly in small cases brought to us by walk-in clients, it still gives me a thrill to introduce myself as a private investigator. Before I landed a job with the agency, I had been unemployed for far too long. A widow and single mom with a PhD and no prospects. Until the morning PW Griffin of Penny-wise Investigations gave me an opportunity to reinvent myself. I've been employed there now for almost two years.

When I arrived, the mall was bustling with activity because of a three-day sales event. There were shoppers moving purposefully through the wide concourse. They all seemed to be carrying shopping bags, pushing their way through the crowd so as not to miss out on any one-time-only bargains. I noticed there were sale signs in the windows of the stores on either side of Penny-wise: Ye Olde Candle Shoppe on the left and Sew What? on the right. Scented candles, private investigators and sewing supplies. An odd trio of goods and services, but today we all had one thing in common. Both adjoining shops announced *50% Off Select Items.* Pennywise didn't need a sale sign; we already advertised ourselves as a discount detective agency. Our motto—*Vigilance You Can Afford.*

I was a little later than usual because I had stopped to pick up dog food on my way to work. The last time I'd gone grocery shopping I'd forgotten to buy any, and I try to follow the vet's instructions about what to feed the dog to keep him healthy. It would devastate Jason if anything happened to his canine companion, but, unfortunately, my son's love for the dog didn't extend to taking care of his day-to-day needs. That fell to me.

As I passed a kiosk with its tempting coffee aroma, my nose told my feet to stop. Every molecule of my body demanded a cup of Guatemalan dark roast. Our office coffee tends to be bland. No specialty beans ground just before brewing. No filtered water or fuss. Just dump some coffee in the filter and hope for the best. Unfortunately—or fortunately, depending on how you look at it—the mall is home to quite a few coffee stands. A costly but satisfying alternative to drinking office brew.

The line was short, so it didn't take long before I was headed for the office, taking my first sip, enjoying both the aroma and the acidic sweetness of the blend, when I heard a loud report that resonated off the high ceilings in the main concourse. The open space runs in a straight line the full length of the mall with the occasional side corridor leading to the outside. I glanced around, looking for the source of the sound. I could have sworn it was a gunshot. But how was that possible? This was a mall in a conservative area outside of the city. Santa's yearly appearance was the most exciting thing that took place here.

Then I saw a young man collapse, falling to the beige vinyl floor without making any attempt to cushion his descent. I started running toward him as a second shot rang out and another man dropped next to the first. Someone screamed. Then another person joined in. And another. A chorus of terrified voices. Accompanied by chaos as people tried to figure out what was happening and which way to run.

Instinctively, I yelled "Run! Hide!" It was the survival strategy I'd been taught if you found yourself in a mass attack situation. The third commandment was to fight, but as a last resort. Not obeying my own command, I didn't try to run away but continued toward what I assumed was a gunshot victim. I was just a few feet away when I saw blood trickling out of his jacket sleeve and across his hand.

The shouting rose to a crescendo as people tried to escape, not knowing which way to go. It's hard to determine the direction of a gunshot in an enclosed space where the high ceiling becomes an echo chamber, amplifying sounds that seem to be coming at you from every direction. Unless you had eyes on the shooter, running and hiding was not an easy thing to do.

I knelt beside the young man to check his vitals just as another shot sliced through the sounds of panic. It crossed my mind that maybe I should be taking my own advice and running away instead of kneeling there in the middle of the mall while someone was shooting at people. I didn't want to make my kids orphans. My mother would never forgive me.

Several more shots were fired in rapid succession. I could feel my own heart racing as I felt for a neck pulse on the victim before me. Out of the corner of my eye I saw someone approaching from behind. Then he was leaning over me, and I glimpsed a glint of metal as his hand moved past me. Before I could react, he reached over and put a gun in the hand of the person whose injuries I was trying to assess. My brain was screaming for me to run. As I started to get up, a hand grabbed my arm and yanked me to my feet. "Let's go," a raspy voice insisted.

I tried to resist, but was dragged along by someone larger and stronger than me. Rescuer or assailant? I didn't know which. But in the midst of the bedlam, getting away seemed like a good idea. Although I couldn't get my mind around why the man who was urging me to leave had put a gun in the hand of a victim. Then something hit me: since that had happened, I hadn't heard any more shots.

Suddenly a man shouted, "The killer is down." Another voice yelled, "Someone call the cops." The first voice repeated, "The killer is down." He sounded like he was announcing the winner of a hard-fought wrestling match. Only in this instance, the stakes had been much higher.

I tried to put on the brakes. Maybe getting away wasn't necessary. But the man grasping my arm wasn't about to slow down or stop. "Keep going," he ordered. "I'll explain once we're outside." It hit me then that I recognized the voice. But it couldn't be. What would he be doing in my mall? He wasn't even from the Seattle area. The last time I'd seen him was on a remote island in the San Juans. He gripped my arm even more firmly, propelling me toward a narrow side exit. I managed a brief look as he hustled me out. He had a hoody pulled over his head, obscuring his face.

"Gary?" I managed to ask as we reached the edge of the parking lot.

"Later," he said. "Got your keys?"

"Yes. But shouldn't we stay ...?"

"No."

My past experience with Gary involved running away from armed survivalists. I knew he was a capable, decisive guy used to being around violence, but I couldn't fathom what that had to do with a shooting in the mall where I worked.

When we reached my car, I was surprised to see Gary's dog, Bandit, in the back seat. As we got in, Bandit briefly nuzzled my face but quickly drew back at Gary's command of "down."

"Start the car and get us out of here." He ducked down out of sight. "Don't speed or do anything unusual," he cautioned. "And keep an eye out to make sure we aren't followed."

I did as he asked while mentally questioning whether I was doing the right thing. Had Gary been the shooter?

Was that even possible? He'd definitely had a gun, one that he had deliberately left behind in someone else's possession. And he was a former soldier and perhaps still did some kind of soldiering from time to time. I couldn't imagine him as a crazed killer though. In fact, I was very much counting on that not being the case. Besides, as we were leaving, someone had yelled "the killer is down."

"Where do you want me to go? Should I just pull over somewhere?" I asked.

"No. Take us somewhere we can talk. A coffee shop. More people around."

"Okay." There was a Starbucks just a few blocks away. I kept going, checking my rearview mirror to see if there was anyone following, like a police car. I suddenly realized that the adrenaline rush I'd experienced had completely drained away. My shoulders were tense, the muscles in my neck stiff, and my mind a battleground of conflicting thoughts. Including how Bandit ended up in my car. "Did you break into my car?" I asked.

"I had to leave Bandit someplace."

"So, you were following me and broke into my car."

"I didn't actually break anything." He didn't sound apologetic, like it was just something he had to do.

"Do you know what happened back there?" I couldn't wait any longer to ask.

"I have an idea."

His short answers were irritating me. I had just survived a shooting incident in a mall where I worked. I didn't know how many people had been injured or killed. I didn't even know if one of my colleagues had been in the main area of the mall when it happened. I hoped that the last voice

I heard as we exited the building was correct and that the shooter had been captured, but most of all, I needed to know why Gary had put a gun in that young victim's hand. Whose gun was it? Where had it come from? I wasn't sure I wanted to know the answers, but I knew I would have to ask.

The thought of going to a coffee shop made me suddenly wonder what had happened to my cup of Guatemalan roast. Had I dropped it when I rushed toward the young man who'd been shot in front of me? Maybe I had tossed it in the air, coffee arcing upward, splattering people trying to get away. I could picture the tiny brown droplets falling like hot rain on the shoppers I passed as they obeyed my command to *run*. If they had managed to avoid being shot, I supposed they didn't care about a few coffee stains on their clothes. Better than blood.

Gary popped up as I pulled into the parking lot. "Over there," he said pointing to a spot away from the main road. "Anyone following us?" He looked around.

"No, I'm fairly certain we're in the clear."

"Stay, Bandit," Gary said as we got out. Bandit had obviously been hoping to join us in whatever we were doing and plopped back down with his head between his paws. "No," Gary said to me as if reading my mind. "You can say hello to him later."

Once inside we didn't talk except to order two coffees. It reminded me of couples I've seen in restaurants, focused on their food, behaving as though they had long ago run out of things to say to each other. As for me, I was about to burst with questions, but I restrained myself until we sat down at a table in a corner, away from windows and from other customers. Gary had pushed his hood back. His bushy blond beard was gone; his face clean-shaven. His thinning hair was well-groomed, unlike the last time I'd seen him. I liked his new look, although I'd also been attracted to the rugged, macho image from the last time we'd met. His dark brown eyes were checking me out at the same time they were taking in the surroundings.

"You look good," he said.

"This isn't a date," I pointed out. No, it was comeuppance time. Time for some answers.

"A man can't help what he sees," he said with a smile. Apparently, the look on my face made it clear that this wasn't a friendly conversation. His smile was quickly replaced by a scowl that caused every muscle in my body to tense up in anticipation of hearing something I was almost positive I didn't want to hear. "Okay, here's what you need to know."

"I don't want 'need to know' information; I want to know everything *you* know."

"We don't have a lot of time." He reached over and put a muscled hand over mine. "I was hoping it would be different when I dropped by today."

Dropped by? Did he consider following me to Pennywise and leaving Bandit in my car a casual visit? Was that why he was in the mall? "Just tell me what happened back there." I pulled my hand back and sat up straight to let him know he wasn't going to charm me into letting him get away with half-truths.

"I shot a man in the mall," he said. "A man who was shooting at me," he added quickly.

"Why was someone in the mall shooting at you?"

"That's the long story. But I swear to you I'm not the bad guy in this scenario."

"That young man I was helping, he was unconscious, bleeding. Did that have something to do with you?"

"Let's just say I was lucky the guy after me was a bad shot; that young man you're referring to wasn't as lucky. Nor was the guy next to him."

"So, someone was shooting at you in a mall full of people. That doesn't make sense."

"Hired killers aren't always smart. And from the way this one approached the job, my guess is he wasn't a professional. More likely a disposable who wasn't intended to survive long enough to collect his pay."

"A 'disposable'?"

"Someone trying to break into the profession, hired for a single job, not intended to be a long-term employee."

"Hired to shoot you?" I was having a hard time getting my mind wrapped around the pieces of his story.

"I knew they would try to follow me. There was someone in Friday Harbor. Different guy when Bandit and I arrived by sea plane at Lake Union. I thought I'd lost the tail on the freeway, but they must have picked it up after I turned back. What I didn't expect is that they would try to eliminate me before ... I'm really sorry. And I sincerely hope no one died because of me. But I think at least one man did. I was running past him toward you when he was shot."

I believed he was sorry, but that didn't change the facts. "Why did you put a gun in that young man's hand?" I asked.

"To make it look like he took out the shooter. To give us enough time to get out of there."

"But assuming he survives, he'll know he didn't do it."

"His wound didn't look serious."

"He wasn't conscious."

"Probably fainted. Not much blood. Getting shot for the first time can be traumatic. Especially in a situation like that, when the bullets come out of the blue. But if all he took was a bullet to his arm, he's going to be fine. I hope he isn't left-handed." For a moment I thought Gary was concerned for the man's future, then he added, "Although I had no choice; I had to put the gun in his good hand. Don't worry, the shooting is over, and the medics have probably arrived already."

"Won't the gun be traced to you? Won't they wonder why you ran away?"

"No, it won't be traced to me."

"Oh." I felt naïve. "You used it to shoot the shooter?"

Gary smiled. "Someone had to."

"Okay. Tell me who you're running from. And don't tell me you're trying to protect me by keeping me in the dark. All that means is that if I don't hear from you once you're gone, I'll have to start from scratch to track you down."

Gary smiled again. He had a nice smile. "You'd try to find me?" he asked, looking amused. It was disconcerting to think that this charming, attractive man had less than an hour ago not only been the target of a hit man but had shot another human being. And here I was, sitting in a coffeeshop, feeling a physical attraction that I couldn't deny, while talking about a tragic event in the mall where I worked as if I had read about it in the news instead of being there when it happened.

"Just tell me." My tone must have conveyed my determination to get at the truth because his smile darkened like a rain cloud. I could see he was struggling to make up his mind about what to say, but if he wanted my help, he was going to have to explain himself.

"Okay, here's the short version. Then we have to get moving." He took a long swig of coffee. "Three friends of mine and I did an undercover job for a government agency about a month ago. Now, one of my friends has gone missing. He sent us a warning minutes before he went off the radar. The other two and I have plans to join up and figure this out. When whoever got to our buddy didn't send someone after me on the island, I thought they were going to wait until we were all together before trying to take us out. That's what I was counting on."

"Do you think your friend is dead?"

"Maybe. But he could have just gone dark."

"And they followed you from Friday Harbor."

"Based on the timing, they had to guess the three of us were going to try to meet up. When I drove in the direction of SeaTac Airport in my rental car, they fell back, undoubtedly assuming they knew where I was headed. That gave me the opportunity I needed to shake them. I wanted to drop Bandit off. That's where you come in."

"You want *me* to take care of Bandit while you're away doing whatever it is you do?"

"He knows and likes you. And this is one time I can't take him along. I could have left him with neighbors, but that would make him too easy to find. They probably know I care about him and might be tempted to try and use him as leverage." He paused and looked at me with his dark brown eyes, pleading. "You'll do this for me, won't you?"

"Finish your story first."

"There's not a lot more to say."

"Let me see if I understand. You're saying there's a government agency who hires, ah …" I was about to say contract mercenaries but thought better of it. "… independent contractors to do undercover work. What's the nature of the job you did for them?"

"You know there are government agencies that sometimes have to deal with undesirables through clandestine operations, right?"

"I'm not sure I approve, but I know it happens."

"Well, in this instance, the four of us were asked to capture someone for what appeared to be good reasons. A real badass involved in terrorist activities. If someone linked to the government got caught going after him in, uh, let's say a non-judicial manner, it would have caused problems with the international community."

"But if you were caught—"

"They would have denied we'd been hired by them. Now, for whatever reason, it appears that someone who knows the four of us were involved wants us out of the picture. We don't know who or why, but we need to find out."

"One of the terrorist's supporters possibly? Surely not our government."

"Like I said, we don't know. But we don't intend to wait around for them to come after us at their leisure."

"What are you going to do?" It sounded farfetched, but at the same time, it did seem like something the Gary I'd had a brief—but, admittedly, gratifying—encounter with might get mixed up in.

He hesitated. "We have to neutralize our enemy. I think what we're going to do is kidnap back the person we originally kidnapped and use him as leverage to get whoever is after us off our backs. If we can't make a deal with them, we'll make his capture public. Turn him over to some other agency, maybe notify someone on the Senate Intelligence Committee, or alert one of our contacts in the press and make arrangements through them for his transfer to the authorities. Maybe we'll give him up to one of our allies since he's wanted by friends and foes alike. The bottom line is we're not going down without a fight."

Gary paused, waiting for a reaction. I didn't know what I thought. *Neutralize our enemy?* This was definitely a situation that was out of my league. I tracked down runaway teenagers and missing pets. I didn't kidnap terrorists or shoot people.

"That's more than I should have told you. But I trust you. And I want you to understand why this might take a while and why you have to stay out of it. You have kids to think of."

"But what if this terrorist's supporters are out for revenge? How does capturing him help?"

"It's possible we'll think of some other way to approach figuring out who's behind this. But right now …" Gary paused again, waiting for my decision.

"Thank you. I appreciate knowing what's going on. And, yes, I'll keep Bandit for you."

He gave me a bright grin that resonated somewhere in the pit of my stomach. Then he wrote down four names on a napkin and handed it to me. "The one with the 'x' is our missing friend. The one at the bottom is my government contact. I'm not sure that's his real name, and he gives me a different contact number for each project. Memorize these."

"And eat the napkin?"

"Glad to see you still have a sense of humor."

"I'm sorry," I said. "Sorry for what happened back there. Sorry for your missing friend. And—"

"And, I hope, you're sorry we don't have more time to spend together. I know I am." He took a cell phone out of his jacket pocket and handed it to me. "This is how I'll get in touch if I need to."

"Can I call you?"

"Not a good idea."

"What now?"

"I say goodbye to Bandit, and I'm outta here."

As we made our way back to my car, I kept wondering if there was something I should ask or say before he disappeared, perhaps forever. I had often fantasized about getting together with him, although it had never seemed like a realistic possibility. I was a single mom living in a carriage house with her mother. He lived in a cabin on a remote island and did who knew what for a living. But he had saved my life. He and Bandit. I owed him. I owed both of them.

He opened the back door of the car and invited Bandit out and up into the passenger's seat. The way Bandit's head drooped, I sensed he knew Gary was leaving him behind. Once Bandit was settled, Gary leaned over and put his face next to Bandit's. I couldn't hear what he said, but I hoped it wasn't "goodbye forever." Then he left, slipping behind a fence at the back of the parking lot and disappearing from view.

I got in the car and put my hand on Bandit's head. "Sorry, fella," I said. "Sorry for both of us." Then I took out the napkin and memorized the names on it and tore it up into tiny pieces. As I drove home, I tossed bits of shredded napkin out the window every few blocks. "Forgive me, environmental gods. At least they're biodegradable."

CHAPTER 2
ALPHA DOG

I DON'T USUALLY ANSWER my phone while driving, but it wouldn't stop ringing. Several times the person on the other end hung up, only to re-dial within seconds. At least I assumed it was the same person. Either that or I had people in a queue wanting to get hold of me. Since there had been a mass shooting at the mall where I worked, it was possible my family was trying to get in touch. My family or my work colleagues. I finally fumbled my phone out of my purse and hit recent calls. They were all from the same person—Yuri. He's a Penny-wise colleague and good friend. When I saw his name on my cell, I was truly mad at myself. What kind of a person was I not to have checked to see if my colleagues were alright after a shooting just outside of our office?

I hit reply. Yuri answered mid-ring. "Cameron, thank God. Are you okay?"

"I'm sorry. Really sorry. I should have called. Are you at the office?"

"Yes. Where are *you*?"

"Ah. I'm in my car on my way home. Something's come up. Is everyone at Penny-wise safe?"

"Yes, we're all accounted for .... except for you, until now. We've been worried. What happened?"

"It's a long story. First, can you tell me about the shooting? Is anyone dead? Did they catch the shooter?"

"Two dead as far as I know. The shooter and one other. A young man took down the shooter. Quite the hero. There's no telling how many people would have ended up dead or injured if it hadn't been for him."

"That's a relief. Were there many injuries?"

"I'm not sure. We stayed inside until we thought it was over. When I went out to see what had happened, several people were already being treated by paramedics. I got the impression that some of the injuries were the result of people crashing into each other while trying to get away. I didn't see any ambulances rushing anyone off, but someone told me they had already taken away the guy who shot the killer. He apparently took a bullet in the arm."

Gary had been right. It sounded like things weren't nearly as bad as I'd feared. Although even one innocent death was one too many.

Based on what Yuri told me, it sounded like Gary had been right about one other thing—his gun gambit. At least for the moment, the young man who'd been shot in the arm was being credited with taking out the shooter. I didn't see that having the wrong person initially identified as the person who saved the day could do any harm. The only problem was what I would tell the police if asked. Although there was the possibility that no one *would* ask. There were cameras in the mall, but I wasn't sure whether my presence near the two victims would have been captured or not. Or whether a camera had caught me leaving the mall with Gary. If it had, how would I explain that? And what if someone had the presence of mind to record some of what had happened on their cell phone? Then what? Was keeping silent a risk I was willing to take? Or did I need to admit to being there but make up a story about why I left?

"Yuri, we need to talk. Any chance you could come by? If not now, after work?"

"Sure. I'll get away as soon as I can. Meanwhile, what should I tell PW and the others?"

"How about the old 'she isn't well,' excuse."

"I can do that; I'll make it convincing." Yuri paused. I could picture the look he gets on his face when he's considering options, his dark eyes behind his thick, black-rimmed glasses staring straight ahead. The only time he is ever completely still.

"Thanks. I'll make it up to you."

"You'd better believe you will," he said, his usual bantering demeanor switching back on. He really was a loyal and supportive friend. I don't know how I would have made it through the first year at Penny-wise without him at my side. My kids adored him. And my mother had finally gotten around to accepting that we were just friends. Not that he would have been her first choice for me in her mission to have me remarry. For the sake of the kids, she always says, but, honestly, I think she simply likes to annoy me.

When I got home, I parked in the alley behind our carriage house. The alley is used by most of the owners to store garbage cans and spillover from garages. It's also choked with weeds, patrolled by cats, and infested with spiders. But I often park there because it's closer to home.

The main house, a large, turn-of-the-century Tudor, is off to the side at the front of the lot. It's been divided into four separate apartment units, but it still retains the elegance of a more prosperous era. There's a wood fence along the sidewalk in front, but none in back on the alley. From the front, we access our home through a tall gate and winding brick path lined with bushes and trees. The carriage house is nestled in trees near the back of the lot. It's very private for a city residence. It was remodeled to accommodate a mother-in-law apartment upstairs that is accessed from the main downstairs living area. It wouldn't suit a lot of people, but it's perfect for our needs.

My mother lives upstairs. My two kids, Mara and Jason, and I live downstairs with a dog that had been abandoned by one of Yuri's neighbors when they'd moved. Yuri had given us the dog as a gift to Jason. A dog I didn't want but couldn't get rid of once Jason and he had experienced instant bonding. It had been several months since the dog had become part of the family, but we were still arguing over what to call him. It must have been confusing to the animal to be called different things by different people, including being called different names by the same person. Jason was still working to identify the perfect name for his friend and kept trying out new ones based on his latest inspiration. I referred to him as "No-name." My mother usually called him "puppy," even though he wasn't a puppy anymore. Sometimes she referred to him as "that dog."

I wasn't sure if Mom was home, but I knew the kids wouldn't be back from school yet. No-name would be there, anxious for Jason's return, possibly amusing himself by chewing up a sock dragged from Jason's closet, knocking over a plant or attacking a pillow for some reason we would never understand. He wasn't consistently destructive, but he wasn't what you would call a well-trained pet. We intended to send him to obedience school; we just never seemed to find the time. Introducing Bandit to No-name might prove challenging. And Mom certainly wouldn't be a pushover. As for me, taking on still another responsibility wasn't something I relished either. But it had to be done.

"Okay, Bandit," I said. "We're here." I opened the door to the car to let him out, then stopped, blocking his exit. "Sorry, but I think we need to call you something else. Bandit is the name of Gary's dog, and we don't want anyone to associate you with him. Even though that *is* you. Hope that's okay." I felt foolish explaining this to him, telling myself I was simply talking out loud. But in my short experience with Bandit, he always seemed to get the drift of what you wanted from him.

I finally let Bandit out of the car, and we headed for what was to be, hopefully, his temporary home. "What would you like to be called?" Bandit looked at me with his big, wise eyes but said nothing. "I think it should be something descriptive. Could you relate to that? Something like Angus or Cinder." He didn't respond. "No? Maybe Midnight. No, you don't look like a Midnight. How about Duffy? I think I remember someone saying that in Old Irish that means black. I mean, we wouldn't want to call you something as mundane as Blackie, would we?" Bandit still refused comment. But I thought I saw him shudder at the possibility that he might be called Blackie.

When we reached the front door, I looked down and said, "This is it. We have to make a decision. I hereby christen you Duffy. Behave now, Duffy. You have to be the adult in this relationship." Then I opened the door. In two seconds No-name was charging the intruder, stopping about a foot away, wary and seemingly inhospitable. Duffy ignored him, obeying my request to act like an adult. Or like the alpha dog that he was.

Duffy looked around, then walked slowly toward No-name and bumped him with his nose. No-name laid down and rolled over. Set-game-match in less than half a minute.

I heard movement from upstairs and my mother appeared wearing a floral apron over her silk blouse and flannel trousers. She was pointing a can of pepper spray at me. "Cameron, what are you doing here at his hour?"

"We have a guest," I explained. "I came home to get him settled."

At that point she seemed to see Duffy for the first time. "Is that a dog?" she asked, making her way slowly down the stairs, as if hoping the image of a second dog in our home would vanish if she blinked enough times.

"Doesn't it look like a dog?"

"But what is it doing here?"

"As I said, he's a guest. He's going to be staying with us for a while."

My mother looked at me as though I was out of my mind. "But he's a large dog." She eyed him with distaste. Duffy stood there, waiting for someone to indicate what his role was in the drama playing out before him.

"Yes. We'll need to buy more dog food. Maybe some grooming tools." I wondered if Gary ever brushed Bandit.

His longish fur had an au natural look. No way he would place in a dog show in his current state.

"Cameron. Be serious. Why on earth would you agree to bring home another animal?" I decided not to point out that I hadn't been responsible for acquiring No-name, but I couldn't deny that it was Yuri who had blessed us with him. Indirectly it was my fault.

"I'm sorry, Mom. I have a friend who is seriously ill. How could I say no?"

"Why don't you put him in a kennel?" My mother is an elegant woman who adores her grandchildren and cooks healthy, gourmet food for all of us, whether we want it or not. She likes things to be tidy, and I had no doubt she could already envision long black hair and big dirty pawprints everywhere. She barely tolerated No-name's good-natured omnipresence and only because Jason was so fond of him.

"Because he wouldn't be happy there."

"How do you know? He'd have good care, other dogs to play with …" She ran out of arguments, aware that she didn't really have a choice. Technically the upstairs was her domain and the downstairs mine. Although the boundaries weren't strictly enforced.

"You can put down the pepper spray," I said. "He's very well-behaved. Duffy, say hello to my mother."

Bandit stood there, unmoving. I put my hand on his head. "Duffy, it's okay." I looked at my mom. "He needs to get used to us."

"Whatever." She turned around and headed back up the stairs. "I'm making something special for dinner tonight. Tell the kids when they get home."

I suppressed a groan. After the day I'd had, all I needed was another one of mother's special, nutrition-packed dinners with their strange flavors and textures and often unidentifiable ingredients. It was at times like this I wished they hadn't remodeled the carriage house to include an upstairs kitchen. The kids wouldn't be pleased either. Jason had some junk food snacks hidden in his room for these occasions. I pretended I didn't know. I had a few items tucked away for emergencies as well, but I probably needed a larger cache.

The kids came rushing in after school and stopped short when they saw Duffy. No-name rushed up to Jason seeking consolation for no longer being an only dog. Duffy suddenly headed straight for Mara. She knelt down and said, "Who do we have here?"

"This is Duffy. We're dog sitting for a while."

Mara rubbed Duffy's head and murmured some dog talk. Duffy rubbed up against her, looking happy. So that's how it's going to be. Well, I couldn't complain; I needed an ally, Duffy needed solace, and if Mara could be one and provide the other, I'd be fine with it. But I had no doubt that I would be the one cleaning up after both dogs. And feeding and watering them.

"He doesn't look like a Duffy," Jason said. He's on the verge of being a teenager and has opinions about everything.

"It means 'black' in Old Irish."

"I like that," Mara said. She's a year older than Jason and tends to disagree with anything he says. Mom says that's normal for kids their age. It may be, but I keep hoping they will start doing less quibbling and more bonding. They'd been best of friends when they were younger, supportive of each other when their father died. I had visions of them becoming best friends again. Maybe because I've always wanted a sibling instead of growing up as an only child.

"Is he Irish?" Jason asked, always the literalist. Jason is a news junkie and is frequently pointing out the difference between fact and opinion.

"No, but he's black," I said, messing up Jason's hair with my hand.

He batted my hand away and backed away out of range.

"I should also mention that Yuri is coming by after work." Both kids instantly looked pleased. "But it's work, not a social visit. Now, go get your homework done before dinner. Grandma's making something special." I struggled to keep a straight face.

Both kids rolled their eyes. They never complained about her cooking directly to her, and Mara was often open to my mother's experiments. But Jason was a picky eater and frequently tried to get me to order a pizza as an after-dinner snack when Mom made one of her special meals. I sympathized, but I didn't want to encourage unhealthy eating habits, so I only relented occasionally. Fortunately, Mom spoiled them, and they loved her. And since I was frequently away on assignments or working late, it was a good arrangement. For all of us.

No-name followed Jason off to his room, dragging along his bright orange pangolin plush toy. Jason had asked for it to replace the two other stuffed toys No-name had chewed apart, a red octopus and a black and white ring-tailed lemur. He'd even chewed up one of Jason's wildlife socks with images of sloths on them. He apparently liked attacking wild animals.

We'd tried buying No-name tough chew toys that were supposedly good for his teeth, but he preferred soft ones that he could slowly rip apart. The lemur had been the first to die. It only lasted a couple of days. The octopus had been made from knotted rope, but it hadn't had a chance either. Jason liked the idea of the pangolin because, he told me, it was the most widely trafficked mammal in the world. He'd explained that in some countries its scales were used in medicines and its meat considered a delicacy. Why any of these facts made it a good candidate for a dog toy was beyond me, but at least it didn't have any long, skinny appendages. I gave it a two- to three-week lease on life. Talk about endangered species.

Mara said goodbye to Duffy and went off to her room. Duffy and I were left alone to contemplate life together, a life without Gary who was off somewhere engaged in some dangerous enterprise. And who might not return.

I had just poured myself a glass of wine and put a handful of dog treats in a plastic bowl for Duffy when Jason burst into the room. "Mom," he yelled, his pre-puberty voice grating like a fingernail on a chalk board. "What happened at the mall?"

"Doing your homework, huh?" That slowed him down, but only for a moment. Nor did he look particularly contrite when he confessed. "Well, I did take a peek at the news."

Having apparently heard her brother's dramatic entrance into the kitchen, Mara hurried into the room, her voice loud in the small space, her accusing glare directed at Jason. "What's going on?"

Before I could respond, Mom too rushed in, sans pepper spray but still wearing her apron. “I just heard on the news that there was a shooting at your mall.”

“Yes, there was, and the killer was one of the victims.”

“My goodness,” Mom said, shaking her head. “It isn’t safe anywhere these days, is it?”

Mom and I agreed on at least one thing.

CHAPTER 3
BROKEN PROMISES

YURI SHOWED UP just in time for dinner. When Mom invited him to join us upstairs, he protested that he had his dinner thawing at home. I instantly knew that excuse wasn't going to cut it. And, sure enough, Mom insisted he stay. His only option was to sit down as ordered while I put out another place setting.

"Sorry," I mouthed. Mara saw me and raised one thick eyebrow in reproof. She hates her eyebrows and the fact that I won't let her pluck them. Well, that isn't entirely accurate. I insist that she's too young to be plucking her eyebrows, but I've noticed of late that they look thinner than they used to. I suspect my mother has been playing beauty advisor.

Jason grudgingly accepted the plate of food Mom handed him, studied it a moment, and asked, "What is it?"

"Fried chicken," Yuri said. "In disguise." He pushed his unruly black hair back off his forehead, so when he wiggled his dark eyebrows for emphasis, all he needed to complete the Groucho Marx image was a mustache and a cigar.

Jason made a face at Yuri, and Yuri made a face back.

"It's a spaghetti squash burrito bowl," Mom announced proudly.

"Burrito," Jason echoed with a question mark in his comment. He looked like he was on the verge of saying that it didn't look like a burrito when Mara jumped in.

"You like everything that's in it. Don't be *extra*. Just eat it." Her use of a trendy word to criticize him lessened the impact of her superior I'm-the-mature-child tone.

"But—"

This time Yuri jumped in. "I bet your grandma made this especially for you." He smiled up at my mother as she put a plate of spaghetti squash burrito bowl in front of him.

"As a matter of fact, I did, Jason. It's a healthy version of the burritos you usually eat."

Her announcement silenced all of us. We obediently dug in, literally, since the squash bowl required scooping out the contents, one spoonful at a time.

"Stella, this is delicious," Yuri said after his first bite, sounding sincere if a bit surprised.

"It *is*," I agreed. It really *was* good, an interesting combination of tasty vegetable tidbits served with a side of fantastic homemade salsa.

"What did you expect?" my mom said. I couldn't tell if it was a rhetorical question or she was mocking us for past comments.

Meanwhile, Jason was trying to separate the beans and roasted vegetables from their squash base. I glared at him to let him know that he was going to have to eat some of it, and no amount of reorganization was going to change that.

After dinner Mara stayed behind to help Mom clean up, Jason escaped to his room and probably to his junk food cache, and Yuri and I settled in at the kitchen table on the main floor with our after-dinner coffee. Bandit wandered in and sniffed his temporary food bowl, then turned expectantly in my direction. I had put out dog food for both dogs before we had gone upstairs for dinner. No-name's bowl was next to Duffy's. Both were empty. I wondered if Duffy had eaten No-name's dinner as well as his own. I would have to supervise next time I fed them. And I needed to pick up some dog food more appropriate to Duffy's breed and size.

"You had your dinner," I said, as Duffy continued to stare at me. "I'll take you for a walk later."

Yuri dumped several spoonsful of sugar and a splash of milk into his coffee before saying: "This is when you explain why you have Gary's dog in your kitchen and why you are talking to him as if he were human."

"This isn't Gary's dog—it's Duffy. I'm dog sitting for a sick friend." Duffy plopped himself down next to his bowl, perhaps hoping for dessert, patiently waiting for whatever was going to happen next.

Yuri turned toward him. "Hey, Bandit," he said. "How's it going?"

Bandit aka Duffy looked at Yuri, his tail thumping and ears arched in anticipation of him saying more. When he didn't, Duffy gave up and rested his head on his paws.

"Duffy," Yuri said. "Hey, Duffy." There was no response from the dog. Yuri turned to me: "I rest my case."

"The family doesn't know," I said. "It's better if they don't."

"They won't hear it from me." Yuri motioned toward Duffy. "But you'd better let *him* in on your secret."

I took a deep breath. I had promised Gary I wouldn't tell anyone about what he was up to, but it was going to be hard to keep everything from Yuri. Not only does he have an incredible sense for when someone is hedging the truth, sharing my burden with him would be a real comfort. Besides, if I was going to ask him to help me work through the legal and moral issues I faced from being a witness to the shooting and then skedaddling from the scene with a hooded man, I would have to give him some background. If some time in the future I was able to tell all, I felt confident he would understand.

"It's a long story," I began.

"Isn't it always?"

"It has to do with Gary—"

"Who, as you know, I don't trust."

"Because he's a loner who lives on an island?"

"No, because I have some serious questions about what he does for a living."

I couldn't contain a sigh of frustration. "I trust him, but I confess I also have reservations about what he does for a living."

He narrowed his eyes at me. "So, what's, ah, Duffy doing here? And please don't try to tell me there's no connection between you acquiring a new dog and what happened at the mall this morning."

"What makes you think there's a connection?"

"Let's see. You fail to show up at the office, and, at the same time you're supposed to arrive, there's a shootout in the mall. Then you go off the grid. When I finally get through to you, you tell me you are on your way home and ask me to tell people at work that you aren't feeling well, when you are obviously fine. Now I find you harboring a dog that belongs to someone who knows his way around guns. It doesn't take much of a detective to conclude there's something suspicious going on here. Are you going to fill in the gaps for me or not?"

"I promised not to say anything."

After a long pause during which Yuri turned his coffee cup around at least three times, he said, "I appreciate that."

"Thank you."

"But ... that's not saying I think it's a good idea. I mean, you don't want to get mixed up in something like this. Whatever 'this' is."

"I can't tell you everything, but there are a couple of things I *do* want to tell you. Because I need your advice." Duffy came over and bumped my leg. "I think that means he wants to go out." I stood up. "Let's take him out and then go for a walk."

Yuri finished off his coffee. "Okay, let's step outside. But I'm not picking up anything he leaves out there—I want that to be clear."

The three of us went outside. Duffy nosed around a bit, found a spot he liked, and did his thing. I wondered how he had known to alert me to his need; on the island he'd had a dog door and had been free to come and go on his own. On the other hand, in the past Gary must either have left him with neighbors or taken him along on trips. Maybe he'd trained the dog for those occasions. The more significant question that was haunting me though was whether Bandit, aka Duffy, was going to end up being a permanent part of the Chandler family.

It was a pleasant evening. We took a short walk to stretch our legs and to give Duffy some exercise. He seemed content to obediently pad along beside us on a city street. I'd been worried that after the freedom of island life he might take off if given the opportunity. But he seemed fine. I wondered if he would be okay going on walks with Jason and No-name. I insisted Jason walk No-name on a leash, but my guess was that Bandit had never been on one before. Would Jason feel like I was playing favorites if we let Duffy run free while No-name wasn't allowed to? Perhaps for consistency I would need to see if Duffy would tolerate a leash.

While we walked, I confessed to Yuri what he had already suspected, that I had been in the mall on my way to the office when I ran into Gary. I explained that he had been on his way to Penny-wise to ask me about taking care of Bandit when the shooting happened. I didn't think it was necessary to admit that he had dragged me out of the mall without identifying himself.

"So, he wasn't involved? The fact that he showed up in time for a mass shooting was a coincidence?"

"I didn't say that."

"Okay, assuming for a moment that someone was shooting at him or he was shooting at someone, wouldn't that be information you should share with the police?"

"They have the shooter," I said.

"Can the shooter be connected to Gary?" Duffy's ears perked up each time Gary's name was mentioned, like he was tracking our conversation, hoping to learn the whereabouts of the companion who had abandoned him.

"I honestly don't know."

"Well, let's say, as a hypothesis, that Gary was the target. He was damn lucky there was a kid with a gun there to take out the shooter."

I didn't say anything.

"Oh no," Yuri stopped and looked at me. "Don't tell me. No, don't tell me—"

"The guy was shooting people. He'd killed an innocent bystander. What was Gary supposed to do?"

"You're defending him?"

"I guess I am."

"He leads a shooter to your doorstep, endangers you and all of those people in the mall, and you defend him."

"He thought he'd lost his tail. And he didn't anticipate they'd be reckless enough to try to shoot him with so many people around."

Yuri stopped walking and turned toward me. "Let me get this straight. Gary knew someone was out to get him. But he still comes to see you. Whoever wants him eliminated tails him to the mall and shoots up a bunch of innocent people. Then you and he run off together. And now you have Bandit here as an unpaid guest. Does that about sum it up?" He was angry, whether at Gary or me or both of us, I couldn't tell.

Bandit was standing at alert.

"In case you've forgotten, he saved our lives when we were being chased by men with guns on his island. How could I say no?"

"But having that dog here is an admission that you've been in touch with him."

"The shooter is dead. Of course, there's the possibility that he had a back-up, but there were so many frantic people running around and streaming out of the mall that it would have been hard for someone to keep track of Gary's movements. Or it's possible they thought the shooter succeeded. In which case, they would have been making tracks. And, unless there was an entire back-up team, it would have been impossible to cover all the exits. Besides, Gary exchanged his jacket for a hoodie. So, he didn't look the same going in as he did going out, and there were two of us leaving together."

"Exchanged? You mean he stole one."

"Things were chaotic. What would you have done?"

Yuri frowned. "I'll give you that."

"Furthermore, I'm fairly certain no one followed us after we left the mall."

"Fairly certain or certain? There's a difference."

"There was a lot of traffic and I did a couple of maneuvers as a precaution. Anyway, back to your original concern about me harboring Gary's dog—that's why I'm calling him Duffy."

"Maybe you should paint white blotches on him. Or dye him red. Something. Anything."

"The kids might think that was strange at this point."

"I suppose I could take him …"

"No. That's not necessary. Besides, you're hardly ever home. He'll be fine here. Really."

We turned and started back, walking in silence for a few minutes. Then Yuri stopped and turned to me again. "One more question. I heard that the alleged hero who everyone thinks nailed the killer with a lucky shot to his head had a gun. If Gary shot his attacker, won't they discover they have the wrong 'hero' as soon as they test his gun?"

My promise to Gary to stay mum was about to take another hit, but I didn't see what choice I had. Yuri was used to connecting the dots, and in this instance, he was doing it a lot faster than I could think up new dots. "It's Gary's gun."

"This just gets better and better. You mean to say, Gary took out the shooter, planted the gun, and the two of you took off?"

"It happened so fast—"

"I can imagine. But what I don't understand is why the kid is going along with it. Unless it's because the media is treating him like some sort of folk hero. That's it, isn't it? They're acting like he's a gun-toting Spiderman. He had the gun in his hand, so he must have shot the bad guy. But *he* has to know he didn't do it. At some point that's bound to come out."

"Maybe. Maybe not. Although I think he's going to have a hard time explaining why he was in possession of an unregistered gun."

Suddenly Yuri switched to the faux hero's side, trying to figure what he could say to get away with the charade, then poking holes in his own argument. "I suppose he could say he found it. That's probably the easiest explanation. Although it seems a bit fortuitous that he just happened to find a gun in time to ward off a mass shooting. I mean, when did he find it? Where? And does he even know how to shoot? If not, that wasn't a lucky shot, it was a miracle. And I bet not too many police officers believe in miracles."

"Maybe they don't believe in miracles, but won't they be pleased to have things resolved so easily? Let's say he doesn't contradict their assumption that he shot the killer.

For whatever reason. I can't imagine that they will do more than fine him or give him a slap on the wrist for the unregistered gun, even after his 15 minutes of fame has expired. That's a pretty good incentive for maintaining the lie."

"If they try to prosecute him for possession of an unregistered gun, I bet his hero story folds in a hurry. Any lawyer would urge him to tell the truth."

"The truth isn't always simple though, is it? And it's pretty embarrassing to admit you aren't the hero everyone thought you were." I was starting to buy into my interpretation of events.

"What about you? What's *your* story? How do you know someone wasn't snapping pictures or making a video? How do you know you weren't caught on camera? The mall has security cameras all over the place, you know."

"That's why I need your advice."

"And what are you going to do if whoever is after Gary figures out why he was at the mall?"

"Gary's name wasn't in any of the news coverage when we rescued that girl from the island survivalists. He didn't want credit, remember? And we kept his name out of it."

"I still think they will wonder why he came to the mall, this particular mall."

"My guess is they are more concerned about where he went afterwards."

Yuri chewed on my comment for a while before conceding I was probably right. Then he said what I knew he would eventually say, "Of course I'll help you weather this mess, but you are going to owe me big time."

CHAPTER 4
THE "TELL"

THE WEEKEND WAS FILLED with soul searching, bored children, a complaining mother, and two dogs constantly underfoot. I found myself wanting to escape—from my family responsibilities, from my two needy pets, and, most of all, from my moral dilemma.

Before I was up, Mom had apparently slipped downstairs and left a list of the "7 Best Jobs for Single Moms Starting Over" on my refrigerator. Private investigator did not make the cut. When my mother first started putting articles on the front of my refrigerator, stretched between two magnets, I had simply glanced at the titles, taken them down and tossed them in our recycle basket. I'd found them annoying, but I'd refused to let their implicit criticism of my marital status, my parenting, and my life choices get to me.

At one point in the past, I had come across an article on how to cope with a controlling parent and considered buying a couple of magnets and pinning the article to the front of *her* refrigerator. But no matter how I played out the scenario in my mind, I couldn't see it as a win for me. Eventually I gave up on the idea of a counterattack and focused on ignoring her messages. Over time, however, just seeing articles appear on my refrigerator had a cumulative impact. I came not only to resent her indirect lectures, I developed an intense dislike of the two magnets that held them in place—the arrogant bonnet-wearing goose and the smirking pig with the blue scarf around its neck. If Mara hadn't purchased the magnets for me, they would have been consigned to the garbage.

Yuri called twice on Saturday, and three times on Sunday. He kept going over and over what could happen and how I could end up in the middle of the mess Gary had brought down on me. He insisted that the longer I waited to tell the police I'd been at the mall during the shooting, the more guilty I would seem. Guilty of what, he couldn't decide. The rationale I'd landed on was that just because I happened to be there when the shooting occurred did not mean I had a responsibility to report my presence to the police. No more than did any of the shoppers who had been there.

He finally gave in after the fifth call and agreed that I should wait until the police got in touch with me to say anything. In my mind I was thinking *if* they got in touch. That would depend on whether I showed up on any mall cameras or if, as part of their investigation, they went around interviewing employees of nearby businesses. Still, if that happened, I didn't see that I had to explain why I'd left. Everyone had been trying to get away. Leaving the scene made sense. Even the desire to get away from the mall could be defended. The only hitch might be explaining who the person was I left with—*if* I had been seen leaving with someone.

The real sticking point was whether a camera or someone with a cell phone had taken a picture or made a video that proved the alleged hero didn't have a gun in his hand when the shooting took place. And what if I'd been caught on camera kneeling by the wounded young hero? Worse yet, what if Gary placing the gun in his hand had been recorded for posterity? How would I explain taking off if that came to light? Did I pretend I hadn't seen the gun? Did I claim the person I left with was a stranger who for some unknown reason dragged me out of the mall? Was there a parking lot camera that would show him getting into my car and me driving him away? Yuri was right, there were too many ways things could go sideways.

I kept checking news updates on my cell and tuning in to TV coverage to see if anyone mentioned a video or photos from the shooting. If someone had captured scenes from the tragedy, surely they would have sold or given them to some news media outlet right away. Unless the police had managed to confiscate everything and were, at that very moment, reviewing the footage. Still, I couldn't imagine the police being quick enough or motivated enough to suppress all photographic evidence. There were too many enterprising reporters looking for a scoop and too many bystanders seeking attention or a reward for being Johnny-on-the-spot. If something incriminating existed, there should at least be rumors floating around.

Neither my kids nor my mother seemed to have connected Duffy coming to stay with what had happened at the mall. Nor had they pressed me about why I wasn't at the office when the shooting occurred. Something Mom said made me think that they assumed I had missed being there because I had gone to pick up Duffy. I didn't correct that impression. I was, however, concerned with the potential aftermath if Mom found out I had deliberately misled all of them.

The weekend dragged on. I hung around the house and moped. My only break was a run to the grocery for more dog food.

Sometimes not making a decision is a way of making a decision. The longer I waited, the more obvious it became that I wasn't going to proactively admit to anyone other than Yuri that I had been in the mall concourse at the time of the shooting. Not to the police, and not to my family. I would play the odds and hope to win. Like the cliché of an ostrich sticking its head in the sand when frightened, hoping whatever had threatened it would be gone when it popped its head back up. Although I knew from one of Yuri's trivia rants that the real reason ostriches dug holes in the sand was to create nests for their eggs. As is so often the case, the myth was more appealing than the reality.

In spite of my decision by procrastination not to tell anyone about being in the mall at the time of the shooting, I knew that on Monday morning, reality would surround me like a ring of fire. I would be compelled to tell colleagues *something* about where I'd been. There was no way to avoid it. They were bound to talk about the shooting and ask where I was when it happened. They might even ask why I hadn't answered when Yuri called. Or, given my cover story, they might assume I'd taken ill on the way to work and ask if I was feeling better. Should I stretch the truth a little? Bend it? Manipulate it? Or go for the outright lie and beg forgiveness if caught? To this point I'd had an open relationship of trust with colleagues. I didn't want to ruin that. But I was trapped between revealing an unpleasant truth that wasn't mine to reveal and making up some near-truth they could accept. The question was how *near* and what happened if I was outed by some unforeseen witness or circumstance.

Yuri agreed in principle that explaining Gary's involvement to colleagues was way too complicated. They were people used to reading between the lines and figuring out connections. It would be easy to make a mistake, to drop one tiny clue that could morph into questions I didn't want to answer. In his opinion, it was far better to dance around the facts, sidestepping the most incriminating ones. Even though I had a reputation at Penny-wise for staying calm under pressure and not running away at the first sign of danger, he thought it would sound credible if I simply said that I wasn't thinking straight when I left. That I had been close to the two victims when it happened and was shaken by the experience. Credible if not embarrassing. Not the image I was trying to portray as an investigator. But under the circumstances, perhaps my best alternative.

Jason took both dogs for a walk on Saturday. Duffy submitted to being on a leash, although it was clear to me as I watched them take off that the dog thought Jason was the one on the leash, not the other way around. At least Duffy's presence seemed to be having a positive influence on No-name. Instead of his usual random misbehavior, he trotted alongside Duffy like a dutiful servant, ready at a moment's notice to do Duffy's bidding.

Mara spent Saturday night at a friend's house. She came back exhausted on Sunday mid-morning and disappeared into her bedroom, reappearing late afternoon to ask what was for dinner. I didn't see her again until the pizza arrived that evening. I hadn't felt up to cooking. My mother thinks I give the kids pizza for dinner way too often, but it's something we all like, and I figure that, in the long run, her healthy meals make up for my lack of domesticity.

Mom went out with friends on Saturday evening and out to brunch with still more friends on Sunday morning. Unlike me, she has a busy social life. Always watching her weight, she declined my invitation to pizza Sunday evening.

On Sunday the dog walking fell to me. I didn't bother putting Duffy on a leash, and if No-name felt put upon, well, that was just too bad. He was always eager to chase after a squirrel or explore some interesting smell; he couldn't be trusted off leash. Duffy, on the other hand, seemed unimpressed with city wildlife and couldn't even be bothered to turn his head to see what No-name was barking about.

When the pizza arrived Sunday evening, Mara and Jason each grabbed a couple of slices and asked if I minded if they ate in their rooms. Usually, I resisted having the family eat meals separately, but that evening it seemed like a good way to keep the topic I didn't want to discuss at bay, so I agreed. No-name went with Jason, his pangolin dangling from his mouth, and Duffy stayed with me. He glared disapprovingly when I poured dry dog food into his dish until I relented and topped off his meal with some sausage from the pizza. I should have asked Gary what he fed him at home. Chunks of deer meat? Wild salmon filets? Maybe Bandit was used to hunting his own food in the woods, a discomforting thought that I quickly suppressed.

All in all, it was a quiet weekend, except for my tumultuous thoughts.

By Monday morning, I still hadn't made a decision as to how I was going to handle questions about where I had been during the shooting. I knew that the first person I would see was W. Blaine Watkins, our receptionist and Man Friday. I didn't have to worry about being asked anything challenging by him; he never engaged in chitchat. A brief greeting and a flash from his penetrating blue eyes would be about it. Unless he had a message to pass on from PW Griffin, our stylish and mysterious boss. I refer to her as stylish because she is a fashion-plate. I always look forward to seeing what she is wearing and checking out the latest hat to grace her ornate, wrought iron coat rack. She's mysterious because no one in the agency knows anything about her background before she started Pennywise. In fact, we don't even know where she lives or what PW stands for. Not for want of trying. There is an on-going effort to learn more about her past as well as about her current situation.

It would be in the "pit," our collective office area, where I could anticipate running into trouble. These were people who had my back on assignments. People whose support and trust I rely on. People I care about. I didn't necessarily know all of their personal secrets, nor they mine, but my actions during the shooting could have repercussions for them and for the agency, so I needed to tread lightly. Yuri had advised that I say just enough but not too much. Lie by omission rather than with distorted facts. And keep it simple.

As I approached the familiar mirrored storefront with our mascot in a small display window left of the entrance, I saw Jenny Perry coming toward me from the other end of the mall. She'd created our mascot, a stuffed bear wearing a Sherlock Holmes deerstalker hat and a coat with a cape across the shoulders. He held a magnifying glass in his right paw. Above the toy sleuth was a flier that read: "For the man or woman who has everything—give them the gift of vigilance. Special rates for gift certificate detection services."

Jenny was approaching rapidly with her usual long stride. She was wearing her signature outfit, a long skirt and laced leather boots. Her long sandy hair jutted out from her head in kinky waves. She could have come straight from a rock concert in the 70s. She definitely didn't look corporate, but even our conservative clients responded favorably to her warm, lively personality. Just being around her made life seem a little brighter. When she saw me, she waved, a spirited welcoming gesture. I waited for her at the door.

"Hey, it's good to see you," I said.

"Nice of you to say that before asking, 'So, what do you need money for this time?'" She laughed, a row of even white teeth peeking out from a wide mouth that smiled a lot. Jenny was a farmer who only worked for Penny-wise when she needed extra cash, unless it was as a favor for PW. PW was good to her, finding her work whenever she needed it, and Jenny was loyal in return.

"I'll leave that to Will." Our gadget-loving, trench-coat-wearing colleague, Will Bishop, always gets right to the point when Jenny comes in. "Need a new gen set?" "Buying some goats?" "Building a new chicken coop?" Jenny is fond of teasing Will, especially about his retro beige detective coat since it was his faux noir look that was the inspiration for our mascot. Will doesn't always seem to appreciate Jenny's jibes, although I think he secretly likes the attention.

I opened the door and held it for her. She gave W. Blaine a cheerful hello and hurried past. "I need coffee," she said over her shoulder. I nodded at Blaine, and he nodded back as I followed Jenny into the pit. Will, Norm and Adele were there already. As soon as Will saw Jenny, he opened his mouth to say something, but before he could, Jenny said: "I need a new tractor." Norm, Adele and I exchanged smiles as Will clamped his mouth shut.

Yuri appeared just as Blaine popped his head in and said, "Jenny, Cameron, as soon as you have your coffee, PW wants to see you."

"Me, too?" I asked, not sure I'd heard correctly.

"That's what I said." Blaine's words were abrupt, but I didn't take it personally. He's all business with us pit dwellers. Although I've seen him console upset clients, and I've often suspected that he and PW are friendlier behind closed doors than they let on. Like our most experienced investigator, Grant Hunter, W. Blaine Watkins had been with the agency from the beginning. His professional demeanor and classic attire adds a touch of class to the office, and he's also extraordinarily efficient. It isn't necessary for him to also be a warm fuzzy personality.

Jenny grabbed her large yellow mug with its dragonfly design and poured coffee up to the "choose happy" motto inscribed on the inside rim of the mug. My green mug with its stenciled leaf design seemed drab by comparison. I poured myself some coffee and hurried after Jenny, thankful that, at least for the time being, I didn't have to worry about talking to colleagues about the day of the shooting.

PW was wearing an unusually demure suit, dark brown with an embroidered geometric design on the lapels. Her white silk blouse was V-necked, showcasing the butterscotch amber carved pendant.

"Wonderful necklace," Jenny said. "Is it an antique?"

"Yes, a family heirloom. I'm very fond of it." She reached up and touched it with her fingertips. I've read that genuine amber is slightly warm to the touch. That's one way you can distinguish it from fake amber that is made of glass. I'm not sure I could tell the difference, but I had the feeling that PW would be able to.

I agreed with Jenny that it was a wonderful piece, Russian perhaps? Maybe from the Baltics? The Dominican Republic? Its origins had to be exotic. I would hate to think it was purchased from an import shop in Miami or a wholesale jewelry market in the Midwest. It was definitely distinctive. If it really was an heirloom, maybe it was a clue worth following up on in our quest to learn more about PW's past. I tried not to stare, surreptitiously studying it so I could give an accurate description to Yuri for him to research.

"Our client should be here shortly," PW said, ending the brief personal exchange. "I wanted to give you a head's up and explain what I want each of you to do for our new client so you can ask whatever questions you feel appropriate. It's a time sensitive situation. That's why I want the two of you on it right away.

"It seems Mr. Bondo got separated from his dog during the shooting on Friday. He's hoping we can find him. Mr. Bondo is apparently very fond of his dog and says price is no object; he just wants his pet back. He came to us because of our location. He feels that we have an advantage since we are familiar with the mall and the surrounding area.

"My idea is that you, Jenny, can check with animal shelters, put up signs, and canvass the nearby neighborhood. Cameron, you can talk to owners of the mall businesses and perhaps check with some of the mall regulars you recognize."

The idea of a man looking for a missing dog definitely set off alarm bells. He wasn't coming after me, I told myself. He was looking for his dog which just happened to be at the mall at the time of the shooting. Coincidences *do* happen. But still ....

She looked from me to Jenny. "How does that sound?" We both nodded. "Mr. Bondo insists that time is of the essence, so put anything else you are doing aside and concentrate on this, understood?"

We both nodded again, and Jenny giggled. "Is his name really 'Bondo,' like the all-purpose putty?"

I was tempted to add, "professional strength," but PW wasn't smiling. Or was there a hint of amusement underneath the schoolmarm look of disapproval?

"Just don't tell me his name is *James* Bondo," Jenny continued. "I can hear it now—'My name is Bondo, James Bondo.'"

I will never know whether PW found her humor inappropriate or hilarious because Blaine interrupted. He came in and said solemnly, like an undertaker announcing the body was ready for viewing, that Mr. Bondo had arrived. PW said, "We're ready. Send him in."

When our new client came in, PW got up to shake his hand and make introductions. He gave Jenny and me a head nod to acknowledge us before taking a seat. He was a tall, dark-haired, middle-aged man with no laugh lines around his eyes. It seemed to me he was making an effort to be personable. The operative word was "effort." His stiff manner and dark suit did not suggest empathy or warmth. Nor did he look like someone who ordered his martini shaken, not stirred. Maybe he wielded a mean putty knife.

PW told him that she had already explained the situation to us and that we were prepared to start immediately. "Did you bring a picture of your pet?" she asked.

"Oh, no. I'm sorry, I forgot. But I can describe him."

He 'forgot" to bring a picture but was willing to pay big bucks for us to search for his pet? My heartrate increased. I knew that for most of our clients, it was their first experience with a detective agency, but not having a picture of a lost pet seemed a bit off. Then he described his dog. And warning signals erupted in my mind like fireworks shooting into the sky as he gave a perfect description of Bandit.

"What's his name?" I asked, trying to keep my tone neutral.

"Ah, Ben. His name is Ben."

"Ben disappeared during the incident last Friday?" Jenny asked to confirm. "Can you describe what happened?"

"I was headed to the Pet Shoppe inside the mall to buy Ben a new collar. His old one was frayed. I had him on a leash, but when the shooting started, he became extremely agitated and jerked the leash out of my hand and ran off."

"Which way did he head?" Jenny asked.

Mr. Bondo thought for a moment. "West. He went west."

"Did you try to catch him?" I asked.

"My only concern at the time was to avoid being shot."

"Understandable," PW said.

"I assume you searched the mall afterwards," Jenny said.

"I spent hours wandering around, looking for him. When I didn't find him, I thought perhaps he would make his way home on his own. I understand dogs can do that. But when he didn't turn up this weekend, I called and left a message on your voice mail. It was good of you to get back to me right away."

Under normal circumstances, breathing is automatic. You don't think about whether you are breathing too slow or too fast. But when stressed, monitoring your breathing becomes a mechanical process, and you have to pay careful attention in order not to betray how upset you are. That's what I was doing, concentrating on breathing in and out in the most normal way possible. Although when forced to actually think about your breathing process, nothing feels normal.

PW looked from Jenny to me. "Any other questions for Mr. Bondo?"

I shook my head.

"Just one," Jenny said. "You will send us a picture, won't you? That would be helpful when asking people if they've seen him."

"Certainly. When I return home this evening. First thing."

Sure you will, I thought. Because I was convinced beyond a doubt, that Mr. Bondo wasn't who he said he was. He hadn't brought a picture with him because he didn't have one. But he had his cover story down pat. Too pat.

"You've checked with the mall police, haven't you?" I

asked. "Was his flight caught on any of the mall cameras?"

Bondo's slight hesitation sent up another red flag. "They told me he could have left with a group of people fleeing the mall, but there was nothing definitive on any cameras."

Really? Did he really check with the mall cops? That was something I could follow up on. Although maybe I didn't want to encourage having them study camera footage. Mr. Bondo went with Blaine to fill out some paperwork, and Jenny and I made our way back to the pit. I immediately excused myself and headed for the "closet," the smaller of our two conference rooms, waving for Yuri to follow me. Once inside, I closed the door and motioned for Yuri to sit down and keep quiet while I pressed the familiar speed dial number on my cell.

"Mom, I'm glad you're there. I have a strange request." I went on to explain that it was imperative that she keep Duffy inside, out of sight. And if anyone came by asking about him, she was to deny his existence. As soon as I could, I would come home and deal with the situation. One of my mother's strengths is that she can sense when something is too important to either question or push back on. She quickly agreed to do what I asked. I thanked her and hung up.

"What's this all about?" Yuri asked, sounding concerned.

"There's a 'Mr. Bondo' who has hired us to find his pet. He claims he lost him during the shooting, doesn't have any pictures, but described Bandit perfectly. He said he came to us because of our location. That makes sense, but I think there may be more to it than that. Do you think I'm overreacting?"

Yuri got an "I told you so" look on his face. "No, I don't

think you're overreacting. I also think it's no longer safe for you to have Bandit at your house. Even if you keep him inside. Which you can't do 24/7 anyway."

"Bondo apparently called PW last night and made an appointment for first thing this morning. What I don't know is whether he's aware of my connection to Gary or not. It could be he's hoping to trick me into contacting Gary. Or it could be there's a missing dog that happens to look like Bandit. I mean, there are a lot of large, shaggy black dogs in the world."

"You're right, it could be a coincidence. Or a fishing expedition. In my opinion, it doesn't matter why he ended up here, you need to get Bandit out of there, now." He jumped up, hurried into the pit and brought Jenny back with him. When she sat down at the cramped table, Yuri turned to me and said, "You explain this to her."

I took a deep breath. "Jenny, we have a problem." When someone begins an exchange with those words, you know that whatever comes after will not be something you want to hear.

Jenny leaned forward and locked eyes with me. "Hit me with it," she said.

Fortunately, Jenny catches on fast and doesn't have to chew a problem into submission before taking action. All it took was a high-level overview for her to suggest next steps. "You can give me details later," she said. "I'll go to your house, pick up Duffy and take him to the farm. He'll be safe there."

"You can't be seen," I said.

"Really, Cameron, you think I'm going to let someone tail me to your house?"

"Sorry." I gave her directions and suggested she go in through the alley. She took down the address on a scrap of paper she dug out of the bottom of a large, crocheted handbag covered in yellow flowers.

"Call your mom and tell her I'm on my way. After I get Duffy settled in, I'll look for Mr. Bondo's lost dog, okay?"

"I don't know how to thank you."

"One thing at a time." She grinned. "And don't worry, I'll find a way."

"You'd better get it in writing," Yuri said to Jenny as she hurried off.

I called my mother back and explained that Jenny would be coming by to pick up Duffy and suggested she give her the new bag of dog food and the food bowl I'd bought for him. If someone came by, we didn't want it to be obvious that we had recently had two dogs. Also, could she figure out some way to tell the kids not to say anything about Duffy? Maybe that there was an ownership dispute or something. Whatever she thought made sense. "I promise to tell you the whole story later, but it would be better if the kids didn't know."

"I certainly hope you can convince me of that this evening," was all she said before hanging up. I had been warned.

"What now?" I asked Yuri, as if he had a magic eight ball with answers to all of our problems.

"You should probably talk with PW about this."

I had been fairly certain that was what he was going to say, but I had clung to the hope that he had another alternative. Before I could respond, we saw Blaine headed in our direction. He opened the door to the conference room and said, "PW wants to see you." He was looking straight at me.

"Sit down," PW said to me when I entered her office. "Now, what is it you want to get off your chest about this assignment?"

"Uh ..."

"Don't bother saying 'nothing.' You have a tell." She smiled. "I find that helpful."

CHAPTER 5
BLOND STREAKS

"A *TELL*—" I REPEATED.

"Don't worry, I'm sure the client didn't notice."

"Didn't *you* find him, ah, suspicious?" I asked. I wasn't really trying to avoid confessing. At this point it seemed inevitable that I would have to explain the situation with Bandit and Gary. But I was curious what she thought of our client. We all assume PW has a keen sense of intuition, but in this instance, I knew—or thought I knew—our client's hidden agenda. It would be interesting to find out what she was able to discern based on limited information. A kind of Sherlock Holmes test.

"Fair enough," PW said. "First, few if any men in his age group are comfortable being called 'Mr.' But our James Bondo seemed to prefer it."

I couldn't control myself. "His first name is actually James?"

"I would suggest you not tell Jenny, but I assume that suggestion is pointless." She smiled. "Because he referred to himself that way, that's how I introduced him to you. Second, I didn't sense any real feeling for his pet, especially given how much he's willing to pay us to look for it. Third, not having a picture to show us seemed out of synch with his expressed urgency for finding the animal. Fourth, he had a slight hesitation before responding to your question about the dog's name. As well as about the mall cameras. Those were the main things that stood out to me. Do you have anything to add?"

"Well, just one thing. The dog he described? He's at my house."

PW actually looked surprised for an instant before regaining her usual dignified composure. "I confess, that wasn't what I expected to hear. I don't suppose you kidnapped his dog."

"No, my guess is that he's trying to find its owner by hiring us to supposedly locate the dog. What I'm not sure of is whether he knows I have the dog or not."

"I think you need to start at the beginning."

It didn't take long to cover the highlights, leaving out the specific details I'd forced Gary to reveal about why someone was after him. I also left out the fact that Gary had been the one to shoot the shooter. Withholding that kind of evidence from the police, if she were questioned, might not be something she would be comfortable with. And, although PW hadn't met Gary or Bandit, she knew about the role they had played in our former missing person's case, so she wasn't surprised I'd been willing to take the risk of keeping Bandit.

"I don't suppose you want to tell me more about why someone is trying to eliminate Gary?"

"I promised him I wouldn't. But I can tell you it's fairly complicated."

"Being the target of a hit man usually is." The matter-of-fact statement was made without a hint of irony. But her hand was fingering the thin, Russian import cigarette in her vintage ashtray made by Faberge. We never saw her actually smoke, but reaching for the Kazbek Papirosi cigarette was *her* tell.

"This is problematic," she said after a brief silence. "I assume you haven't talked with the police about any of this."

"No. One of the things I haven't figured out yet is what I should say if asked. I mean, someone may have pictures or even a video of me kneeling next to the young man who was shot. Nor am I sure where the mall cameras are located. I could have been caught on camera with Gary on the way out. I just don't know."

"I don't believe there are any cameras aimed directly at the location where the two men were shot. You're probably okay that way. But one may have caught you on the way out. Not that they will necessarily be trying to identify everyone who took off. Which exit did you take?"

I explained where we had fled the mall, down a narrow side corridor through an emergency only exit. PW smiled. "It looks as though your friend chose wisely. There's only single camera coverage there. If you kept your heads down, they may not have face photos." It hadn't occurred to me that PW would know all of the camera locations in the mall. But that made sense; she would want to know about the mall's security. What I didn't know was whether Gary and I had just been lucky, or if he knew enough about mall security to make a calculated spur-of-the-moment decision as to the best way to escape with minimum exposure.

"Even so, you're in a bit of a bind," PW acknowledged. "Let's start with the immediate problem—the dog you've been sheltering."

"That's being taken care of—Jenny is on her way to my place right now. My mother will have Bandit ready to go. Jenny is going to run him out to her farm for safekeeping."

"Good." She fondled the cigarette. "I think it's best if you continue with the investigation as if you think you are looking for a dog named Ben, Mr. Bondo's imaginary pet. He knows you are supposed to be questioning businesses in the mall. If he's watching, that will perhaps throw him off, at least for a time. He could have expected Jenny to leave since she's supposed to focus on outside sources. Although it's possible he will have her followed too. I'm assuming she'll keep an eye out for a tail." The latter wasn't a question, but I responded to it anyway.

"Yes, she's aware there could be someone tailing her."

"Good. Meanwhile, I'll ask Adele to check on Mr. Bondo's bona fides, see what we can find out about him. I'm sorry to say that Gary has put you in a bad, perhaps dangerous situation. I won't pressure you to tell me anything you are uncomfortable sharing, but I feel I have the right, and an obligation, to do whatever I can to protect you. And the agency."

"I'm sorry this happened—"

"You did what you thought was right. Life sometimes comes at you with unforeseen and unavoidable complications. How you deal with them is what's important."

"Thank you." I stood up. "I'll get out there and start canvassing the businesses." I started to leave, then turned back and asked, "What would you suggest I tell the others?"

PW didn't hesitate. "Just that you're looking for a lost pet for the moment. We can always bring them up to speed when we have a better handle on what's going on."

"And should I admit I was here during the shooting?"

"They are bound to ask. Keep whatever you say close to the truth. You were on your way to the office, and when the shooting broke out you ran for an exit. You were shaken by the experience and didn't feel great to begin with, so you decided to go home to recuperate. You called Yuri and let him know you wouldn't be in for the rest of the day."

"That seems a bit strange, doesn't it?" I wasn't fishing for a compliment, but I wanted to hear that she thought I was stronger than that.

"Remember, you weren't feeling well, and this was a traumatic event. It's not unusual to feel anxious or upset afterwards. There was nothing you could have done, so why hang around? Leave it at that for now. I have the feeling this may get messy. If so, we'll deal with that when it happens."

I started my assignment with Ye Old Candle Shoppe. The faint smell of candles often seeped into our office, but I was overwhelmed by the mix of scents as I entered the small shop. Cinnamon and vanilla, cedar, a spice blend and something that conjured up the image in my mind of wet moss on a decaying log. I considered buying one of the latter as a joke for Yuri, but the thought that he might actually like it was disquieting. Like last Christmas when I gave him a picture of a bullfighting matador painted on black velvet as a joke and he hung it up in the office, until Blaine made him take it down. I wasn't sure if he put it up as a reverse joke or he actually liked it. With Yuri, it was hard to tell.

The young clerk in the candle shop was very friendly. When I introduced myself and explained that I was looking for a lost dog, she said she had always wondered about what kind of cases we handled. "Not homicides, then?"

Since I'd been at Penny-wise, we'd found ourselves mixed up in a homicide or two, but only after a small investigation morphed into something much larger. It wasn't something we sought out. "We leave those to the police," I assured her.

"I've read the sign in your window," she said. "Accidents, surveillance, missing persons; it all sounds so interesting. Especially the part about 'private matters.'" She turned her head to the side and pretended to twirl a mustache she didn't have.

I laughed. "Mostly mundane stuff, actually, like finding someone's lost dog."

"Sorry," she said. "I didn't see a thing. I stayed crouched behind the counter the whole time. I didn't even see them haul off the guy who took out the shooter." She sounded disappointed, like she'd missed the end of the movie. I thanked her and exited the shop, the aroma of candles chasing me to my next stop.

I was coming out of a jewelry boutique that catered to young girls who wanted their ears or other places pierced when my cell rang. It was Jenny.

"I'm in a strip mall down the road. I checked for our missing dog at an animal shelter here. No luck; no one's seen Ben. But there's a hair salon here that looks good, and I need a cut. What do you think about me getting my hair streaked blond—would that look good?"

"Well, it would definitely be a new you."

"So that's a yes?"

"Why not?"

"Okay, I'll drop in and make an appointment. I can ask if they've seen the dog, so it will be on the client's dime."

I was 95 percent certain she was talking about changing Bandit's appearance, but there was a 5 percent chance that I'd given her bad advice about her hair. It surprised me that she might consider talking in code. Maybe I needed to be more careful about such things. I mean, I knew not to text or email someone with details. Or leave phone messages that revealed anything I wanted to keep secret. But if I was right about Jenny's implicit agenda, maybe I also needed to be worried about one-time conversations. I knew there were remote listening devices. Our agency occasionally used them. Still, it hadn't crossed my mind that our Mr. Bondo would go so far as to eavesdrop on a private conversation I was having.

I casually looked around, slowly, thoroughly but hopefully not as if I was checking out who was in the vicinity. Once you get an idea like that in your mind, everyone looks suspicious. That man over there with the newspaper—who reads newspapers on a bench in a mall? That woman supposedly eating a cookie at that table in front of the coffee kiosk. Where was her drink? Maybe she carried cookies in her purse to whip out when she wanted to look like she had a reason to be occupying a table. The young man with the earphones. Was he really listening to music? Given all of the possibilities, I was glad I had gone along with Jenny's stratagem.

My cell rang again. This time it was my mother.

"I wanted you to know I'm going out to do some shopping," Mom said. I assumed that was code for *everything is under control and Duffy is gone*. Even my mother was being super cautious. "Want me to pick up anything for you?"

"No, I don't think I need anything." Code for, *everything is under control at this end, too.* "Will you be there when the kids get home?"

"Yes, I might take them out for ice cream. I have an urge for an ice cream cone." More code! Mother never has an urge for ice cream. Well, perhaps she does, but she rarely gives in to it; she's too calorie conscious. I had no doubt that was her way of letting me know she was going to talk to the kids about Duffy and thought it would make more of an impression if she took them away from home to tell them about it.

"I doubt the kids will refuse ice cream, and it sounds good to me. How about bringing some back?" Perhaps I should be worried about the calories like Mom was, but given how hectic my life is at times, I often find myself succumbing to food cravings rather than making sound heath choices. "And thanks," I added before hanging up.

I spent the next few hours going from store to store, asking whether they'd seen a dog matching Bandit's description, either during the shooting or since then. I knew Bandit had been in my car the entire time, so I didn't expect anyone to say "yes" and wasn't upset when they didn't.

What was interesting was that each person I talked to had a story about that day—where they were when it happened, what they had heard from others about the event, and their concerns about future attacks. And, almost to a person, everyone commented on the young man's fortuitous shot. What a hero! They were also eager to know more about the shooter. I'd been surprised to learn he was a young, local man. But then, Gary had said he might be an amateur.

At a tiny health food shop just beyond where Gary and I had left the mall, the woman behind the counter asked, "Were you there?" For an instant I thought maybe she had seen me leave, then I realized she was simply hoping to hear some juicy details.

"I'm thankful it wasn't any worse," I said, sidestepping the question. "One of my colleagues was there when they took the guy who shot the shooter away. Said he was barely conscious." My attempt at diversion worked.

"Wasn't that something? I mean, a young guy with no training getting off a lucky shot like that." After she was done reveling in the miracle of a novice shooter taking out a killer, I thanked her and left.

A clerk in a small shoe store mentioned that there was a movement afoot to get the mall administrators to issue a plan for what to do if something like that happened again, comparable to our earthquake evacuation plan.

"I didn't know we had an evacuation plan," I said.

"It's supposed to be posted in every store."

"Where's yours?" I asked, glancing around.

The clerk's eyes frantically darted from wall to wall, like he'd suddenly remembered he'd misplaced his car keys. Finally, he pointed and said, "On that wall." I went over and checked out the map showing all of the mall's exits alongside a detailed list of dos and don'ts if an earthquake occurred. Even though we were in a major earthquake zone, I hadn't given it much thought before now. Seeing these official recommendations made me think that this was a conversation I needed to have with my family. Maybe even develop a plan of our own.

In between going into stores, I also stopped the

occasional shopper or walker who looked like they would be willing to take a few minutes to chat about what had happened. If there was anyone watching me, I would look like I was doing exactly what PW had said I would be doing. Although my search was unproductive. No one had seen Mr. James Bondo's dog, Ben. Surprise!

Out of all the clerks and shoppers I talked to, only two people had actually been in the main concourse at the time, and they had been near the edge of the crowd. They told me how terrifying it had been, how loud the shots were even at a distance, and how shoppers were running every which way. Nothing I didn't already know.

I grabbed lunch in the food court, a tasty chicken Pho topped with green onions and cilantro. One of the healthier of my food court favorites. I appreciate good food and fine dining but have no problem eating things loaded with carbs or that are deep fried or laden with excessive amounts of sugar. I'm an eclectic eater. I even like mac and cheese out of a box! I often fed it to the kids when they were younger because it was one of the few things Jason would eat without a fight.

After lunch I went back to the office to give PW an update. "Smart thinking," she said with a smile when I described Jenny's message.

Just as I was about to leave, Blaine buzzed PW to let her know that Adele had a report on Bondo. PW indicated I should stay and hear what Adele had to say. She came in carrying a slim manila folder and sat down next to me. "Cameron," she said. "You doing okay?" Adele is a middle-aged woman with reddish brown hair and sharply honed research skills. She's our go-to person for background checks and a whiz at tracking down bits and pieces of information about almost anything and everything.

"Yes. Thanks for asking." I was still not looking forward to elaborating on the story Yuri had told everyone about why I had gone home on the day of the shooting, hoping that I could avoid having to say more indefinitely.

Adele handed the file folder to PW. When she opened it, I saw that it contained a single sheet of paper. "I looked in all the usual places," Adele said. "His PayPal account is good, but other than that, he doesn't seem to have a history of any kind. It's like he doesn't exist."

PW and I exchanged meaningful looks.

Noting our exchange, Adele said, "I take it that was what you were expecting?"

"Let's just say it doesn't surprise us."

"Want me to keep digging?"

PW didn't have to think about it for more than a moment. It was not time we could bill, but she undoubtedly didn't like clients who lied to her. "Yes. See what you can find. He may not be from around here. Check to see if he rented a car under 'Bondo.' 'James Bondo,'" she said with the hint of a grin.

Adele went off to continue her online search for our deceitful client, and I went back to performing my part in the pretend investigation. If the stakes hadn't been so high, I would have been enjoying myself. I'd never had time or a reason to go out of my way to meet other mall tenets before. Now I was putting faces to the individuals who worked in the shops I walked by every day, as well as getting a better idea of the types of businesses we had as neighbors. In addition, I'd indulged myself in more than one good cup of coffee along the way. I even snagged a peanut butter cookie at one of the kiosks. With so many coffee stands in the main concourse, some affiliated with big box stores, others stand-alone businesses, it was too tempting to grab a cup to go. Just like I had the morning of the shooting. I still wondered what had become of it.

The afternoon went by quickly. By the end of the day, I was a bit hyped from all of the caffeine, but other than that, the day had been uneventful. Neither Jenny nor I had turned up anything encouraging to report to our client. We were no closer to finding Bondo's missing dog, Ben, than we had been at the start of our search.

Just before closing, Bondo checked in to see how we were doing, and PW gave him the bad news. She added that we had one lead that we would follow up on first thing in the morning. It had been Jenny's idea to tell him that. Make it seem like we were taking his assignment seriously and stay one step ahead of him. We still didn't know if he suspected I might be involved, although there was no indication so far that he did. Either way, we didn't want him taking over the search on his own or hiring another agency for the job.

Of course, Bondo wanted to know why we couldn't pursue our lead right away. PW was ready for that demand and explained that the people we needed to question wouldn't be available until tomorrow during business hours. Then she put him on the defensive by reminding him about the photo he was supposed to give us.

"If you don't have time to drop off a picture of Ben, could you scan one and send it to us?"

That effectively put an end to the conversation. Bondo promised he would send a copy of a picture of his beloved Ben shortly, and quickly signed off.

PW and I both smiled. We suspected there would be another excuse rather than a photo forthcoming. But we were wrong.

CHAPTER 6
A WELCOME FAILURE

THAT EVENING WE ATE dinner upstairs with Mom in her small but tastefully furnished dining room. Her rectangular table seats six, if you sit close together. It has slightly curved sides and curved corners. The titanium base looks like it could be a standalone sculpture with a sleek and glossy Marmi ceramic top. The chairs are also modern but with just enough padding and contour to be comfortable. There is a narrow sideboard along one wall. It's perfect for putting out anything that didn't quite fit on the table or for setting aside used dishes.

At one end of the sideboard, Mom keeps a vintage tea set that belonged to her mother. It's displayed on a two-level wood stand that looks like it was made for the purpose. The tea pot on top is nestled into a round indentation to keep it in place. There is a space below for saucers. Next to the stand is an ornate cup tree that holds four cups. Extra cups and saucers along with matching cream and sugar containers are stored inside the sideboard. The tea pot is only used on special occasions. I couldn't remember drinking tea from the set until I was an adult. But Mara has mentioned several occasions when she and my mother have enjoyed drinking tea from the delicate blue and white tea set.

Mom fixed salmon with a lemon sauce that even Jason liked. She served it with brown rice flecked with tiny pieces of vegetables and roasted asparagus. Jason won't eat the stalks on asparagus, but he likes the tips. I noticed that his asparagus didn't have any ends. My mother really does try to accommodate his preferences while at the same time trying to educate his palate. She probably chopped up the stalks from Jason's asparagus and put them in the rice with the other veggies.

"So, Duffy went home already?" Mara said, sounding sad.

"I know you liked him," I acknowledged.

"He was a smart dog," she said.

"King is smarter," Jason chimed in.

"King?" Mom, Mara and I echoed.

"Why not? Better than being a Duke."

"He doesn't look like a King," Mara said. "Even *you* should know that."

Before they could start arguing, I changed the subject back to Duffy: "You do understand that if anyone asks, Duffy was never here."

"Yeah, Grandma made that clear," Jason said.

"What I don't understand is why people who were once in love can be so mean to each other." Mara sounded distressed.

"Divorce can be messy," I said. Mom had apparently decided that in order to make sure the kids didn't cave in to pressure if approached by someone trying to find "Duffy" that she had to make the situation sound serious. I had no choice but to carry on with the story she had spun, adding details I hoped explained the situation rather than making Mara even more upset. "I think Mom told you that my friend's husband was terribly upset by their separation. There were problems in their marriage for some time, but it still came as a shock to him when she finally said that she wanted a divorce. He lost his temper and flew off the handle." Had I really used such a trite cliché?

"Does that mean he hit her?" Mara asked.

"Ah, he didn't hit her, but she felt unsafe. That's why she was trying to stay as far away from him as possible. Also, he knew how much she loves Duffy, and my friend feared he would try to take him away to get back at her."

"So why did she take him back now?" Jason asked.

"She's found a safe place to live," I said, hoping they would accept such a simple answer to the complex problem we'd made up.

I didn't like using scare tactics on my kids; in truth, I was scared enough for all of us. However, once I'd accepted responsibility for Bandit, I had unintentionally involved colleagues, friends, and family in a dangerous game of hide and seek. There was no way to know how far the shadowy figures threatening Gary would go to find him. If keeping my kids safe required lying to them, then that's what I'd do.

Our dinner conversation lightened up when Mom asked Jason about school and he gave more than his usual monosyllabic response to that question. He actually provided some details about a STEM class he was taking. What had him excited was that he was part of a team that was building a robot.

"Doesn't that require using math?" Mara said. She's the

math whiz in the family. Given how literal Jason can be, it's surprising to me how little aptitude he has for math.

"You have to use math and science *and* be creative," he said, as if she didn't already know the answer to her question. "The math is hard, but the design part is fun."

"It's nice that there's a team working on the project," Mom said. She always worries that Jason isn't social enough.

"Yeah, the teacher says that together we have all the skills we need to be successful."

I couldn't help but smile. It was nice he was learning such a critical lesson at a young age.

Later that evening Yuri checked in to see how we were doing. Even after I assured him that I was fine and that Mom and the kids were fine, Yuri couldn't resist a dig at Gary. "He shouldn't have put you in that situation," he said for the umpteenth time.

"He didn't think he was," I responded for the umpteenth time. "He just wanted to keep Bandit safe. He had no way of anticipating how things would evolve."

Yuri sighed. "Maybe. Although when someone is out to get you—" He didn't need to finish his thought; this was ground we had covered very thoroughly. "I just think he shouldn't have imposed on you like that."

"Well, it's done. We're safe, and Bandit is safe."

"What if he doesn't come back. Have you thought about that?"

"Then Bandit will live out his days as a farm dog."

"And what happens the next time your kids go to Jenny's?" We had held a Penny-wise picnic there last summer, and my kids had been out there several times since to hang out with Jenny's daughter, Caitlan, and to ride horses. Like many young girls, Mara loved being on a horse.

"I'll have to figure something out."

Yuri wasn't going to let me off the hook that easy. "Are you going to ask Caitlan to lie to your kids about 'Duffy' spending time on the farm? The topic is bound to come up at some point. And what if the dog ends up living there permanently? How do you plan on explaining that?"

When Mom had come up with her story to cover Duffy's departure, she hadn't thought about that particular twist. If she had, she could have told at least one truth—that Duffy had gone to live on the farm. But she hadn't, and the lie had become more complicated. At some point we were probably going to have to come clean with Mara and Jason. Mom wasn't going to be happy about having to confess to her grandchildren that she had made it all up. Just as I wasn't going to be happy about having to admit I was part of the deception. Well, not just "part," but the *reason* for the pretense in the first place.

"You realize those are two different scenarios. We'll have to figure out something that satisfies all three kids. What that is, I don't know. Jenny, Mom and I will put our heads together and come up with something when Gary comes back for Bandit."

"*If* he comes back for Bandit."

"He will." I didn't like to think about the alternative … for several reasons.

Tuesday morning Jenny was already at her desk when I came in. There were no blond streaks in her hair. "Coffee's ready," she called out. Then she looked up, saw it was me, and waved me over. "I hesitated to take a picture, but I want you to know that Duffy is definitely a transformed animal. I even think he likes his new look. Although he still doesn't respond to his new name. But I've decided it's best to keep trying."

I was relieved that I had decoded her message correctly, but I still had some concerns. "Do you think he'll try to run away? I mean, you don't have him tied up or anything, do you?"

"No, he's free to roam, but I think he understands that he's there for a reason. And Caitlan adores him. Our golden retriever passed last year. She misses him a lot. The minute she met Duffy she wanted to know if she could keep him. I explained that he's merely a guest for a while. After this, I'm afraid I see a puppy in our future."

"That brings up something I'm worried about." I explained how my mother had made up a story about a phony divorce to keep the kids from mentioning Duffy to anyone. "It was to protect them, but they may be upset when they find out it isn't true."

"Maybe we can all fess up before the next time the kids are together. That would be my recommendation. They're smart; they'll understand."

"I hope you're right." She made it sound so simple.

Jenny stood. "Meanwhile, I need to hit the road and keep up the charade. I have to admit, it's the first time I've courted failure on the job."

"It is strange asking questions you know they can't answer. Still, it's been fun from this end. I've never had the chance to say more than a few passing words to our mall neighbors. Although I also feel guilty—some of them were pretty shook up by the shooting."

"Not your fault," Jenny said firmly. "Just pick up the pieces and move on." She started to leave, then turned back. "It's none of my business, but is there more to your relationship with Gary than …?"

"Than …?" I laughed. "Subtle."

"I notice you're not answering."

"There can't be. Two different worlds. But he does happen to be very appealing."

"If he's as attractive as his dog, I believe it." Jenny laughed swirling her long, fringed shawl around her shoulders as she headed for the door.

Blaine spoiled her dramatic exit by appearing as she opened the door, blocking her departure. He waved at me to come along, too. PW wanted to talk to us.

PW was standing up at her desk when we came in. The pattern in her shirtwaist dress with its pleated skirt reminded me of a Klee painting. The matching wide belt had an embossed silver buckle that complemented her large silver earrings and her silver ring with its deep blue stone. She reached down and picked two pieces of paper off her desk and handed each of us one. "Our client sent these pictures this morning." There were two pictures of a dog on the page, the same breed as Bandit, but not quite Bandit. In one photo the dog was playing with a young boy. The other was a shot from the side with the dog standing there, posed.

"I take it this is Ben." Jenny said.

"According to our client."

"Photoshopped or from a new wallet?" I asked.

"Hard to tell. But he obviously wants us to keep looking. What do you think?"

"I think we need to ask him to pay up front," Jenny said.

"He already has three days covered."

PW hadn't mentioned that before. But it made sense. She had been suspicious from the start, even before she knew the score. Under the circumstances, he could hardly have tried to negotiate a better deal with her.

"Great," I said, "It gives us something to show people."

Jenny looked thoughtful. "I keep wondering if Bondo knows the connection between Cameron and Gary. I mean, he probably knows that Gary came to the mall with his dog even if he doesn't know about Cameron. But if so, he must wonder *why* he came here."

PW sat down and her hand reached for the cigarette in the antique ashtray. I was never sure if it was an unconscious act or not. Why would you have a cigarette that you never intended to smoke in plain sight on your desk? Yuri and I had spent far too many hours speculating about the possibilities.

"I wish I knew the answer to that question," PW said. "And I wish I knew for sure that Gary managed to get the dog into Cameron's car without being seen. If he did, he must have lost the tail at least for a while."

"You're right," Jenny said. "They wouldn't be trying so hard to be subtle if they knew for certain Cameron had him."

"They might think there was something Gary could buy here that he couldn't get elsewhere. He could have googled it while driving, and that's why he turned back."

"I'm sure they've considered that," PW said. "But there are other places on the way where he could have purchased anything I can think of."

"There's another thing that bothers me," Jenny said.

"What about his car? If the shooter had an accomplice, wouldn't they have been waiting for him there after the shooting? Just in case? Although, I don't suppose Bondo would have hired us if Gary hadn't managed to escape."

I'd had the same thought and didn't care for some of the possibilities. "He might not have wanted to chance going back to his rental car. He could have hopped a bus or called a taxi." Or, I thought, he could have disposed of whoever was waiting for him at the car. The word "disposable" would never quite have the same meaning for me again.

"Based on the fact that we have a client trying to trace him through his dog, I think we can assume he got away. And, just so you know, Adele is still trying to learn more about our client. Who he works for might tell us whether it's a coincidence or not that he came to us for help. Meanwhile, we carry on like we would with any client."

We took that as our cue to quit speculating and get on with work.

What used to be considered anchor stores in malls are having a hard time surviving. But our mall still has two major department stores. In spite of the overall downturn, they are a big draw for shoppers. I spent about an hour talking to clerks on the main floor of one of them. When I was finished, I decided to talk to the barista at the coffee stand out front, and get a cup of coffee too, a double win. I had just got in line when my phone rang. It was my mother. She very seldom called me at work. Under the circumstances I felt instantly alarmed. I stepped out of line and away from the tables scattered in front of the coffee kiosk, glancing around to see if anyone was watching. It was hard to tell, so I started walking.

"Everything okay?" I asked before even saying hello.

"I'm not sure." Mom usually sounded like the confident, independent woman she is, but this time her voice quavered slightly, a leaf moving in a light breeze.

"Tell me." I picked up my pace and looked back to see if anyone was following me. There was no one that stood out, but, as a precaution, I suddenly crossed over to the other side of the concourse and headed in the other direction. No one else changed course.

"I heard someone knock on your door, so I went out on my deck to see who it was," Mom said. "It was a man wearing what looked like a UPS uniform. I called down to him to ask what he wanted, and he held up a package and said he needed a signature for it. You usually tell me when you are expecting a delivery, but I assumed you had just forgotten, given how chaotic things have been lately. So, I went down to pick it up.

"I had written the first few letters of my name before I noticed the package wasn't for you. The name and address on the label was for someone whose last name was Johansson. At first, I thought it was an honest mistake. When I pointed it out to the carrier though, he didn't really react. He simply reached out and took the package back, as if that was something that happened all the time. Our dog was, of course, begging for attention. The man knelt down and petted him, then casually asked if we had other pets. That's when I got worried. 'Just the one,' I told him. I added that I wasn't a dog person and wouldn't even have the one if it weren't for my grandson.

"How did he respond?'

"He said that it's nice to have two pets so one can keep the other company when there's no one around. I replied that it was better to have 'none,' but he didn't give up. He mentioned seeing a big black dog next to our house when he came down the walk and asked if I knew who it belonged to. I said that I didn't think any of our neighbors had a large black dog. Then I added, 'If you see it on your way out, chase it away.'"

"It sounds like you did exactly the right thing."

"The right thing? I shouldn't have to be doing 'the right thing.' What if he comes back? What if he comes when the kids are here?"

"He obviously went to a lot of trouble to ask about the dog without calling attention to his interest in it. And he doesn't have any reason to not believe you at this point."

"You think this is over?" She sounded hopeful.

"Well, if I were him—" I hesitated, but I didn't want to offer false assurance. "I'd probably make one more try, to be absolutely certain. Maybe send someone else, someone looking for a big black dog. He's already laid the groundwork for that scenario."

"See what being a detective has done to you?! You're starting to think like a criminal."

"I'm sorry, Mom." I should have realized that she didn't want to think about what the guy *might* do next. She wanted me to tell her everything was going to be fine. Unfortunately, I couldn't do that. "We can talk about this later, okay? I'll try to come home early."

"Maybe Yuri can come for dinner."

"And stay overnight as a house guest?" I knew she felt safer when Yuri was around, but I didn't think it was a good idea.

"Why not?"

"Because it isn't necessary," I said. "And we don't want to alarm the kids. There's no reason to worry them about this."

Mom seemed to calm down, perhaps believing my flimsy assurance, perhaps just desperately wanting to believe it. At the same time, my anxiety started to build as "what if" scenarios played out in my mind. What if someone did come by and poked around while the kids where there? What if they came by again when my mother was there alone, this time more determined to look inside our house for Bandit? What if they decided to come after me directly instead of using subterfuge? What if—?

Without consciously making the decision, I made my way back to the coffee stand. I needed both a shot of caffeine and time to think. Unfortunately, having time to think doesn't mean you will actually think of something worthwhile. Standing there in line trying to get my brain in gear reminded me of learning how to play chess when I was in college; I knew I should be able to envision at least five moves ahead when I couldn't even decide on the very next move.

One disturbing thought did break through my brain fog: what if I had been intended to see through their charade all along? What if they had been sending me a not-so-subtle message? We know you are Gary's accomplice, and we can get to you or your family any time we want. If that was their message, what was their next move?

Yuri was right—knowing I had kids, Gary shouldn't have asked me to take care of Bandit for him. Although I knew he had intended to drop Bandit off and leave before anyone was aware he had been there. It was just his—and *my*—bad luck that things had turned out like they had.

Thoroughly shaken by the possibilities, I decided that it would be wise to tell PW and Yuri about the bogus delivery. For the second time, I left the coffee line. If someone *was* watching, they must think my behavior inexplicable, if not downright bizarre.

Since starting with Penny-wise I've always carried pepper spray and an ear-splitting keychain whistle, but I didn't know what, if any, devices Mom kept close by. It might be advisable for her to have pepper spray and a whistle with her at all times, too. Another thing we could both do was to park out front instead of in the alley for a while. Less chance of someone taking us by surprise. Making recommendations about taking extra safety precautions was probably going to upset my mother, but under the circumstances, I felt it was essential.

When Mara and Jason were younger, I'd had the usual parent conversations with them about what they should do to protect themselves. Things like using the buddy system and not going off on their own. Assuring them that it's okay to be rude to strangers if they make you feel unsafe. Telling them not to answer the door if they were home alone. Simple things designed to make them cautious but not overly fearful. They were older now, more independent, but still vulnerable in so many ways. It was the parental dilemma, how to keep kids safe without making them paranoid. Unfortunately, because of my actions, it seemed to me that induced paranoia might be the only safe solution.

Yuri wasn't in the office, but PW was. When I described to her what had happened, she said, "I'd like to tell you to go home right now, but someone could be watching. You need to act as if nothing unusual has happened. Keep looking for Ben until quitting time."

"That makes sense, but what about my family? What do you think Bondo and his cohorts will do next?"

She thought about my question for a moment. "If I were them, I'd wait until later, watch for your kids to come home and ask them if they've seen the dog. Kids aren't as good at covering up the truth as adults are. Well, most kids aren't. How do you think yours will respond?"

Great. Gary's fate might be in the hands of my children. They were smart and tough, but they were also just kids. "I *think* they will be okay .... Mom and I have done a pretty thorough job of making it clear that they need to deny Bandit, ah, Duffy was ever at our house. But you never know for sure, do you?"

"No. It depends on the person they send and how good they are at charming and manipulating adolescents."

"My concern is that it might get, ah, physical. Do you think I'm overreacting?"

PW suddenly picked up her phone. "It won't hurt to make sure we have your kids covered."

CHAPTER 7
WHEN IS A LIE NOT A LIE?

GRANT IS NOT ONLY OUR most experienced investigator, we all look up to him and trust his judgment. He has also interacted with Mara and Jason on several occasions; they know and like him. That's partly why PW sent him to their school to talk with them before they went home. In addition, Grant has a calm and reassuring manner and can make something sound both serious and not alarming at the same time. Even so, I was nervous. It's a huge burden to put on a young person to be careful about what they say when asked about something, and, at the same time, to try not to sound like they're lying.

After talking to them, Grant called me to report—and reassure me—that he thought they would be fine. He had decided against following them when they left school, in case they were already under surveillance. No use exposing our hand, he said. Instead, Grant instructed Mara and Jason to stay together on the way home. He told them that if things went as we expected, someone would approach them before they went inside. If that happened, it was up to my kids to convince them that Duffy had never been there. *If* they were approached. It was only a guess that they would be. But it's what we all agreed we would have done if the situation had been reversed.

It was really hard to go about business as usual while wondering whether some stranger was going to accost my kids on their way home from school and try to trick them into revealing information we didn't want shared. I was confident that Grant had them well prepared for the situation, *if* it happened. But I was weighed down by guilt for putting them through something like that. As their usual time for returning from school approached, I became anxious and kept looking at my watch and checking my phone for messages.

When Mom finally called to let me know that the kids had arrived safely and that our guess had been right on the mark, I had mixed feelings. I was relieved the kids were fine, but I was angry someone had waylaid them on their way home. I started to ask Mom for details, but she quickly shut me down by saying that she didn't have time to talk and would see me later. Was she seriously worried about phone taps?

Jason met me at the door when I got home. "Mom, we were sooo good," he said. "You'd have been proud of us."

I gave him a hug. "I'm always proud of you." I didn't add that I would rather have been proud of him for something other than being a good liar.

Mom and Mara came down the stairs together. They both started talking at once, and then Mara graciously let her grandmother go first. "This woman looking for her dog showed up just as the kids were starting down the walkway," Mom said. "I saw her from my deck." She was letting me know that she had been on watch while at the same time radiating disapproval. Mara, on the other hand, looked almost as pleased with herself as Jason had with himself.

"Grant came to school to warn us," Mara said.

Jason had been waiting impatiently, clearly dying to be the one to tell me the details. "Mom, it was just like Grant said it would be. Only it was a woman and not a man. He thought it might be a man."

Interesting. I wondered if she was supposed to be posing as Mr. Bondo's wife. Or, if I had shown up, would they have come up with still another layer of subterfuge?

"She looked nice," Mara added. "Designer jeans, matching denim jacket. And she sounded really sincere."

"But we knew she was lying," Jason said proudly. "So we pretended we hadn't seen any black dog in the area."

"We asked her to describe him," Mara said. "That was my idea."

"She showed us a picture. Said it was her dog's litter mate. It did look a lot like Duffy." Very clever of her, I thought.

"Did she mention the dog's name?" I asked.

"She said it was Ben," Jason said.

"Why would she call him Ben?" Mara asked. "I don't get that."

"She was just trying to trick you into saying you saw a black dog." I could hardly admit that Duffy was neither Duffy nor Ben. I hoped Jenny was right and that some day, I'd be able to tell them the real story. And that they'd understand and forgive me for lying to them.

Mom interrupted. "Dinner is almost ready. Cameron, kids, wash your hands and come on upstairs."

It made me smile to be included in the order to *wash your hands*. I wondered if I would be saying similar things to my kids after they became adults.

Dinner wasn't fancy, pasta and vegetables, a meal that both Jason and Mara liked. I silently thanked my mother for going easy on us that evening and for being kind enough to make dinner on a night I was exhausted from stress.

"Mom," Jason said at one point, pausing to get attention. Both my mother and I responded "yes," causing Jason to giggle. "I meant *my* mom, not you Grandma." For several years my mother had tried to get the kids to call her something cute or clever rather than Grandma. She'd rejected Mara's suggestions of Grammy or Grandmama, preferring something less obvious, like Amma. When that didn't work, she'd encouraged them to call her Nonna, Italian for grandma. Nothing stuck … she was destined to be "Grandma."

"Mom," he began again. "You always tell us lying is not only bad, but that it can lead to more lying and that it may be hard to keep track of your lies, so it's best not to lie."

I was living proof of that, I thought.

"Yeah," Mara interjected. "You're always quoting Mark Twain: *If you tell the truth, you don't have to remember anything.*"

"Hey, don't tell me you actually listened to one of my lectures."

"But today, you asked us to lie. So, today's lie was a good thing, right?" Jason asked.

"Today's lie was to protect someone," I said.

"So, it was a *good* lie. But it was still a lie."

I had the feeling that to my literal-minded son that this was a crucial teaching moment. But my mind was a blank.

"It was an 'alternative truth,'" Mara said with a smirk.

"There was nothing 'true' about it," Jason argued.

"There are different types of lies," Mom said, coming to my rescue. "There are lies of exaggeration, equivocation and omission. They are all forms of intentional deception, but they vary in their delivery, and in their relationship to the truth. Then there are 'white lies.' They are told to keep you from hurting someone. That's what you did, you told a 'white lie.' So, yes, it was a lie, but it was a special kind of lie."

"So white lies are okay to tell?" Oops, he'd caught her on that one.

"Not always," Mom said slowly, perhaps hoping her little gray cells would kick into gear and provide an answer that would satisfy Jason without encouraging him to lie. "You need to analyze the situation and make an informed decision. My point is that lying is not always a black and white choice; there may be shades of gray."

Jason is not fond of shades of gray under any circumstances, so I wasn't surprised when he sat there frowning at the food in front of him. But after a few moments of reflection, he perked up. "I'm okay with that. As long as I can identify the type of lie, I'm fine."

Silently I blessed my mother for giving Jason the structure he needed to live with a lie while not condoning lying.

"I haven't told you the best part yet," Mara said.

"Oh?"

"While we were talking, I pretended to see a dark-eyed junco. So, I took out my phone and snapped a picture. I got the woman supposedly looking for her dog in the corner of the shot."

"She was pretty convincing," Jason reluctantly admitted. "I asked where the bird was and she pointed. I said I couldn't see it. She told me what to look for, and we stood there and watched for a long time."

"Then I said I'd probably been mistaken and pretended to delete the picture just as the woman asked to see it. 'Too late, sorry.' I said."

"That was smart thinking," I said, secretly wishing she hadn't taken a risk like that.

"I sent it to Grant. He seemed pleased."

Later that evening Grant called. "Sorry to bother you at home. But I thought you might be worried about Mara taking that picture of the woman asking about Duffy."

"I am. I almost called you to ask your opinion. I can't decide whether to say something about the risk she took or to let it ride."

"I'd let it ride for now. What she did was quick-witted and helpful. I praised her for doing it rather than telling her the reasons she shouldn't have done it; I didn't want to diminish her feeling of accomplishment."

"But she needs to understand that there can be consequences for taking a chance like that."

"We know it was a bad move. The problem is that she has no idea how potentially dangerous the situation might be. And you don't want her to start jumping each time she hears a noise. There's a fine line between being careful and letting fear dominate everything you do."

"You're right, of course. That's another problem with lying—it puts the person you've lied to at a disadvantage."

"And it makes it difficult to tell a kid that lying is wrong when you ask them to lie in a particular situation. Been there, done that."

"Jason brought that up. My mother helped him label different types of lies in an attempt to understand why lying is generally bad, even though sometimes you find yourself in a position where it's necessary."

"Like lies of omission," Grant said pointedly. "For example, I know this situation you're dealing with has to do with some dangerous people hoping to track down someone by locating his dog, and I don't need the details unless you think it would be helpful for me to know more."

"I really don't want to lie to colleagues. Even with a lie of omission. But—"

"No problem. Just keep PW in the loop as much as possible, okay? She'll know if you need more help."

"Yes, I'm doing that."

"Then I'm okay with you lying to me." He chuckled. "But as Mark Twain once said—"

"*If you tell the truth, you don't have to remember anything.*"

"From a parent lecture on lying, right?"

"I wonder if anyone has written a book on moral lessons for kids."

"I think it's called *Grimm's Fairy Tales*."

"Oh, that's right, scare them into being good."

"It beats trying to reason with a partly-formed brain. And sometimes it's the best approach for a fully functioning adult brain, too."

"Still, it's hard to argue that there are consequences for behavior when it often seems as though there are consequences for your own actions, but that others get away with things you wouldn't dream of doing."

"Grim indeed. But the good news is that with the picture Mara took, we may be able to track down one of the villains in *this* story."

CHAPTER 8
CONSEQUENCES!

SHORTLY AFTER ARRIVING at the office Wednesday morning, I got a call from Mara. She was crying so hard it was difficult to understand what she was trying to say.

"Slow down, Mara. Tell me again what's happened." I felt like someone was standing on my chest. I struggled to breathe.

"I was pushed down—"

"Are you hurt?" I interrupted before she could complete her sentence. "Where are you?" I was half out of my chair and was reaching for my purse when I felt Grant's hand on my arm. "It's Mara," I whispered.

"Put her on speaker."

I sat back down. "Mara, I'm putting you on speaker. Grant wants to hear what you have to say." Yuri and Adele also came over as I switched to speaker. "Mara, Yuri and Adele are here, too."

"Mom," she said again, obviously struggling to stop crying. "I was pushed down."

"Are you hurt?" I asked again, this time more calmly.

Mara sniffed loudly and exhaled. "I'm fine. Just a few bruises." She sniffed again. "It was such a shock though."

"Did someone attack you?" I asked. My voice didn't sound like mine; it was someone else's, far away and hollow. Yuri pulled up a chair alongside me, his face full of concern.

"A guy on a bicycle ran into me while I was taking pictures of Shelly and me on her new phone." She spoke rapidly, as if wanting to get it all out at once.

"Is Shelly okay?" I asked.

"Yes, we're both okay. But he stole her phone." She started crying softly. "Sorry, I just feel so bad about what happened."

Grant asked, "Where are you now, Mara? Is there someone there with you?"

"We're at school." She took a deep, audible breath. "We're waiting to talk to the principal."

"Okay. Listen to me," Grant said. "Stay there. Tell the principal that your mother is on her way. Don't leave the school. And keep your own cell phone out of sight. If someone asks, you left it at home. Understand?"

Mara was suddenly silent. "You don't think—" She was a quick study. Grant didn't need to say more for her to get his message.

"We're on our way. You can answer questions about the bicycle incident, but don't bring up anything else, okay?"

Yuri and Adele said they would tell PW and to call if we needed anything. Yuri managed a quick hug while saying several times, "It will be okay. It will be okay." Then Grant and I took off.

Grant drove. He had recently traded in his red Rav4 for a newer model in a dark blue. "What do you think of my new car?" he asked, obviously trying to distract me. Which was good. Even knowing Mara hadn't been seriously injured, I was still badly shaken. I needed to get control of my emotions. Mara would need empathy sans hysteria.

"I thought you loved your red car," I said.

"I did. But this one has updated electronics," he explained. "And it's not as flashy. My wife was tired of me borrowing her car each time I had to do a stakeout or follow someone. A black sedan would have been better. People have difficulty distinguishing one black car from another. But blue is less eye-catching than red."

"This PI stuff seeps into every aspect of your life, doesn't it?"

"It's not unlike other jobs in that respect, you know."

"I do know that, but when it touches your children—"

"Cameron, I know this is hard for you, but we need to talk about what you're going to tell Mara. You need to make your cover story about the dog consistent with the seriousness of what's happening."

"How do I admit that I've put her and Jason in danger again?" I didn't have to remind Grant that it wasn't that long ago that Will had to escort my kids to and from school because of threats made against me. This time was worse though. This time the target had been Mara.

"You have to explain that you didn't realize how aggressive the man looking for Duffy was going to get. That he has enlisted the help of some loose cannon friends, people whose behavior is out of control. That's why she and Jason have to take extra precautions." Grant glanced in my direction. "Don't worry. She knows there are bad people out there. She won't blame you for that. She got through a tough situation like this before, and she'll get through this one just fine."

"But what kind of a mother knowingly puts her kids in danger?"

"Cameron, take a deep breath and put your situation in perspective. Being an investigator means you sometimes come in contact with unsavory types. The instinct to protect offspring is primal. But no matter what you do for a living, you can't keep your children 100 percent safe. The best thing you can do for them is to acknowledge that the real world is neither Disneyland nor an episode from The Sopranos. Explain that when things go wrong you have to pick yourself up and dust yourself off—it's the resiliency model for living."

"They were after her phone, Grant. It's just a fluke that kept them from getting it. And if they had, they would have discovered she hadn't deleted that picture. Then what would have happened?"

"Then they would have upped the pressure on you. She was lucky. *You* were lucky. Let's go from there."

"But—"

"You can't dwell on all of the bad things that could have happened but didn't. That will drive you crazy. We'll talk to Mara, get the details of what took place from her, make a plan to ensure everyone's safety, and then you go on with your lives."

Grant was so practical and matter-of-fact. I could feel the edges smoothed off my anxiety, my mind starting to focus on problem solving rather than simply reacting with a mother's concern for her child. No matter what I did in the future as a professional and as a mother, my immediate focus had to be on how to deal with the situation at hand. To do what was best for my children, as well as for everyone else involved.

We got to the school in record time. Even not going over the speed limit and without advice from his GPS, Grant seemed to have a knack for finding the shortest route with the least traffic. The principal's admin was waiting for us at the front door. She explained that Mara and her friend Shelly were in the student lounge. A school counselor was with them. She emphasized that the girls were both fine, just a bit dazed by the incident, and added that the principal wanted me to know that the school would look into the matter. I resisted telling her they shouldn't bother.

As soon as we entered the student lounge, Mara rushed over to give me a hug. The counselor waited until she went back to sit down next to Shelly before introducing himself. I explained that Grant was a colleague who had kindly driven me to the school to keep me from having an accident on the way. We shared a light moment about stressed parents, and the counselor assured me that both girls were fine. It had been a random accident, and the bicycler had taken advantage of the situation to rip off an expensive new phone. The girls both nodded. Shelly most likely accepted that interpretation of events, but I was acutely aware that Mara's nod was fake.

"These things happen," he said.

"My mother is still going to be upset," Shelly said.

Right on cue, a harried looking woman in a bright blue running outfit came whooshing into the room. Her hair was windblown, like she had just completed a five-mile run.

"Shelly, are you alright?" She hurried over to Shelly and enclosed her in a crushing hug. It was a good thing her daughter hadn't injured an arm or cracked a rib.

When she finished reassuring herself that her daughter was not in need of emergency treatment, she turned to us and explained that she was Shelly's mother, as if we hadn't already guessed. Then she turned to *my* daughter. "Mara," she said, moving quickly forward, wrapping her arms around Mara before Mara could retreat. Shelly rolled her eyes while her mother gave Mara a big squeeze. "I'm so glad the two of you are okay."

"Sorry about the new phone," Mara said, taking a step back.

"Oh that. We'll get her another one." Shelly's mother turned back to her daughter and started examining her more closely. Shelly seemed uncomfortable with the scrutiny, but she didn't try to stop her mother's inspection. Not that she could have done so; her mother was in full mom mode.

"Do you want to go home?" I asked Mara.

"I'd rather stay at school. I just skinned my knees and scraped my hand on the sidewalk when I fell." I resisted embarrassing her by checking out her knees and hand like Shelly's mother had done with her daughter. "I had turned away just before impact, so Shelly got hit harder than me. She has a bump on her head from the fall as well as some other scrapes and bruises. But neither of us broke anything."

Mara's comment about Shelly getting a bump on her forehead resulted in Shelly's mother focusing her attention on her daughter's forehead. "I'm okay, Mom," Shelly protested, leaning away.

Grant turned to the counselor and asked, "Is there some place we could talk to Mara in private?"

"You can use my office. It's to the right and down the hall about three doors. I'll stay here with Shelly and her mother."

As soon as we were alone, Mara asked, "There's more to this than a bicyclist accidentally running into us and stealing Shelly's phone, isn't there?"

"Your mother didn't want to worry you and your brother, so she didn't tell you the whole story."

"A lie of omission?" Mara asked. Her question sounded less like an accusation than someone proud of getting a question right on an exam. Her eyes were still red from crying, but she had regained her composure and was homing in on what Grant was saying.

"A bit more than that," Grant said. "Even I don't know the whole story at this point, but what I can tell you is that the person searching for the dog you know as Duffy is pulling out all of the stops trying to find the dog's owner. It involves a Penny-wise case, so your mother couldn't give you the details, but she had to tell you something to let you know this was a serious situation. Duffy's owner is in some serious trouble, and the people after him are determined and ruthless. Your mother had no way of knowing they would make the connection between her and the guy she's trying to help. That's why she agreed to take the dog."

"So, it isn't about a divorce?" Mara turned from Grant to me to verify that I had made that part up.

"I'm sorry," I said.

"Does Grandma know the truth?"

"Part of it. The part I could share. She went along with the story to protect you and Jason."

Mara seemed to be taking in the new information. Then her eyes lit up with an *aha*! "I think I know who Duffy's owner is," she said, "It's the guy from the island, isn't it? Duffy isn't Duffy. He's the dog who saved your life. The one you told us about." How she had made the leap from Duffy to Bandit, I wasn't sure. But then, we had talked at some length about Bandit at the time.

"Yes." I didn't see how I could deny her conclusion.

"His name was Bandit, wasn't it?"

"Yes."

"That's why he never responded to Duffy."

Grant smiled. "You are quite the detective."

"Where is he now?"

"On the farm, with Jenny. And Caitlan."

"We had a client who hired us to look for his dog, a dog named Ben who looked a lot like Bandit," Grant continued. "We think he's responsible for what happened to you today, but we can't prove it. At this point our only goal is to keep the dog and everyone safe."

"But if you know who's after him ..."

"He was using a false name. That's why having the picture you took is helpful. We're trying to figure out who specifically is trying to find the dog, so we know what we're up against."

"But what about, what was his name, the island guy?"

"Gary," I said. There seemed little point in withholding his name after she had already pieced most of it together.

"Doesn't Gary know who is trying to find him?"

"It's complicated. He didn't anticipate they would think of looking for Bandit here, so I didn't get a lot of details when he dropped him off. And I can't get in touch with him."

Mara gazed off into the distance, a sign she was busy processing. Before I could say anything, she vocalized what had been worrying me. "As soon as they realize they didn't get my phone, they're going to come after me again, aren't they?"

"I'll be back to keep an eye on you after school," Grant said.

"But you can't stay with me all the time." Mara had a look on her face I knew all too well. She was scheming. "I've got an idea. I'll let them steal my phone. All I have to do is delete that picture. When they see that I really did delete it, they will think I was telling the truth, right?"

"I suppose you have an idea about how to set that up?" Grant clearly thought she was onto something.

"I can hang out with some kids at that outdoor food truck after school. I'll make sure they see me putting my phone in the pocket of my jacket, then I'll leave it on my chair while I go get a snack."

"That might work," Grant said to me. "That just might work."

"If they are watching you, you'll most likely lose your jacket and your cell," I pointed out, then quickly added, "But I'll buy you new ones."

"That only seems fair," Mara said, like a judge declaring compensation to a victim.

Grant asked to see her phone. Mara meekly handed it over and gave him her password, glancing at me with that look teens get when they're hoping to keep something from a parent.

"Don't worry. I'll let Grant handle this. I don't need to see anything on your phone."

"In addition to deleting the picture you took," Grant said, "... we need to remove the email you sent to me. The normal delete function is sufficient for the picture since that's what you told the woman you did. But I need to have someone at the office do a better job of eliminating the email. Okay if I take this with me?"

Mara nodded "yes," clearly already thinking about her new phone. Then she quickly went off to class, excited to be part of a new plan to trick the tricksters.

Grant and I returned to the office. He had Will permanently remove the email from Mara's phone, and then returned it to her before school was out. The rest was up to her. And to Yuri. Yuri seemed to us like the best person to keep an eye on the operation. He would fit right in with the afternoon food truck crowd from the nearby satellite high-tech campus. And he would happily serve as spy and bodyguard, especially if the food was good.

I spent the rest of the day canvassing mall businesses situated along exits to the mall, occasionally finding a shopper willing to chat about the shooting. As expected, no one had seen a large black dog in the mall the day of the shooting or since then. Even so, if Bondo bothered to verify what I put in my final report, he would find I had done my due diligence. In spite of all of the roadblocks he had thrown in my path.

It was almost quitting time when I put the final finishes on my half of the report. I had just hit send to PW with a cc to Jenny when the call came announcing that "operation cell phone" had been a success.

What can I say—sometimes a plan goes exactly as planned. In my experience, that's very rare, but in this instance, it did. Of course, Mara took credit for operation cell phone's success, and, since it had been her idea and she was the one who carried it out, I felt she'd earned bragging rights. Although Yuri did a lot of bragging on her behalf, describing in some detail what he had observed.

Mara told us how she had set it all up. She said it was easy to convince four classmates to go with her to the food truck after school. Everyone liked the idea. When they got there, she steered them to a table as far away from the food truck as possible. Fortunately, no one objected. Then she took off her jacket and carefully hung it over the back of her chair. Several other kids also left some article of clothing or a backpack behind. Then, after starting toward the truck with the other kids, Mara explained how she had stopped and said, loudly but not overdoing it, "Just a minute." Then, as she had planned, she turned and went back to the table. In plain sight of anyone who was watching, she slipped her cell phone into her jacket pocket. She said she did it that way so none of her friends blocked the view of her action from any angle. Afterwards, she went to place an order and hang out with the others in front of the truck until their food was ready.

While Mara was with her friends buying snacks, Yuri was keeping watch over her jacket. He said it was only a few minutes before a man casually approached their empty table and knelt down next to Mara's chair as if tying his shoe. While pretending to be reading his email, Yuri aimed his phone in the general direction of the kneeling man. He didn't want to be obvious about taking a picture, aware that the target was glancing around in anticipation of lifting the jacket. Unfortunately, Yuri clicked a shot at the very instant the man chose to stand up. He managed a second shot just as the man grabbed the jacket and quickly made his getaway. It happened so fast Yuri didn't get any other pictures.

Both of Yuri's pictures missed the mark. The first was blurry and off-center. He caught the man's lower body and one of his shoes. The only thing you could make out perfectly was the fact that the man was pantomiming tying a black leather slip-on. The second snapshot captured the empty space next to the chair.

We were all disappointed about the pictures, but everyone still considered operation cell phone a victory for the good guys. No one was hurt. The trap snapped shut on the intended target. And Mara was looking forward to shopping for a new jacket and an upgraded cell phone. "Why not get a new model?" she asked when I challenged whether she needed an upgrade. "And they have some new cool metallic colors." She knew this was one time I couldn't say no, and she intended to take full advantage of the situation.

That evening after dinner, Mara, Mom and I had a conversation about "operation cell phone" while Jason was watching the evening news in the living room. Mom managed to restrain her irritation with me in front of Mara, but I could feel her anger simmering beneath the surface. I had put her granddaughter in danger and let her participate in a sting. Assiduously avoiding looking in my direction, she focused instead on praising her granddaughter for coming up with an ingenious con and for keeping her cool in a tense situation. My turn would come later. Undoubtedly to be followed by a barrage of articles posted on the fridge about the responsibilities of being a parent.

Not that I blamed my mother for being concerned about me being a single mom and having a job that brought a fair amount of uncertainty and disruption as well as intermittent danger into our lives. Although I was happier than I'd been in a long time and loved my job, I frequently questioned whether it was right to put my family at risk to satisfy the Nancy Drew fantasies of my childhood. I was all too aware that there are consequences for every choice made, for good and for bad decisions.

When my husband, Dan, was alive I'd come across something Isadora Duncan had said about marriage: *Any intelligent woman who reads the marriage contract, and then goes into it, deserves all the consequences.* That's how I'd felt at the time, like I should have known what I was getting into when I married Dan and therefore deserved what I got. It wasn't that he was a bad person; he just wasn't a satisfying life partner. Being married to him was like watching a hamster running around and around the same wheel, day after day, never questioning his routine. And always on the run.

To be honest, initially I'd been satisfied with being a stay-at-home mother while he spent most of his time at work. Once the kids were in school, however, I was bored. That's when I decided to finish my degree and fulfill my dream of becoming a college professor. With a PhD, I thought I could have a life of my own while, at the same time, fulfilling my dual roles as wife and mother. I thought that if I had my own career, I wouldn't mind if he spent more time at work than with his family. I thought that it might make me care less that he didn't want to take up any new interests or travel somewhere exotic or add some exciting adventure to a bucket list. And, if Dan hadn't died unexpectedly of a heart attack, leaving us with no life insurance and very little money in reserve, maybe there would have been a "they lived happily ever after" ending. But he died, so I'll never know.

Yes, there are always consequences. And given the way things were going with my job and my life, I was having some serious doubts about whether I could live with the consequences of my current actions. It was becoming increasingly clear to me how *my* choices were impacting my entire family. Maybe my mother was right after all.

CHAPTER 9
WHY?

THE FOLLOWING DAY I had to drag myself into work. Depression hung over me like a gray fog, obscuring even the tiny joys of life. Like the kids getting off to school without a hitch. Lack of traffic on the roads. The sun breaking through the clouds. I had a headache from spending half the night tossing and soul searching. The mall was practically empty, a reminder of what had happened there less than a week ago. The coffee I bought to cheer myself up tasted bitter, like it had been left too long at the bottom of the pot. I discovered a big stain on the front of my jacket, probably coffee, one that would be impossible to hide. And I hadn't bothered to iron my blouse. I had the choice between displaying wrinkles or a giant splotch.

The only thing Mom had said the night before as she headed for her upstairs apartment was, "We'll talk tomorrow." Something definitely to look forward to.

Yuri was already drinking coffee out of his cup with the fornicating penguins cavorting around the base. You had to look carefully to realize you weren't seeing some sort of cartoon characters. Initially I'd thought it was amusing, but today it struck me as repulsively cutesy. I don't care for anything cutesy when I'm in a bad mood.

Blaine wasn't at his desk when I came in, but he appeared in the doorway just as I sat down at my desk. "Cameron, front and center. The others are already in there with PW."

"The others" turned out to be Grant and Adele. When I sat down, they all turned to me with "I'm so sorry for you" stares, like I was an Ebola victim. Maybe they just felt bad about the giant spot on my jacket.

"Adele has made some headway," PW said.

"From the looks on your faces, I take it that it's not good news."

"More like 'ominous.'" She nodded toward Adele. "Tell her what you've learned so far."

Adele adjusted the papers in front of her and frowned at them and then at me. "Your Mr. Bondo is a freelance investigator from DC named Drake Dick. Of DD Consultants." That almost made me smile, almost. When Jenny heard his real name, she was going to flip out.

"It seems he does a lot of work for various government agencies. Just what kind of work isn't entirely clear. He markets himself as an expert in Intelligence and Mediation. There are also references to being a Security Analyst. I suspect he is one of those consultants who asks what needs to be done and then says 'Yes, I can do that for you.' When I started really probing into specific contracts he's had with the government, I ran into some serious firewalls. I immediately backed off."

"Firewalls?"

"He's not your ordinary freelance investigator," Grant explained.

"Like ....?"

"Probably does some dirty work for one or more government agencies is my guess," Grant said

That was consistent with what Gary had told me about what had led up to his problem, but I didn't know how much I should admit. Maybe it didn't matter; we already had enough to worry about.

"Well?" PW said.

"I'm not surprised," I said. "But I'm not sure I understand what this means for us."

"It means we have to be very careful what we're stepping in," Adele said. Her tone sounded accusing to me. I wanted to defend my actions, but I wasn't sure I could. She was right; by agreeing to help Gary, I had brought some very bad people into our otherwise low-key business.

PW was staring at her cigarette, her hands folded on the desk in front of her. Perhaps as a way to prevent herself from finally lighting her lone cigarette. After a few seconds, she looked at us and said, "It is what it is. I know that's a cliché. Unfortunately, I think we have no choice but to act as though we believe Mr. Bondo is who he claims to be. I will forward the report you and Jenny put together, and hopefully he will accept that we were unable to find his beloved Ben and move on."

"What about the woman Mara took a picture of? Do we have anything on her?"

"Not yet," Adele said. "I ran it through a few facial recognition search engines, but nothing came up. We'd have to call in a favor to put it through a more powerful database. Besides, she probably works for DD Consultants. There are no employee pictures or names on their website."

"They have a website?" I asked.

"It provides a veil of legitimacy," Grant said. "It's likely they take on some standard projects as a cover. And maybe so that some of what they earn can be run through a seemingly legitimate source."

"We're going to hold off on looking for her," PW added. "If she's connected to our client, we don't want to call attention to our suspicions."

"My concern at this point is that this Bondo guy could get even more aggressive with Cameron." Grant directed his comment to PW as if Adele and I weren't there.

"From what you've told me, she and the kids have done a good job of deflecting their inquiries." PW turned to me, "What do you think, Cameron? What would you like us to do?"

"If he seems satisfied with our report, I say we let it go."

"You will need to watch your back," Grant said. "Make sure your family stays alert."

"Mara gets it at this point," I said. "We're still soft-pedaling a little with Jason. I'll see that he doesn't go off on his own for a while. Mom will back me up on that. She's more than a little upset about all this. But I think she'll be okay."

"Alright then," PW said. "I'll call our Mr. Bondo today and tell him that we've been unable to find his dog and ask if he wants to receive a paper copy or an online copy of our report. We need to end our association with him while demonstrating that we've made a good-faith effort."

Once back in the pit, Grant asked me to join him in the conference room. "I have a bad feeling about this," he said. "These people are slick. If they don't have any other leads, they might try to lean on you. I want to make sure you don't underestimate what they might do to get you to talk."

"You mean like kidnap one of my kids or threaten my mother? That sort of thing?"

"Yes, *that* sort of thing."

"If he's a freelancer, he doesn't have direct skin in the game, does he? Won't that make him less likely to do something that drastic?"

"Being freelance doesn't make him any less dangerous. And I think you know more than you're saying about what kind of trouble your friend is in. Don't hesitate to ask for help. At the slightest hint of trouble, call me. Got that?"

"Thanks, Grant." I could feel myself getting emotional. Grant and my other colleagues at Penny-wise were each special in their own way and consistently supportive. That meant a lot to me. If there was any way I could rationalize remaining in my job at Penny-wise, I wanted to stay.

I'd barely had time to sit down at my computer before Blaine came to tell Yuri and me that we had a new client, a husband and wife, and PW wanted us in her office to meet them. Yuri had been working solo on an assignment that was winding down, so he was pleased to have a new opportunity. I was pleased too; it was just too bad that I would meet our new clients wearing a jacket with a large spot on it. Maybe if I took a yellow pad in with me I could hide the spot under it. It would be awkward, but it was worth a try.

The man and woman seated across from PW were in their 40s. He was going bald, his high forehead featuring a shiny spot highlighted by the overhead, recessed lighting. He had sad eyes and a pointy chin. He stood up as we entered and reached out to shake hands, first with me, then with Yuri. Even though I'm left-handed, I shake hands with my right. That meant I was able to hold the yellow pad in place with my left hand, keeping the spot out of sight.

The woman remained in her seat, staring down at her lap where her hands were cupped, one on top of the other, as if they were ready to catch something falling from above. Her hair looked permed, and not by an expert. The curls were kinked and held back from her face by matching silver barrettes shaped like dragonflies. Maybe both the perm and the barrettes were a new trend, but I doubted it. When she didn't look up it struck me that she was someone used to having her husband take the lead. Or maybe I was being unfair. Maybe she was simply too upset about whatever they were there to talk with us about to be social. I would know soon enough.

PW said, "Cameron, Yuri—this is Frank and Gwen Goldberg."

Goldberg—the name sounded familiar. Yuri pulled up a couple of chairs from the back of the room so both of us could sit off to the side of PW's desk. Frank turned toward us and nodded, but Gwen continued to look down at her hands.

"These are the two investigators I'm going to assign to your case," PW said to the Goldbergs. "Why don't you tell them what you told me."

Frank cleared his throat. "Our son, Callum, was the only person who died during last Friday's shooting." OMG, I thought, their son's body had been just a few feet away from the young man Gary planted the gun on. I regretted that I hadn't looked over at him and acknowledged the life that had been so abruptly taken away.

"I'm sorry for your loss," I said. It was a perfunctory comment, echoed by Yuri, although it was meant as heartfelt. The words seemed to awaken Gwen Goldberg from her trance, and she looked up at us with round, light-brown eyes. It was as though she had suddenly become aware of our presence. As our eyes met, I had the urge to reach out to put my hand on her arm. But you have to be careful with gestures like that, no matter how well intentioned. Some people do not like to be touched by strangers.

Frank Goldberg patted his wife on the knee and continued speaking. "Callum played basketball in high school." He lowered his voice and added, "Callum loved basketball." Then he paused to regain his composure. "Timothy Lee, the young man who killed the shooter, played for a rival school. The same school the killer attended, I believe. Although according to press coverage, they didn't know each other."

I had been so distracted by what had been happening with my family that I hadn't paid much attention to the bios of the victims. Now it crossed my mind that maybe I should have looked at them more closely.

"I don't think Callum knew him either. At least I don't remember him ever mentioning the name." He took a deep breath. "We are, as you might imagine, devastated. He was our only son. And although there is some satisfaction in knowing the person who shot Callum has received the ultimate punishment, that isn't enough."

Gwen spoke for the first time, her voice soft and scratchy. "We need to know *why*." Then she looked down again, clenching her fingers into two tiny fists, holding tightly to her sorrow and anger.

We all waited for her to say more. When she didn't, her husband said, "We would like to know about the shooter as a person, to perhaps better understand what his life was like. To get past the image of a cold-blooded killer randomly taking the life of our son. It was suggested by our therapist that seeing him as a human being will help us find closure."

"It takes times to find peace with a loved one's death," PW offered.

"We understand. But we need to know more about why he died, why someone came to a public place with the sole purpose of taking the lives of innocent people."

"The police will be searching for motive," Yuri said. "They do a psychological postmortem on shooters; they dig into everything—their childhood, friends, associations, everything." I knew that Yuri, like me, was thinking about all the reasons why we should not take this case.

"We're aware that reporters and police will be all over this, building a profile that they hope fits with the other profiles they've developed over the years. But that's the point. Reporters and police have their own agendas. Reporters want to sell papers. They tend to rush to judgement and sensationalize events like this. They can't take time to reflect, the news has to be in-the-moment. The police also want to act quickly so they can close the case and make the public feel safe again. Maybe some writer will dig deeper into the shooter's psyche in order to include the incident in a book on mass shooters, but that will take time. None of that will help us come to terms with this now."

Frank Goldberg glanced at his wife. "The guy had parents, and a brother. He wasn't born to kill. We want to know how he got there, how he found himself standing in a mall with a gun. I know the police will ask whether anyone saw it coming, but people talk differently to the police than they might to someone representing us. People feel sorry for us. We figure we might as well take advantage of that."

"We need to know why," Gwen repeated.

I was fairly certain the real "why" would not help them find closure; I needed to convince them it wasn't worth pursuing. "Even if people are willing to talk to us, even granting that both reporters and police sometimes rush to conclusions and filter what they find through specific agendas, I'm really not sure we'll be able to discover more about the shooter than they can." I was surprised how matter-of-fact I sounded, while all the time my roiling stomach was warning me that there was a *conflict of interest*. I wondered if PW was as worried as I was about that.

"We understand. But people don't always open up to reporters or cops. They don't necessarily trust them. If you approach people on our behalf, they might tell you things that, oh, I don't know what. We just feel like we owe it to Callum to try to understand why this happened." He paused, then added, "Penny-wise did some work for a friend of ours. She said you were thorough, honest, and, ah, not too expensive."

PW smiled at the couple. "We try to be all of those things. And I understand your desire to learn more about the shooter. But I want to make sure you understand that we won't necessarily find anything that will explain why he chose to come to the mall that day with a gun. Nor why your son was the only one to die." It was a harsh statement delivered with compassion.

They said they understood, and that anything we discovered would be appreciated. Maybe the therapist they had talked to thought it would be good for them to take some action, any action, to feel like they were doing something positive to solve the mystery of their son's death. I could imagine how helpless they must feel standing on the sidelines, waiting to hear from the police. By paying us to take on an investigative role, they could at least count on receiving frequent progress reports.

In spite of having brought Yuri and me in to listen to the Goldbergs' request, I half expected PW to turn them down. Instead, she waited while we asked a few more questions about Callum. Then she handed them off to Blaine to sign our standard fee and expenses agreement.

It's our practice after meeting a new client to go over deliverables, timelines and strategies with PW. She doesn't micromanage, but she likes to make certain we understand what is expected of us. In this instance, I definitely felt we needed some clarity around expectations.

"Are you sure we want to take this on?" Yuri asked as soon as the door closed on the Goldbergs. He usually doesn't question PW's judgment, but he was obviously baffled by her decision to take the case.

"I'm afraid we need to." She glanced at me. "Do you agree, Cameron?"

"What I think you're suggesting is that if we don't take their case, someone else will. But isn't it a classic conflict of interest?"

Yuri jumped in. "Isn't there an ethical issue here, too? In addition to being a potential conflict of interest, we're already withholding information from our clients."

"I agree there are some gray areas here," PW said. "But let me put it in perspective. You will be investigating the shooter, not the shooting. There's a big difference. If you focus on the psychological makeup of the young man and not why he committed this particular crime, you can sidestep the conflict of interest and ethical issues."

"But—" Yuri began.

"No," PW said, "let me continue. I realize Mrs. Goldberg said several times that they want to know 'why,' but again, it's his motivation for *becoming* a killer that they are interested in. They're unaware that there might have been an intended victim other than their son. The fact is that Gabe Miller shot Callum Goldberg. Callum's parents want to try and see Gabe as a person in the hope that it will ease their own pain. Furthermore, Cameron, you don't know for a fact that Gabe intended to kill Gary, do you?"

"No, but—"

"Is there *anything* you're aware of about this assignment that will interfere with the police investigation?"

Yuri and I exchanged looks. "Isn't it my obligation to tell the police what I *think* I know?"

"In my opinion, you are under no legal obligation to go to the police with unsupported theories. If, however, they ask you something directly, you should tell them the truth as you know it." PW looked at Yuri, waiting to see if he was going to push back on her position. When he didn't, she turned back to me. "This is going to be a delicate assignment." She tapped the cigarette in her antique ashtray with two fingers. That told me she knew just how delicate the assignment was. "If at any time you feel you are crossing the line between investigating the shooter and the shooting, back off immediately. Keep in mind, the people behind all this are both unscrupulous and very dangerous. Our goal is simple, to help the Goldbergs find peace. Nothing more."

Maybe not all that simple, I thought. In addition to helping the Goldbergs find peace, I desperately wanted to maintain my distance from whoever was after Gary. And if we started asking questions about the shooter, they might not make the distinction we were making between investigating the shooter rather than the shooting. At the same time, if we let some other agency take the job, we would relinquish control of the inquiry. And that could be equally disastrous.

Delicate, yes. Simple, no.

CHAPTER 10
A NICE GUY

YURI AND I SEQUESTERED ourselves in the closet to brainstorm how we were going to approach our investigation of the shooter for the parents of the victim. Before I could make any suggestions, Yuri glanced at my jacket and asked, "You do know you have a rather large spot, don't you?"

"This splotch, here?" I asked. "Part of the design. It goes with the wrinkles in my blouse."

"I bet Blaine has something that would take it out."

Normally I would have resented fashion advice from Yuri, but if we were going to be interviewing people later, I would need to look more professional. I told him to wait while I went to see Blaine about a spot.

Yuri was scribbling ideas on a yellow pad when I returned wearing a sweater jacket that wasn't a bad fit or match with my pants. "He took one look at my jacket and insisted on sending it out for cleaning. Then he gave me this sweater. It's something PW keeps in her office, in case she gets cold, I assume. Not up to her usual standards."

"It'll do."

"You mean, it will do for someone who isn't a stylish dresser?"

"I feel like any answer I give will be the wrong one. But I think you look better without the spot." I couldn't argue with that.

We would normally approach a request to profile an individual in much the same way the police would—find out who the individual knew and talked to, check out their presence on social media, find out what groups they were affiliated with, run background checks, and talk to neighbors, friends and family members. Sometimes, depending on the age of the individual, we also talked to teachers and classmates. And, if we had access to their electronic devices, which we seldom did, we would search them for information. That is what we would have done if we had been asked to put together a complete profile on an individual. But, given the parameters set for our investigation, we intended to pursue a level of understanding that was more personal than thorough.

In my opinion, there was nothing we could learn that would help the Goldbergs find closure, no matter what their therapist had suggested. Furthermore, I was worried about Mrs. Goldberg's repeated comments about wanting to know "why." I felt like her "why" had to do more with the shooting than the shooter. In fact, I felt like it was a larger existential "why," a quest to understand the whims of the universe in selecting who lives and who dies. Unfortunately, an answer to a question like that was definitely beyond our pay grade.

Setting aside our concerns about the assignment and its potential for going sideways, we began strategizing. We agreed that the Goldbergs were right about people sometimes being reluctant to talk to reporters or police.

We also agreed that working on behalf of the victim's parents would very likely open some doors. Especially since we could truthfully offer assurance that we weren't going to go public with anything they told us. Perhaps most importantly, in our report to the Goldbergs, we needed to package what we learned in a way that would help them feel like they better understood the who and the why.

"Based on what I've read in the newspaper coverage, the shooter was a single, 20-year-old construction worker who liked to hunt and had a closet full of guns in his apartment. He lived in a low-income neighborhood and was described by neighbors as a 'nice guy.'" Yuri rolled his eyes. "How often has that been said about a killer?"

"I thought the pictures of him in the newspapers and on TV made him look like a reject from Duck Dynasty. Wonder how hard they had to look to find those?"

Ignoring my comment, Yuri changed the subject. "The thing I keep coming back to is that Miller must have had a particular skill set if he tailed Gary to the mall without Gary knowing he was there." I couldn't decide if his comment was praise for the shooter's skill or indirect criticism of Gary. Then he added, "Under the circumstances, no matter how good he was, I can't understand why Gary didn't notice he was being followed."

"Keep in mind that he thought he had a head start," I countered, trying not to sound defensive. I did agree, at least in part, with Yuri's assessment, but I still resisted the idea that Miller had managed to outwit Gary.

"Yet somehow Miller caught up with Gary at the mall."

"But not until after he had put Bandit in my car. Otherwise they would have known for sure that I had him."

"That makes the argument for two people being involved, one to follow Gary from the airplane and one to take him out."

"That makes sense, especially if Gary was right about him being a disposable asset. They could have considered it a longshot but worth a try."

"What bothers me is that there was no way they could have known Gary would try to get Bandit to you. Even with a tag team that wouldn't have given them much time to set up the hit."

"Well, it wasn't as if it was a smoothly executed plan. They were lucky Miller didn't survive."

"Maybe Gary's right," Yuri said. "Miller was a 'disposable.' Maybe someone was waiting to take him out if he somehow managed to get away."

"If you think about it, burying Gary's death in what appeared to be a random mall shooting was a smart move. Shooter kills Gary. Then someone kills the shooter. Then .... who knows? The more degrees of separation, the harder it is to trace the source, the people who wanted Gary out of the picture."

Yuri took off his glasses, gripped one side of the frame between two fingers, and twirled them around several times. "I wonder if we could get a look at the mall camera footage."

"That doesn't seem like something you'd do if your goal was to develop a personality profile of the killer, does it?"

"You're right." He put on his glasses and held his pen over the yellow pad I'd put down on the table. "So, we begin with the usual: talk to parents, friends, and neighbors."

"I say we also talk to a couple of reporters covering the case. They would undoubtedly be sympathetic to the parents of the victim. They might share something that didn't find its way into the media."

"There may be a good-looking male police officer who might open up to you. Maybe that Detective Connolly from Major Crimes? I seem to remember you thought he had nice eyes? What do you say? Maybe you'd get a date out of it."

"How about you talking to a female police officer?"

"Ouch, that's sexist."

"No kidding."

"Okay, after we talk to some of the more obvious sources, if we feel like we need more data, let's figure out who's working the case and decide which of us would be the best for the approach. Based solely on an astute personality assessment, of course."

I glared at him, but I knew he was right. There are times when you have to set aside your beliefs and go with what works. "We also need to review the online stories and interviews with people there that day or people who knew the shooter. We can either site them as sources or follow up on our own."

"I have a friend at a local TV station I could call."

"Is she good looking?" Yuri ignored my comment, so I let it drop. "If we do all of this, it would take more time than I think we should be putting on their tab."

"I agree. Let's prioritize and do what we can do from the office first."

Yuri got a cup of coffee and began making calls. He was supposed to get in touch with his TV acquaintance and see what she could tell him about Miller and ask who she would suggest we talk to. I wasn't at all surprised that particular call had made the top of his priority list. His female reporter friend was next. They were both good sources though, so I wasn't complaining. Then he was also going to see if he could arrange a meeting for the two of us with Miller's parents.

Meanwhile, I was to do a background check on Miller and compile names and information on his parents' neighbors. It was always helpful to know in advance who you were dealing with.

It was 12:15 when Yuri came over to my desk and said, "Let's go. We'll just have enough time to grab something to eat before our meeting with Miller's parents."

I grabbed my purse and off we went. Yuri has a dark green Volvo station wagon that he claims is a classic; to me it's just old. But it isn't the car that's the problem—Yuri is a terrible driver. Sometimes I am brave enough to let him drive, or foolish enough. Today I was thinking about Gary and Bandit and all of the unknowns associated with Gary's predicament and agreed he could drive before I was totally aware of what I had done. As I was getting into the Volvo, I noticed that the mirror on the passenger side had duct tape wrapped around it. As if it had been knocked off, and he'd repaired it by taping it in place. It was a bit cockeyed.

"You can see out of your side mirror, can't you?" I asked as we got under way.

"Sure."

"You *do* use your side mirrors, don't you?" I knew I shouldn't ask. And I knew I shouldn't have agreed to let him drive.

"Where do you want to stop for lunch? There's a Pho shop at a strip mall on our way."

"Sounds good to me. So tell me, how did it happen?" It was more of a glutton-for-punishment question than an expectation that there might be a reasonable explanation.

"What?"

"The mirror. Did you have a duel with another car?"

"Oh, I bumped a column in an underground parking lot." He sounded like it was something everyone does on a regular basis.

"Like a cement column?"

"Yeah. It was nothing."

"Well, obviously it was something. And you really should get it fixed. You could get a ticket."

"Really? You think they would stop me for that?"

No, I was thinking, they will stop you for erratic driving and add that to your other crimes. But I kept my mouth shut. For his birthday everyone had pitched in to get him a gift certificate for a safe-driving course. When he unfolded the certificate and read what it said, his only comment was, "Very funny." Grant had urged him to take advantage of it, explaining that taking the course would lower his insurance rates. I hadn't followed up to see whether he had done the course or not. The damaged mirror suggested he hadn't.

To prove he had either tossed the gift certificate or lost it amidst the pile of paperwork on his desk, he suddenly slammed on the brakes as the stoplight ahead turned red. He'd just stepped on the gas, miscalculating what it would take to get through the intersection before the light turned. The car skidded a few feet into the intersection, breaks squealing. "Sorry—I was distracted."

I had to bite my tongue to keep from pointing out that he was often distracted while driving; that was the problem. He would tap the gas to the beat of the music he was playing or turn almost completely sideways to talk to the person in the passenger seat. Or he would suddenly slow down to get a better look at something alongside the road or in a store window. And he was usually oblivious to the cars behind him, unless he was looking out for a tail. I knew these things and still let him drive. You need to take responsibility for the consequences of your actions, I reminded myself. I just hoped he didn't find another cement pillar to run into on my side of the car.

As we sat down with our bowls of vegetarian Pho, Yuri said, "Just don't spill any on PW's sweater." I knew he was giving me a bad time and didn't bother commenting, although I admit to being nervous about the possibility. While we slurped noodles and broth, we compared notes on what we had learned so far. It wasn't much. Neither of Yuri's sources had provided new leads, and nothing unusual had popped up on the background check I had done. I asked Yuri what he knew about Miller's parents and how he had convinced them to talk to us.

"I don't know much. They are in their early 50s. He's a car mechanic. She works in the office at the same car repair shop where he works. They have one other son who is in the army, stationed in Afghanistan."

"Maybe his father can fix your mirror," I said, kiddingly.

Yuri ignored my comment. "What I told Mrs. Miller when we talked was that we were hired by the Goldbergs to put together a more sympathetic picture of their son than was being portrayed in the papers and on TV. I explained that the Goldbergs were hoping to find it in their hearts to forgive Gabe for the life he had taken and that they felt learning more about their son might help them do that."

"If I were them, I'd be worried we were gathering information to use in a lawsuit."

"She sounded like a nice person."

"Oh? Not-so-nice people are the skeptical ones, huh?"

"That's not what I meant. Hey, we shouldn't be arguing about this. We're on the same side."

"I know. Sorry. Obviously, I'm a bit stressed by all of this."

Yuri reached across the table to put his hand on mine and accidentally knocked over my water glass. I jumped up as water slipped over the edge into my lap. "Oh no," he said. "I'm so sorry." Still mumbling apologies, he rushed off to get more napkins.

Once we had cleaned up the mess, and I had sopped up enough of the spilled water to not look like I had wet my pants—the sweater was, thankfully, unharmed—we headed for the Miller residence. According to their tax records, the Millers had owned the house for twenty-five years, so it was probably the house Gabe had grown up in. The neighbors I'd researched spanned several generations. Quite a few had lived there for a long time. It was a nice location, if not a particularly upscale neighborhood. For younger residents it was likely a first home, a stepping stone to something better once they could afford to move on.

The neighborhood consisted of older homes that all looked alike. Probably built around the same time. The Millers' house was in the middle of the block, a one-story, square house painted in off-white. There were cobalt blue faux shudders on the 3 windows facing the street. The door was painted a matching cobalt blue. There weren't many ornamental plants or flowers, but the lawn was mowed. A nicely shaped dogwood tree that was just starting to blossom dominated the area off to our right next to a row of rhododendrons. These were people who might not have much money, but they cared about appearances.

Yuri pulled into a space in front of their place, the right front tire of the Volvo climbing the curb. The gate in the low fence that surrounded their front yard was open. We followed the narrow cement walkway up to the three cement steps that led to a tiny landing. There was so little overhang that I couldn't imagine it would offer any shelter when it was raining. A lot of older houses seemed to have been built like that. Maybe it didn't used to rain as much. Then again, men used to wear hats and women carried umbrellas. So why not save a little money on a front porch?

The Millers must have been waiting for us to arrive. They responded immediately, ushered us inside and offered us coffee. Yuri accepted for us, readily adapting to the Millers' friendly hospitality. As if we were welcome guests rather than two investigators who had come to talk about their murderous son. The whole set-up made me uncomfortable. The Millers might behave as if everything was normal, but that didn't change the fact that their son was not only a disturbed young man but possibly a paid assassin. An assassin who had tried to shoot a friend of mine and had instead killed an innocent bystander.

"Is that a picture of Gabe?" Yuri asked as Mrs. Miller put a cup of coffee on a coaster on the low wood coffee table in front of the overstuffed couch where we were seated. He was pointing to a framed photo on the wall of a young man in waders proudly displaying a large trout. Next to it was another photo of the same young man holding up a pair of antlers. In both photos he was smiling for the camera.

"Yes," Mrs. Miller replied. "Gabe loves fishing and hunting, any excuse to get out of doors."

"That's 'loved,' past tense," Mr. Miller corrected his wife. "They're using that against him, you know. Reporters think that anyone who owns a gun is somehow suspect."

I hesitated to point out that their son had apparently had an arsenal in his apartment and that he had gone to a mall and shot at people. *That* set him apart from your average male who liked to hunt. Before I could say the wrong thing in response, Yuri jumped in again and said: "It's our constitutional right to own a gun."

The Millers both nodded vigorously in agreement. I didn't disagree, but I wasn't feeling the love the way the three of them seemed to be.

"That's a picture of him with his older brother," Mrs. Miller said, pointing at another picture on the wall. The older brother was wearing an army uniform, his arm around Gabe's shoulders. "Gabe idolized him," she added.

"The papers described your son as a loner; is that how you would describe him?" I asked.

Yuri gently kicked my ankle. I was apparently jumping into our reason for being there a little too quickly, not respecting the need for chitchat to create a bond first. But the Millers were prepared for the question.

"They imply that because he didn't socialize a lot that he wasn't normal." Mrs. Miller dabbed at her eyes with a Kleenex.

"I'm sure that's not how his friends saw him," I said, trying to show Yuri that I, too, could suck up. "We would like to talk to a few of his friends if we could, to get a better picture of what he was like from a peer's perspective. Can you give us some names?"

"He moved out about a year ago," his father said. "I'm not sure who his current friends were."

Maybe I was hung up on the loner stereotype, but I couldn't let it go that easily. "What about former high school buddies. Any of them we should talk to?" Yuri kicked me again.

Mr. Miller frowned. "I'm not sure."

"There's nothing wrong with not being a party guy," Yuri said, easing the awkwardness of the moment. "I'm not much of a party goer either."

"Gabe always preferred doing things on his own," his mother said. "Or with family members."

"Did you take your two sons fishing and hunting?" Yuri asked Mr. Miller. I noticed he didn't look at Mrs. Miller when he asked the question. I could picture the three "boys" out doing male things while mom stayed home baking cookies.

"Yes, we did both lake and stream fishing. And we never missed a deer or elk season opening. It was a family tradition." Probably a *male* family tradition, I thought. Mrs. Miller's part had most likely been to cook what they brought back from the hunt. Like early caveman society.

"Elk meat is one of my favorites," Yuri said. I didn't remember him ever mentioning that before. He was going full macho on me. Next, he would be referring to the taxidermy in his man cave.

"I have a great recipe for elk jerky if you'd like it," Mrs. Miller offered.

"That would be wonderful. Let me give you my email address." Yuri took out a card and handed it to her.

She studied his card and said, "I've seen your storefront in the mall. It's right near where . . ." Her voice wavered and seemed to dry up before she could complete her thought.

"I was there that day. It was tragic. But he's still your son, and you knew him better than anyone." Yuri's comment was matter-of-fact, gently easing into the conversation we were hoping to have with the Millers.

"Everyone asks, but we have no idea why he did it," Mrs. Miller said, practically shredding the Kleenex she had used to wipe her eyes. "He didn't drink much or take drugs. He wasn't a gang member. He wasn't into violent online games." She paused. "And he has always been good to us."

Mr. Miller nodded. "Police and reporters wanted to know if we anticipated this was going to happen. Do they think we wouldn't have tried to stop him if we'd known?"

Redirecting the conversation, I asked, "I understand he worked in construction. Did he like his job? Was he having any problems at work? Stress can do strange things to people." There, Yuri, see—I can offer up excuses for a killing spree, too.

"He never complained to us about anything wrong at work." Mr. Miller got up, went over to a table and came back with an advertisement for a building project. "He was working on this. Proud of being a part of it. And he was making good money. That's why he was able to get an apartment on his own."

"Anyone he worked with that you think we should talk to?" Yuri asked.

"He talked about the work but not the people he worked with. Sorry."

"Did he have a girlfriend?" I asked.

Mrs. Miller frowned. "I kept hoping. But no, there was no one special in his life."

"He hadn't broken up with anyone recently? That can be upsetting."

"No."

"Did he have a pet?" That seemed like something that might soften his image for the Goldbergs. Unless it was a hunting dog.

"No, he was never much interested in pets."

"What about school. Did he have any favorite subjects or teachers?" Yuri was kicking me again, more vigorously. Maybe I sounded like I was trying to interrogate them. That wasn't what I intended, but none of our questions were encouraging discussion. It was starting to feel as though the Millers didn't know much about their son's life.

They looked at each other before shaking their heads in the negative.

We chatted about a few random things. I kept trying to build a picture of his life before the shooting by bringing up topics related to how he might have spent his leisure time. What movies he liked—they didn't know. What TV shows he liked—they didn't know. Where he shopped for clothes—they didn't know. Which restaurants or bars he went to—they didn't know.

I exhausted my list of questions and turned to Yuri to wrap things up. He asked if there was anything else that they wanted to share with us that might be of interest to the Goldbergs.

"He was a good kid," Mr. Miller said. "He never caused us any problems when he was young. His older brother on the other hand— One fight after another. That's why we encouraged him to join the army to get his GED and some job training. But Gabe, never a moment's worry."

Back in the car, Yuri summarized what we'd learned: "No friends, no girlfriend, no pets, no membership in any groups, and no problems .... just one lonely guy who was good to his parents, looked up to his brother, and liked to hunt and fish."

"Well, he didn't decide to shoot Gary on his own. Someone hired him. The question is how they managed to find him. According to one newspaper article I read, he didn't have an online presence. I still tried looking, but couldn't find anything. That doesn't mean he didn't troll some sites or groups. Maybe he saw an ad for mercenary work or private soldiering and thought, 'Hey, I'm good with a gun.'"

"Remember," Yuri said, "we're looking at the shooter, not the shooting. Figuring out if he was acting on his own falls outside of that stricture. Our clients want to know about his softer side. So far, the only positive things we've learned are that he was good to his parents and was fond of his brother. That's not much of a start."

CHAPTER 11
50 SHADES OF ANONYMITY

YURI STARTED HIS CAR, then switched off the engine. "Since we're already here…"

"Isn't that a bit tacky?" I knew what he was going to suggest because I'd had the same thought.

"They're going to know we talked to their neighbors whether we do it now or later. Remind me what you found out about them."

I got out my notes. "Quite a few are older, own their own homes, have lived in the neighborhood for years. Only a few houses have changed hands recently."

"So, there are at least some who would have known Gabe when he was growing up."

"Yes. But only one or two seem to be the right age group for having kids who Gabe might have played with. The newcomers probably won't have a lot to say about him. In general, nothing unusual popped up. No arrest records or sexual predators or drug busts. Just your average, lower-income neighborhood."

I glanced out the window at the Millers' home. The curtains were pulled shut in all of the front windows. Maybe they wouldn't even see us talking to their neighbors.

Although Yuri's car was right out front. Still, he was right; we had to do it sometime. "Let's do it," I said, handing Yuri a map of the neighborhood on which I'd marked the names of the neighbors on both sides of the street. "There may be more we should talk to around the other side of the block, but this might do it."

"Looks like enough of a sampling. We can always add some if we don't get enough information."

Back on the sidewalk, I said, "You go right, and I'll go left? When we get to the last house on the block, let's cross the street and work our way towards the middle, until we meet up."

"Sounds good. I'm thinking it's best not to go inside anyone's home, even if they ask you to. Takes too much time. Just ask a few questions and move on. Okay? This shouldn't take more than a half hour tops." He headed off to the left. I almost yelled at him that the plan was for me to go left, but it had been a random choice anyway.

The houses on both sides of the street looked like they'd all started out as boxy structures. Over the years, some owners had built additions and, from the look of things, they'd not always hired professionals. One had a slope-roofed sunroom off to one side. Another had an enclosed front porch with siding that didn't match the rest of the house. Still another had what appeared to be a garage or workshop dropped into a space between two trees. Unlike the house, there was no moss on the roof of the newer structure.

The house next door to the Millers badly needed paint, but the yard was filled with spring flowers and potted plants. There was a gnome with a chipped beard next to the front steps. As I was about to knock, I saw a woman peek out from behind a lace curtain. I waved to let her know she'd been caught. Then I knocked politely.

She opened the door about two inches. She was either short or bending over. All I could see was one eye peering out from under a patch of curly white hair.

"Mrs. Hillier? Hi. My name is Cameron Chandler. I'm with Penny-wise investigations." I poked a card at her through the narrow opening. "I just have a couple of questions about your neighbor's son, Gabe."

"I've already talked to the police." Her voice was firm, but she didn't shut the door.

"I'm not involved in the criminal investigation. We're putting together a profile of Gabe for the parents of the young man who died. We're trying to get a feel for what happened to make a normal, friendly young man do something like he did."

"Normal? Friendly? Where did you get that idea?" The door opened a bit wider. I could see most of her face now, but I was still looking at the top of her head. At five foot ten, I'm taller than most women, but she was a good seven inches shorter than me. I resisted scrunching down so as not to tower over her. It's a difficult stance to hold for any length of time.

"In the newspapers, they said neighbors described him as a 'nice guy.'" I stopped talking, hoping she would take it from there. She hardly missed a beat before giving me an earful.

"He used to torment my cat, pull its tail, chase it around. One time he took her up on the roof and dropped her. Said he wanted to see if she would land on her feet. She had a limp after that."

"I'm sorry. Did he dislike cats? Or your cat in particular?" Or was he simply a nasty little boy?

"Whatever. But he was old enough to know better. He called me an old bat one time when I complained to him about what he was doing to my cat."

"Kids are sometimes like that," I said. At the same time, I was thinking that if either of my kids were caught tormenting an animal they would be grounded for months, maybe years, and definitely sent to a therapist.

"Well, my kids were never like that and my grandkids certainly aren't like that now. And they"—she pointed at the Millers' house—"they should have disciplined him instead of letting him run wild."

"Was he part of a gang of neighborhood kids?"

"No, that's not what I meant. I seldom saw him with other kids. I don't think he was well liked."

"What about lately? I understand he moved out about a year ago."

"I think he visited his parents from time to time, but I didn't talk to him."

"I take it you aren't particularly fond of the Millers in general."

"They're okay. They keep to themselves."

"Anything else you think I should know about Gabe?"

"I guess just that I wasn't surprised to read about what he did."

I waited a moment to see if she would add anything. When she didn't, I said, "Well, thank you for your time. And if you think of anything else, give me a call."

At the next house, no one answered. There were no lights on inside and no cars in the driveway. I made a note on my map to remind myself I didn't talk to anyone at this address and moved on.

The last house on that side of the street had a fenced in yard with two dogs who immediately came running over to greet me. Or attack me. It was hard to tell which. All I knew was that they were making a lot of racket and didn't look all that friendly. The house belonged to a couple who had owned it for twenty-two years, so it was likely they had some impressions of Gabe. I was trying to decide how to get their attention without going inside the fence when a man stepped out onto the front porch and yelled at his dogs to shut up. To my surprise, they immediately quit barking and moved away from the gate.

"Mr. Allen?" I called.

"Who's askin'?"

"Is it okay if I come up to your porch to talk to you?" It wouldn't be a very effective interview if we had to shout back and forth.

"You trying to sell something?"

"No, I'm a private investigator." Sometimes people find that intriguing, but not always. In this case it was enough to get me an entry ticket. He waved me in. The dogs watched as I opened the gate and started toward the house. I kept an eye on them, fearing they might make a flank attack.

"They won't bite. Just make a lot of noise." I wanted to believe him, but the larger of the two dogs was crouched down, his tail motionless, his lips pulled back in what didn't look like a smile. The second dog was standing just behind his friend, waiting for his cue.

"I just have a couple of questions," I said, hurrying to the top of the steps. Then I gave him my opening spiel and handed him a card. He didn't react negatively to the "nice guy" label. Instead, he said,

"He was okay. Kinda quiet. I went hunting with him and his dad a couple of times."

"So you know the family?"

"Not that well."

"But you knew Gabe as a kid. What was he like back then?"

The man thought about my question before replying. "Can't say that he was a happy kid. Kind of a misfit, you know? But not exactly a weirdo. Didn't play sports. Didn't seem to have a lot of friends coming and going. But I never heard of him getting into any trouble."

"Did it surprise you when you read about what he did?"

"I have to admit that it did. But they say it's always the quiet ones, don't they?"

I pressed for more observations about Gabe when he was younger as well as anything he'd noticed more recently, but I had apparently drained the well in a very short time. I thanked him and turned to leave, wondering if I could make it back to the sidewalk in one piece. The dogs watched as I came down the steps. When I heard the door on the house shut and realized it was just them and me, I thought for sure they would take that as a sign their owner was saying I was fair game. They fell in behind me as I passed by but didn't bark. My hand shook as I opened the gate and stepped through. Once safely on the other side it was all I could do to keep myself from slamming the gate shut and shouting *neener-neener*. But then I wasn't entirely sure the dogs weren't capable of jumping the fence. It seemed like the wise thing to do was to make tracks.

As I crossed to the other side of the street, I looked around for Yuri. He had already crossed over and was talking to a woman at the first house on the opposite corner from where I stood. He was gesturing with his hands, like they were having a lively conversation.

No one responded when I rang the doorbell next to the bright red door at the corner house, although there was a light on inside, and I thought I could hear someone moving about. Glancing at my map I noted the house belonged to a couple who had moved in three years ago. I was sorry I had tried the doorbell because I hadn't heard it ring inside, and I didn't want to be pushy by knocking if it they were deliberately ignoring me. On the other hand, I felt like I had to try, just in case the doorbell was inoperable, so I rapped a few times. I could almost feel the residents inside trying to be quiet, hoping I would go away. So I did.

A young boy came to the door of the next house and announced that his mother was taking a shower. I asked if he knew Gabe Miller and he said he didn't. I thanked him and moved on.

Yuri was approaching the house just to the other side of the one I was about to call on. I glanced at my watch. It had been exactly 22 minutes since we started canvassing the neighborhood. Yuri's estimate of how long it would take was right on.

The walkway leading to the door of the last house on our list was lined with plastic flower pots. Some contained spring flowers; others were lying empty next to a flower already in the ground. It was a project in process. I glanced at my map. The house belonged to another couple who had lived in the neighborhood for a long time. I hoped they had something helpful to say. I didn't feel I had much to show for what I'd done so far.

When I knocked, I heard a male voice yell for someone to answer the door. Moments later, a middle-aged woman in jeans and a navy-blue sweatshirt opened the door and said, "Yes?" Her tone spoke louder than her words. It was clear she meant "What do you want?" I explained and handed her a card. She studied it a moment, then asked, "You really a PI?"

"Yes, I am. Do you have a few minutes to answer a couple of questions?"

"Do you like being a PI?"

"Yes, it's an interesting job. Lots of variety." Before I could change the topic, she hit me with still another question.

"Did you have to go to school?"

"No, I got on-the-job training, but there are programs you can take." I wanted to tell her I wasn't a career counselor and had a job to do. Yuri picked that moment to join us.

"Hi," he said, holding out his hand. "I'm Yuri Webster, Cameron's colleague. Sorry to interrupt, but this is the last house on our list."

"Our house is on your *list*?" It was clear she didn't want to be on anyone's list, no matter what it was about.

A man came up behind the woman and glared at us. "What can we do for you?" he said. Again, the tone was much less polite than the words. I repeated my explanation while Yuri nodded in agreement.

"Can I have your card?" the woman asked Yuri. He handed her one. Before she could start quizzing him on the PI profession, I asked the "nice guy" question.

"That's not how I would describe him," she said.

"How *would* you describe him then?"

"Our son was a year ahead of him in school. He thought Gabe was a loser. You know, didn't participate in activities, not one of the popular kids. The kind of boy that didn't have anything but his major under his picture in the high school annual."

"Did you see him around the neighborhood with other kids?"

"No, he was usually alone."

"Did you ever talk with him?"

"No reason to."

"Was he a troublemaker?" Yuri asked.

They looked at each other, then shook their heads, no.

"Is there anything you think we should know about him?"

Again, they shook their heads, no. The interview obviously wasn't going anywhere. We thanked them for their time and headed back to the car. It was almost rush hour. I was wondering whether I should suggest we avoid the freeway or hope that good karma would keep us safe.

"Learn anything worthwhile?" I asked when we got underway. Yuri animatedly began summarizing what he had learned. I was sorry I'd asked. I listened, trying to stay alert to what was happening around us. Just in case I'd have time to warn him and avert disaster.

Basically, the neighbors had told him the same stuff they'd told me. As a youngster Gabe didn't seem to have any friends, but he'd never been in trouble with the law as far as anyone knew. On the one hand, no one had anything positive to say about him. Except for the woman whose cat he tormented, no one had anything particularly negative to say about him either. He'd been a sleeper. No one had anticipated he would make the front page as a mass shooter.

I continued to struggle with conflicting thoughts about my responsibility to "tell the truth" versus keeping my promise to Gary. From Gabe's parents' perspective, for instance, would they rather think of their son as someone who flipped out and shot innocent people for some unknown reason or would they prefer to know he may have been an assassin for hire? Either way, he would be condemned for what he had done. We were skirting the line between what was ethical and what wasn't. Still, I couldn't think of anything positive that would come from telling the truth, other than easing my own guilt.

By some miracle, we made it back to the office without running off the road or colliding with another car. There were a few times when a chorus of honks should have made Yuri pay more attention to his driving and less to his analysis of what we'd learned from the Millers and their neighbors, but he remained blissfully oblivious. By the time he pulled into the parking lot at the mall, I was experiencing a borderline panic attack and the side mirror on his car had slipped down another inch.

That evening, my mother went out to dinner with friends, so the kids and I were left to fend for ourselves. "I want pizza," Jason announced. I was about to point out that we'd had pizza recently, but Mara agreed with him before I could say anything. Then the fight began as to what toppings to order.

"Half and half," I said. "Like we always do." I could have added "after you two fight about it for 20 minutes." That was another thing they "always" did. But not tonight; I was too tired and too hungry.

Mara asked to use my cell and called in our order with Jason pointedly listening to make sure she didn't cheat.

"I'll make a salad to go with it," I said.

"No mushrooms," Jason said.

"Don't be weird," Mara said. Then, "I'll help." Apparently, my mother was doing a good job training Mara to be a cook's assistant. That was one thing I couldn't complain about.

"Want to join us, Jason? As you may already know, more than three-quarters of chefs are male." Although he has a fondness for statistics, I doubted this particular fact would impress him, but it was worth a try.

"Nah. But can we have ice cream for dessert?" We had been eating a lot of my mother's healthy food of late, so I didn't hesitate. Ice cream sounded like an excellent idea.

The pizza arrived in record time. Our dinner conversation started with Mara showing me pictures of fancy cell phones she thought would be perfect for her.

"What happened to yours?" Jason asked.

"Lost it. But it was due for an upgrade anyway."

I agreed to let her make an online order if she okayed it with me first. She nodded, then added that there was something else she wanted too. Hint, hint. A new jacket. "Just check with me first," I said. Too bad I couldn't put in a reimbursement request for 'operation cell phone' expenses.

While we ate, I told them that Yuri and I had visited the Millers and their neighbors. I asked what they thought *our* neighbors would say about the two of them if someone went around and asked.

"There aren't any kids our age in the neighborhood," Jason pointed out. "So, I don't really know any of our neighbors, except to say hi. But I like the guy in the brown house. The one with the apple tree in his front yard. He lets me have as many apples as I want."

"Do you talk with him while you're scarfing down his apples?" I was curious.

"Not a lot. He sometimes asks about school, if I like sports, that sort of thing."

"Do you tell him that all you do is watch the news?" Mara asked.

"There's nothing wrong with taking an interest in what's going on in the world," Jason said, sounding like a combatant who was ready to fight to the finish to defend his position.

"Mara," I interrupted. "Do *you* have a favorite neighbor?"

Reluctantly she let her attack on Jason's obsession with the news slide. "I like Mrs. Franklin. She's nice."

"Mrs. Franklin?" I realized I didn't know any of our neighbors by name. In fact, I not only couldn't name them, I wasn't even sure I could pick them out of a lineup.

"She lives in the house with all of the flowers in her yard. You know, three houses west of us."

I had a vague recollection of passing a house with a color-filled yard. "Yeah, I know the one."

"She lets me help her in the yard when she's planting flowers."

Lets me help her—had I heard that correctly? Was this my daughter who had to be ordered to clean up her room and refused to do any work in *our* yard? The same daughter who complained when I didn't do her laundry in a timely fashion but wouldn't do it for herself? The same daughter who … I could go on and on. Apparently, I had a lot to learn from Mrs. Franklin and my own mother about motivating my daughter to do anything she could label as "work."

"Okay, so how would these two neighbors describe each of you?"

"Mrs. Franklin would say I was polite and hard working."

"The man with the apple tree would say I liked apples."

"That's it? You like apples?"

"And I'm not into sports."

"Grandma talks to the neighbors," Mara offered. "She likes one of the ladies next door. The one in the ground floor apartment on this side of the house." Then she turned the tables on me and asked, "What would they say about *you*?" It was a fair question, but one that was hard to answer.

"That I have two attractive kids and a black and white dog that needs to be trained not to jump up on people."

"Maybe you'll meet more neighbors now that we have a dog," Jason said, ignoring my comment about our dog's behavior.

"You mean *you* will meet more of them while *you* are walking No-name. Speaking of which, have you decided on a name yet?"

"I'm thinking of calling him Crusher. Or Fang."

"No!" Mara protested. I let them argue about it for a few minutes. I kept quiet partly because I didn't want to tell Jason that I thought those were terrible names for a dog who immediately rolled over when confronted by Bandit, aka Duffy. Nor was I sure he was seriously considering those names; he might just have been trying to get a rise out of his sister for implying that his affinity for news was somehow strange for a boy his age.

Jason suddenly lost interest in fighting with his sister and turned back to me. "What did the shooter's neighbors tell you about him? They said on the news that he fit the profile, you know—a loner with a gun collection and kinda unstable."

Although I wasn't supposed to share work information with my kids, I was the one who had brought up the subject. And I sensed our discussion about our own neighbors had been a learning moment. For them, and for me. I couldn't see how adding a few details about what we had learned about Gabe from his neighbors could hurt.

"The main thing we discovered is that no one knew him very well. Even though some of the neighbors had lived there for most of his life. They knew that he liked to hunt and fish with his father and brother. They knew that he moved out about a year ago but continued to visit his parents on a regular basis. And most of them were surprised at what happened."

"He sounds normal enough," Mara said. "Even if he wasn't very social, what does that really mean?"

"It's hard to say. We're hoping we'll learn something useful from the people we're going to talk to tomorrow."

No-name suddenly yowled, either announcing he was bored with our conversation or making a comment about the state of the world.

"Quiet, Fang," Jason said. No-name yowled again.

"Not Fang," I said. I didn't want to be on our front porch shouting for Fang to come home. That would make quite an impression on our neighbors. “He shall remain No-name until we can all agree on a name. For now, I suggest we call it a night and sleep on it.”

CHAPTER 12
GROUND RULES

HOW MOM KNEW the kids had gone to bed and that I was still up, I have no idea. But the instant I thought I was going to be able to finally have a little time to myself, Mom appeared with a bottle of wine.

"How about a glass of merlot?" She headed to the cabinet containing our wine glasses. Apparently, "no thanks" wasn't an option.

"What's the occasion?"

"I mentioned yesterday that we needed to talk. Well, this is a good time, isn't it?"

"As good as any," I conceded. Although the last thing I wanted to do was talk to my mother about her grievances with me, if there was going to be an eventual confrontation, putting it off a day wasn't going to make it any easier.

Mom poured two generous glasses of wine and set one down in front of me. It looked like it wasn't going to be a short exchange. Or else she thought we both needed a mega amount of fortification for what was about to take place.

"You need to know that I've been giving this some thought," I said.

"You don't know what I'm going to say,"Mom countered.

"No, but I can guess."

"Well, let me admit that I, too, have been giving *this* some thought." An experienced fencer deftly dodging a feint. I couldn't help but smile.

"Should we identify *this* or continue our conversation based on vague references? And do I need to call my lawyer?"

"You have a lawyer?"

"No, but I could find one in the yellow pages."

"Cameron, I don't think they have 'yellow pages' anymore. But if you want a lawyer, try to find an attractive, single male."Then she smiled, a wide, warm smile. "Truce?"

"Truce." I had no idea what I was agreeing to, but a genuine smile is a trustworthy equivalent of a white flag in my opinion. And it sure beat a yell to *Charge!*

"There are times when I've been hard on you," Mom said after taking a sip of wine. "I'm aware of that. But I assume you know I only have your best interests at heart."

"I understand. Still, we may not always agree on what's best for me."

"That's obvious. Otherwise, you would be a professor rather than a PI."

"That's what *this* is about, isn't it?"

"I admit that I've been upset about my grandchildren becoming targets in one of your, ah, situations."

"That has upset me, too." Having just conceded a key point, I knew deep down that this was a dispute I had little chance of winning.

"If this were the first time, I might be able to ignore what happened, but this is beginning to look like a pattern."

Another fact I couldn't contest.

"I know they are at risk each time they get in a car or cross the street or even when they are simply sitting in a classroom. I understand that. And I worry whenever they are out of sight. But those are things over which I have little or no control."

She was covering the same ground I had struggled with in my own mind, weighing the same risks, balancing pros and cons. I could feel my world shrinking, the doors of opportunity slamming shut on my newfound happiness. How could I possibly defend myself when it wasn't just about me?

"I know you weren't happy with Dan," she said, abruptly changing direction.

My eyes widened in surprise. "You knew?"

"It was obvious. At the time I forgave him his obsession with work because I thought he was doing what a good provider needed to do. Then, when he left you almost penniless, well, I don't understand how that happened." She paused. "You've never told me." She paused again.

"I guess I was too stunned and embarrassed to want to talk about it. The bottom line was that he was an addict."

"Drugs?" Mom looked shocked.

"No, that's something I think I would have noticed. He was addicted to a form of gambling—he played the stock market. And he was not only unlucky, he was incompetent."

"Well—" For once she was speechless.

"You never asked."

"I didn't want to pry."

"After it happened, well, I felt like I should have known. I should have kept an eye on our finances. If not for me, for the kids. But I'd trusted him."

After a brief silence, my Mom said, "Your father wasn't perfect either." She took a sip of wine and added, "But that's a discussion for another time."

I was dying to know what she meant by that comment, but I wanted to get on with our talk about *my* situation even more.

Mom took a long drink, almost draining her glass. "What I want to tell you is that I support your decision to work for Penny-wise as a private investigator."

I almost dropped my glass. "You what?!"

"I'm not saying it's what I would have chosen for you, but I can see how much it means to you. And the people you work with appear to be competent and caring. It's rare to find that combination in a workplace."

To my surprise, I tried but failed to choke back a sob. My mother reached into her pocket and handed me a Kleenex. "I didn't think my support would make you sad. Or are these tears of joy?"

"It's just that, well, since this thing with Gary happened, I've been questioning whether it's fair to you and the kids to continue doing a job that is sometimes dangerous."

"You do realize that Mara and Jason don't understand the risks involved. They see what you do as glamorous."

"Really?" My Mom was full of surprise statements this evening.

"That's not how I see it, however. I'm more realistic. Not that I would try to dissuade them from their romanticized view."

"I did think Mara was a bit overly enthusiastic about suggesting the set-up to have her phone stolen. But it was a good idea and it worked. Although, even at the time, I felt like I shouldn't be encouraging her, and afterwards, well, afterwards it was too late. Even *you* praised her for it."

"That's also a topic for another time. The reason I wanted to have this talk tonight is that I want to set some ground rules. As long as you continue in this profession, I require two things from you.

"First, I want you to promise me that going forward you will be super cautious. Not just a little bit cautious, but constantly vigilant about what could go wrong. Don't try to do things on your own. Make sure you always have backup. *Super* cautious. That's rule number one.

"Rule number two is that I want you to keep me better informed. You don't have to give me a daily report, but you need to let me know when you have a new assignment and what it involves. I can keep a secret; you don't have to worry about me telling someone something I shouldn't. And if I know what's going on, I'll be better able to support you and protect my grandchildren.

"Can you agree to these two simple rules?"

I didn't have to think twice about them. It was a reprieve I hadn't seen coming, and I wasn't going to give her time to change her mind. "Yes. They seem fair."

"Let me be clear, they are not only 'fair,' they are a requirement of our living arrangement."

"I understand." I was a child again with my mother in charge of my life. But I didn't mind. She wasn't telling me I had to give up my new career. She wasn't asking me to reinvent myself still another time.

Mom stood up, leaving her empty glass on the table but taking the bottle of wine. "That doesn't mean that I will no longer make suggestions about things when I think it's appropriate. It's a truce, not an end to the battle." She couldn't help but smile at her clever closing line.

I got up and gave her an awkward hug. Then I drained my glass and went to bed.

Friday morning, I had a spring in my step as I headed into the mall, and it wasn't only because I'd put new athletic performance insoles in my walking shoes. My mother had almost given me a seal of approval. It had been wrapped in an unconditional demand, but it was an act of acceptance that had both surprised and delighted me. Since it was only a truce, I realized she wouldn't be retiring her spot on my refrigerator any time soon, but it made the goose and the pig less loathsome.

The coffee I bought at the kiosk closest to the office smelled like a slice of caffeine heaven. I even picked up a pastry, a danish with cream cheese filling. Life was looking good. Until I opened the door to Penny-wise and caught a subtle but distinct heads-up signal from the expression on Blaine's face.

"I was about to call you," he said.

Out of the corner of my eye, I saw someone moving toward me from behind. I almost responded with a defensive maneuver but caught myself just in time.

"Mr. Bondo," I said, somehow managing to regain my composure. "How can I help you?"

"I would like to go over your report with you."

Blaine said, "I explained that we didn't expect Jenny in today and that I would make an appointment for the two of you to meet with him later."

"You'll do just fine," Bondo said, looking directly at me, ignoring Blaine's suggestion. "I'm sure you can answer my questions."

"It's okay, Blaine," I said. My mind was racing. What on earth was the man doing here, grinning like the villain in *Willy Wonka & the Chocolate Factory*. "Have you told PW that Mr. Bondo would like to talk about his report?"

"Yes, she was waiting for you to arrive. I'll let her know you're here now." PW usually came to work earlier than the rest of us. Today, I was particularly thankful for that.

Before I could think of anything more to say to Bondo, PW emerged from her office. She was wearing a mint green dress with spring flowers of different sizes and colors artistically spaced from the midriff to the wide, dark green expanse of border hem. It made me think of English gardens and running through meadows. Not that I have ever run through a meadow wearing a floral dress, but that image was floating around somewhere in my head.

She invited the two of us to join her in her office. As we approached, she stepped aside to let us precede her. Then she said, "Just a minute" and closed the door behind us. My heart skipped a beat as I took a seat a few feet away from Bondo. How long would we be left alone in PW's office? Should I mention the weather or ask if he and his family were thinking about getting a puppy to replace Ben?

It was, fortunately, only a few minutes of strained silence before PW returned. "Sorry, I had a message for Blaine to pass on."

I guessed that was code for "Grant and Yuri have been alerted to Bondo's presence." Not that I could imagine him doing anything untoward in PW's office. Unless she knew something I didn't.

"You've had a chance to go over the report, I gather." PW sounded very matter-of-fact. "What questions do you have?"

"I'm very disappointed," he began. "Ben was part of the family."

"I'm so sorry," I said. "Jenny and I did everything we could to find him. The people and places we checked out are listed in the report. It seems like he simply vanished." Take that, you deceptive creep.

"No one in the mall saw him?"

"As covered in the report, I talked to all of the nearby business owners as well as a number of shoppers who were here that day. I know it's hard to believe that no one saw him running away, but then it was a chaotic and stressful situation."

"I understand, but no one? Not a single person?"

"Did you ever see the video of the two teams playing basketball when a man dressed in a gorilla suit walks right through their game?"

"No." Bondo was staring at me with a blank expression on his face.

"It's used as a training video to demonstrate the weakness of eyewitness testimony. When people are shown the video and instructed to count the number of times one team bounces the basketball, that's all they see. No one notices a man in a gorilla suit walking on the court. In other words, they see what's important to them, what they're looking for. In this instance, everyone's focus was on escaping, getting away from a shooter, and no one saw your dog. At least that's what I think happened. Because obviously he was here with you and ran off when the shots were fired." It was hard not to broadcast how pleased I was with myself for coming up with such an apt example on the spur of the moment.

"I wish we could have had a different outcome," PW added, a sympathetic tone in her voice. "As I said in our initial interview, we can't guarantee success, although we can promise to make a good faith effort at a reasonable price. I believe we did that."

Bondo looked at us as if we were both crazy. The gorilla story had apparently thrown him off his game.

"Again, I am truly sorry. I know how upset my son would be if our dog ran away."

That got him back on track. "You have a dog?"

"Yes, he was a gift to my son from a colleague. Not my favorite family member, but he's been totally integrated into our lives. I really do understand what you're going through, and I want to assure you again that Jenny and I did everything we could to find Ben."

Whatever Bondo had been hoping to accomplish by talking to me didn't seem to be materializing. Maybe he'd thought it would be just the two of us. Perhaps PW's presence kept him from trying to pry a confession out of me. Although in order to do so, he would have had to reveal that he was more than a man with a lost dog.

When he ran out of things to ask and say, he took his leave. I stayed behind to debrief with PW. We waited until Blaine assured us Bondo had left the office. Then she called Grant in, motioning for me to stay mum. Without saying a word, he checked for bugs. When he found none, he said he would also make sure there were none in the lobby.

"You thought Bondo came by to bug us?" I asked when Grant left.

"It crossed my mind."

"That makes more sense than what actually happened. What do you think he was trying to accomplish?"

"I think he was testing you one last time. Or maybe he heard that you and Yuri are looking into Gabe Miller's life. If so, I assume he knows we were hired to do that. Make sure you stay on message when you're talking to people. In case he follows up."

"Will do."

Suddenly PW laughed, a hearty, open mouth laugh. "I loved the gorilla story."

"It occurs to me that Bondo is a little like the gorilla in the video, wandering through our investigations, hoping to distract us from our goals. Although in some ways, he's more like Godzilla, rising up again and again only to be beaten back into submission."

"Well, let's hope this time we've sent him back to the depths for good."

CHAPTER 13
SOLDIER OF MISFORTUNE

"GABE MILLER'S MOM sent me her elk jerky recipe," Yuri announced. "Wonder if it would be good with flank steak."

"No elk in the freezer?"

"Maybe next season."

We'd already discussed Bondo's visit and decided the only thing to do was wait and see if he popped up again. Although we were hopeful that he had at long last given up on using Bandit to trace Gary and moved on. Meanwhile, we were planning *our* next moves for gathering information about Gabe Miller on behalf of the Goldbergs. Taking into account that we needed to stay on message.

"Maybe we're approaching this all wrong," I said.

"What's wrong with what we've been doing?"

"We've been giving people a starting point by mentioning how he's been covered by the media. Seeing if they would describe him as a 'nice guy.' Maybe we need to be less specific. Try to tease out their opinions with more open-ended questions."

"Like start by asking how well they knew him, how much interaction they had with him, that sort of thing?"

"Yeah. Let their opinion of him come out slowly, organically."

"Organically? Without sprinkling growth hormones on their thought processes?"

"You know what I mean."

"My guess is we will end up with the same results no matter where we start," Yuri said with a shrug. "No one seems to have known him well. Even his parents."

"Too bad we can't talk to his brother. But maybe we can find a teacher to fill in some blanks. Kids spend a lot of time in classrooms."

"If he was a mediocre student who didn't make waves, I bet most of his teachers didn't pay much attention to him. Students like that tend to fall through the cracks."

"That neighbor who said he was the kind of kid who didn't have anything to list under his senior picture besides his major really struck a note with me," I said. "Although, given what we've heard about him so far, he might not even have bothered getting a picture taken for the school annual. If he went to a school that's still doing yearbooks, that is. I understand a lot of schools don't anymore. They've been replaced by the digital media and individual albums."

"Did your school do yearbooks?" Yuri asked. "If they did, I bet you were voted the most likely to succeed." He made a noise that I imagined was supposed to be a guffaw, but it came out more like a sick crow coughing.

"Let me guess," I retorted. "*You* were the class clown."

"That would have been an honor. I've often thought about getting a registered clown face. Have you seen how they do it on the Clown Egg Registry?"

"Egg Registry?"

"Starting in the 1940s the International Circus Clowns started a registry of faces on real hollowed-out eggs as a way to copyright facial features."

"Enough!" I said. I should have realized I'd opened myself up to a fusillade of trivia by asking about the egg registry.

"They switched to ceramic eggs at one point for obvious reasons."

"Okay—" I said, holding up one hand in an effort to dodge the incoming hail of trivia facts.

"The collection is in the organ room of the Holy Trinity Church in London. I assume that's 'organ' like in musical instrument rather than a display of human organs. The church is also the final resting place of Grimaldi the Clown. He passed away in the mid 1800's I believe."

"That's all very interesting, but—"

"And it's known as the Clowns' Church. Each year on the first Sunday in February they host the Clowns International service in honor of Grimaldi and deceased clowns."

"That it?" I asked when he finally stopped talking.

"I could tell you about coulrophobia."

"You already have, back when you were on a phobia kick."

"So, you know—"

"That it's a fear of clowns, yes. Now if we can get back to the subject of Gabe Miller and who might have been sufficiently aware of his existence to comment on what he was like."

"I agree with your previous assessment about time spent at school. I suggest we pay a visit to his former high school."

"Should we call first?"

"No, I think this is one of those times when it would be easier to just show up. After all, schools do their business during the day. With luck, we'll find someone there who remembers Gabe."

"Okay, I'll drive today," I said, as if it was just a way of sharing the burden and not an unnamed fear of driving with Yuri. Or maybe I should give it a name. I could refer to it as Yurobia. I remembered Yuri saying on one of his monologues that there were four categories of phobias: natural environment, animals, mutilation/medicine and situations. In my opinion, fear of his driving qualified under several of the four categories.

As we were about to leave, Blaine waved us over. PW wanted to see us in her office before we took off. My second time in one day. Somehow, I didn't think it was to tell us good news.

We stood in front of PW's desk, not sure if this was a sit-down occasion or a quick comment situation. When she didn't suggest that we sit, we assumed it was the latter and remained standing.

"Cameron, I know you're keeping an eye out, but I just want to reiterate that I think you need to continue exercising extra caution for a while. Understood?" That sounded suspiciously like Rule Number One. I wondered if she and my mother were colluding behind my back?

"They may have given up," Yuri said. "There hasn't been anyone lurking near her home the last few evenings." Yuri directed his comment to PW.

I turned to him in surprise. "Have you been spying on me?"

"Not *spying*, just making sure there were no hostiles in the area."

"*Hostiles*?"

"Grant thought it was a good idea," Yuri said defensively.

"That's enough," PW intervened. "I understand why you may not feel Yuri's late-night visits were necessary, Cameron. But I can also understand his concern. I've been giving this some thought. Gary would have done everything possible to cover his tracks after leaving the mall. If they lost him, they might consider you their only lead. In spite of everything you've done to convince them you aren't in touch with him."

"There's another thing that's been worrying me," Yuri said. "We've talked a lot about Bondo and what he might do, but what about the people he works for? They could get tired of waiting around for Bondo to find Gary and send in another team. Or they could start worrying that we might stumble across a connection between Miller and whoever hired him to do the work. Either way, they aren't going to appreciate us nosing around."

"I agree. Both are possibilities," PW said. "I still think we're better off doing the work for the Goldbergs rather than having them go elsewhere. I recommend that you keep a low profile and complete your assignment quickly."

As we left, Yuri said, "She's right, 'It ain't over till it's over.'"

"You quoting Yogi Berra?" I asked. "Or the song by Lenny Kravitz?"

"I'm surprised you know the song," Yuri said.

"We are both full of surprises, aren't we?" I was still smarting over his night-time surveillance of my home.

"Sorry about the surveillance. I didn't want to worry you."

"I appreciate your concern, but next time don't go sneaking around." After a few moments of awkward silence, I added, "But thanks."

Gabe Miller's former high school was an older 3-story brick structure with rows of small windows facing the mostly brown stretch of lawn between the sidewalk and the ornate entrance to the building. It looked big and old and not particularly welcoming. A giant box with no distinguishing features to offset its hulking presence. All it needed to be used as the location for a haunted orphanage in a movie were a few giant trees to cast shadows around the perimeter, their wavery grayness flickering across windows and darkening the entrance.

Just inside the double front doors was a small vestibule with poor lighting. On one wall was a map of the building. I was just getting oriented when Yuri pointed to an arrow indicating "Administrative Offices." It directed us down a dreary corridor lined with framed pictures of sporting events. At the end of the hall was a large wood desk. Behind it sat a pleasant-looking young women with straight blond hair and a clear complexion. She seemed delighted to see us appear out of the gloom. The nameplate on her desk said Anita Vanderbilt.

I let Yuri do the talking. He started by asking Anita how long she had worked at the school. Unfortunately, she had only been there for two years, so she personally wasn't going to be a source of information. However, after explaining why we were there, Yuri tried to charm her into calling the principal to see if she would be willing to talk to us for a few minutes.

"She's already talked to several reporters and the police," Anita said, obviously reluctant to ask the principal if she was available to talk to us. "She may not want to go over what's already been published about him." It was her discreet way of saying that the principal was not someone who liked to waste time, and that she might consider *us* a waste of time. When Yuri finally convinced her to give it a try, I was surprised when the principal asked her to send us in.

The principal was a well-preserved older woman—or a poorly preserved younger woman. She had brown hair streaked with white, a face that was starting to wrinkle but hadn't quite given in to gravity yet. As she came out from behind her desk to shake hands and make introductions, I noted her erect posture and felt somewhat unsettled by the directness of her gaze. This was a woman used to being in charge, and who didn't mind using her presence to intimidate uninvited visitors. That was probably a handy superpower when it came to dealing with unruly students.

Yuri's charm didn't work as well on her as it had on her assistant. When he told her that we were there on behalf of the Goldbergs to learn what we could about Gabe Miller, she quickly declared that student records were private. End of conversation. Yuri tried to explain we didn't want to see any official records, and she countered with a firm pronouncement: she didn't believe in gossiping about former students. For a moment I thought the interview was over before it had begun. It made me wonder why she had agreed to see us in the first place.

"We won't be making anything we learn public," I assured her, hoping to do an end run around what I assumed were her unstated concerns. "As Yuri said, we're interviewing people who knew Gabe to put together a profile for the parents of the victim. They want to get to know him as a human being rather than as some evil caricature. They're hoping that by seeing him through the eyes of people who knew him before his desperate act of violence that they may be able to let go of some of the bitterness they feel and, in turn, find closure."

"The police have already done an investigation."

"But the police were looking for confirmation of criminal intent. We're trying to paint a picture of the person he was *before* he picked up a gun and headed to the mall."

"You can't excuse what he did. No matter what he was like as a child. What his home circumstances were. He was, after all, 20 years old. He made the choice as an adult to go to that mall and shoot innocent people." It was a harsh indictment, but I understood her point of view. And being a principal, she had probably heard every excuse there was for every type and degree of misbehavior.

"If it had been your son that was shot," I said, "wouldn't you want to know everything you could about the person who did it? That's all the Goldbergs are asking for. They may not be able to forgive the man who shot their son, but they want to try to find at least a partial answer to the question of 'why?'"

She looked down at her desk a moment before coming to a decision. "I don't remember him all that well," she admitted. "He wasn't a squeaky wheel. Nor did he do anything in particular to call attention to his presence, either good or bad. He simply came and went, doing barely well enough to graduate."

"Did he have any friends that we could try to find and talk to?"

"Not that I know of," she said. "I've already asked around for the police."

"Any teachers we could talk to who might be able to tell us more about him?"

She reached down and hit an intercom button on her landline phone. "Anita, could you look up Gabe Miller's class schedule and make a copy?" She turned back to us and said, "I'm not sure you will learn much from any of them, but you're welcome to try."

"I assume the police talked to his teachers," Yuri said.

"They held a meeting with teachers and staff. I don't think it was very productive."

We thanked her and were about to leave when she added, "There is one person you might want to talk to—our former school cook, Mila Samberg. She retired last year, but she paid a lot of attention to individual kids and what went on in the lunchroom. I can give you her name and phone number, but I would ask you not to imply that I said she should talk to you. If she wants to, that's fine. It's her choice."

There was a Rolodex on her desk, next to her computer. As she flipped through it, she seemed to realize we were watching her with amusement. "Some habits are hard to break," she said. She stopped at a card in the "S" section and copied a name and number down on a post-it. "My Rolodex never loses its charge or gets hacked. There is no maintenance involved." She was right, of course. I'd be tempted to use one myself if the classic rotary file fit in a pocket or a small purse. I wondered if the card Yuri had given her would end up under "P" or "W."

"I believe the Rolodex was created in 1950 by Arnold Neustadter," Yuri said. Uh oh, I thought. Here we go. On the other hand, we were in an educational institution, so perhaps mentioning historical facts was appropriate.

The principal looked at him and blinked as if he was responding to questions on a quiz that had not been given to him yet.

"It's a registered trademark and still quite popular in spite of all of the electronic devices that store and manage business contact information," Yuri added.

Before he could further elaborate on the history of the Rolodex, I smiled at the principal and said, "My colleague loves trivia. He has a mind like a Rolodex, spin it around and you never know what you'll get."

For a moment we were a frozen tableau of people who didn't really know what our conversation was about. Then the principal stood up, indicating our interview was over. "You are welcome to talk to any of our teachers, but I would ask that you meet with them during their lunch time or free periods. If that can't be arranged, please make arrangements to see them outside of school hours. Our teachers are very busy with their students and classroom responsibilities."

We thanked her again and went back to get Gabe's schedule from her assistant, Anita. We found her studying the printout she had copied for us. One name was highlighted in bright orange. "There is only one teacher he took more than one class from. Mr. Bingham. He took both world history and European history from him. You might want to start there. He should be in the teacher's lounge in about a half hour. That's his lunch break." She handed us the schedule and a floor plan of the school with X's to mark the lounge and Bingham's classroom.

We were about to leave when she said, "We've all talked about him, you know. Even those of us who weren't here when he was. We speculate about whether there was anything the faculty missed about his behavior, any signs that he was capable of something like this. The main concern, of course, is whether there was something they could have done to prevent what happened. And how do we make sure we don't have other unstable students in our midst?"

"As a parent, that's something I worry about," I said. "Someone capable of a mass shooting in a mall could just as easily target a school. My two kids have had instruction on what to do if that happens. But there are no guarantees."

"It's scary," Anita agreed.

"Any particular insights about either his behavior or what could have been done?" Yuri asked.

"Not that I've heard. Most of his teachers couldn't even remember what he looked like. And it's only been two years. Those who did remember him described him as a quiet boy who was almost a non-presence. There are always a few like that. They don't leave their mark, just go through the motions and fade away. It's sad."

She had basically written a paragraph of our report for us. Her comments made me feel sorry for Gabe. But I agreed with the principal that choices made by adults cannot be entirely excused by their past. We thanked her and headed for Bingham's classroom.

"This way," I said.

"You sure?"

"Women's intuition."

"I thought that only applied to the ability to read facial expressions and body language."

"This map is the face of the school," I countered.

The doors to the classrooms had small glass windows, so tiny and smudged as to provide very little visual access into individual rooms. If you got up close to look in your face would fill the space. From the inside it would probably look like a headshot that should have been adjusted for the size of the frame.

When we got to Bingham's classroom, we kept back from the door and were able to catch glimpses of the man we assumed to be Mr. Bingham walking back and forth in the front of the room. He was a compact man in slacks and a tweed jacket. No tie. He was using broad gestures to punctuate whatever he was saying. We couldn't make out who he was talking to without getting closer. We assumed there was an audience for his dramatic presentation.

After a few minutes, a bell rang and a group of students stampeded out of the room. Maybe it was unfair to say they *stampeded*, but it felt like we were obstructions to be navigated around as a herd of kids flowed past. When the flow ended, we went in and introduced ourselves while Mr. Bingham gathered up his notes. We explained why we wanted to talk to him, and he invited us to join him in the lounge while he took his lunch break.

Once in the lounge, he offered us coffee which we both accepted.

"Yes, I remember Gabe," he said between taking dainty bites of a sandwich on whole wheat bread. I couldn't make out what the thin layer of beige filling was. "I can't say that I knew him well, but he seemed to like history. Perhaps he was a bit fixated on war strategy, but then a lot of history emphasizes conflicts between countries or people, winners and losers." He was eating his sandwich as if it was divided into rows, like a flat corn on the cob. I'd never seen anyone do that before.

"Can you tell us your impression of him? What he was like?"

"The most striking thing about him was that he was a loner. I know that's one of the things they often say about shooters after the fact. But at the time he didn't strike me as being a loner in a bad way. Just someone who didn't care for the company of other kids his age. I can't say that I blamed him. Boys can be hard on each other."

"You say he was a loner. Did he have any friends that you remember him hanging out with?"

"No." For a minute I thought he was going to lecture us on what it means to be a "loner," but he was more interested in eating his sandwich than in educating us.

"Did anyone bully him that you know of?" I asked. If he didn't have any friends, maybe he had some enemies.

"We usually hear about things like that and try to nip it in the bud as quickly as possible. I don't remember any situations involving Gabe."

We talked a little longer, then ran out of things to ask. I didn't get to see him finish his sandwich. I wondered whether he turned it sideways when he got to the last row and ate it like a breadstick with filling.

"What do you think?" I asked Yuri. "Want to see if we can find any of the other teachers on this list?

"If his 'favorite' teacher didn't know him, then the others probably wouldn't have much to add. Anita said most of them couldn't remember him at all."

"I'm in favor of calling the retired cook. What do you think? If she's available and willing to talk, we could do it on our way back to the office. Might as well get it done if we can."

Yuri made the call as we wended our way through the cars in the parking lot. We were in luck. Not only was the former school cook at home and willing to talk, she wasn't too far away. As I started the car and headed for the exit, Yuri punched her address into his cell's GPS. The voice that gave us directions was very British.

"Did you customize the voice on your phone?"

"The original woman was too, oh, I don't know …"

"You were going to say 'bossy' but hesitated because you thought I would think that was sexist. The male equivalent voice would be described as 'commanding' or 'authoritative,' right?"

"She sounded disapproving when I didn't follow her directions."

I swallowed my smile. "Instead, you chose a very proper Cambridge professor voice. You don't mind taking orders from a toff, huh?"

"I'm thinking of changing it to a sexy Brazilian woman's voice."

"Don't they speak Portuguese?"

"Funny."

It didn't take long for Yuri's British friend to locate the school cook's home. Mila Samberg lived in a small, modular structure in a row of inexpensive looking, well-cared for houses. She was in the yard when we dove up, trimming some bushes near her front porch. I guessed she was in her late 60s, her light brown hair sprinkled with gray. She had a patch on one knee of her jeans. When she saw us pull up out front, she took off her gardening gloves and set them on the railing of the small front porch.

We introduced ourselves, and I gave her my card. I like having a card announcing my profession as a private investigator for Penny-wise Investigations, *Vigilance You Can Afford*. It makes my job feel tangible. Besides, people seem to expect you to have some sort of identification, as if having a business card gives you legitimacy. In spite of the fact that anyone can print up their own cards and claim to be anyone they want.

"Call me Mila," she said as she led us inside.

"That's a lovely name," I said.

"Beats Amelia," she laughed. "At least that's how I felt when I was younger. Now it's too late to change back." She offered us tea, and even though we'd just had coffee, we both said yes. It had been a long day.

The inside of her small home was as tidy as the outside. The chairs across from the couch looked inviting. We accepted the invitation and sank down into them. Mila disappeared into another room and came back shortly with a tray holding a teapot, three cups, sugar and milk. Yuri immediately doctored his tea with an excess of sugar and a dribble of milk. I took mine plain.

"I like tea the way the English take it," Mila said, smiling at Yuri. "I can see that you do, too." She didn't comment on the amount of sugar he'd added to his tea; that probably wasn't a common British trait. "Now, what is it you want to know about Gabe Miller?"

We explained what the Goldbergs were hoping to learn and added that no one we'd talked to so far felt like they knew Gabe. "The principal told us that you served the kids lunch, knew most of them by name, and that you might be able to provide some insight into Gabe's interactions with other students. Maybe even give us a name of someone who knew him back then. Either would help."

"I suppose the people you've talked to told you he was a loner."

"Yes."

"And that he liked guns and didn't make waves. Right?"

"That about sums it up," I said.

"Did they tell you how he envied his brother because he's in the military?"

"No, no one mentioned his brother. You talked to him about his brother?"

"Given the nature of our relationship, we didn't have long talks. But he usually went through the line at the end, so we sometimes had brief conversations. One time he mentioned that he had an older brother in the military, so after that I made it a point to ask about him, how he was doing, where he was stationed, that sort of thing. Gabe was very proud that his brother was serving in a combat zone and sometimes told me stories that I was pretty sure he was making up, or at least exaggerating."

"That fits with his love of guns," Yuri said. "Maybe his gun collection was partly an attempt to emulate his brother, the soldier."

"Actually, I was a little surprised that he didn't join the service when he graduated. My guess is that he didn't like the idea of living in close quarters with other men and women."

"No one mentioned him participating in any group activities in high school."

"As far as I know, he didn't. He didn't even talk to other students at lunch. Did anyone mention his Soldier of Fortune magazines?"

"No," I said. "No one mentioned them."

"He read them almost every day while he was eating. I think he liked the tough guy image they portrayed. But I also felt like it was his way of letting the other kids know that it was his choice to be alone during lunch. That he was busy reading and didn't have time to talk. Not that anyone noticed."

"Besides you."

"Well, I liked to keep an eye on my kids." I noted the personal possessive.

"I doubt anything he read in a Soldier of Fortune magazine encouraged mass shootings," Yuri commented.

"No," Mila said. "But it's an addictive fantasy world for a young boy who feels powerless. Some kids don't mature mentally or physically until after high school. Gabe struck me as one of those."

"Did you like Gabe?" I asked. It would be nice if we could cite his relationship with the school cook as an indication that he was willing to interact with others if they reached out to him first. That made him seem vulnerable and shy instead of strictly anti-social.

"I'm not sure 'like' is the right word. I felt sorry for him. Gabe was insecure, probably very lonely. I mean, who spends time at that age talking to the school cook when you could be living it up with friends? I didn't think he was a bad kid though, just one that didn't fit in. And it was painful to watch him constantly sneaking peeks during lunch at one of the most popular girls in his class. Lindy Mason. She was a looker and knew it. Flirted with all of the boys. He seemed to have a huge crush on her. She, of course, didn't know he even existed. Really sad."

"Yes, sad," I agreed. "I can picture him pretending to read while checking out Lindy and wishing he were part of her group of admirers."

We sat a moment considering what it must have felt like to always be on the outside looking in. Then Yuri said, "Even though most of his teachers couldn't even remember who he was, they've apparently been agonizing over whether they should have noticed any red flags indicating he had the potential for violence. Looking back, did he ever say anything that you wish you'd paid more attention to?"

"No, not a thing. And when I read about it in the papers, I was surprised. What I wondered was whether he thought he would get away with the shooting, like it was some elite military operation. Or was he depressed and just wanted to go out in a macho blaze of violence? Since he was killed, we will never know the truth of his story."

"It seems like quite a few mass shooters end up taking their own lives," I said. "I guess that's something else we won't know, if he intended to shoot himself at the end. But there hasn't been any mention of a note or a manifesto or anything like that."

We sat quietly, sipping tea, each of us lost in our own thoughts. I was trying to imagine what those last minutes must have been like for Gabe. Did he think that, like a movie hero, he could have people shooting at him but still manage to escape? Or had he been looking for a posthumous fifteen minutes of fame before fading into permanent anonymity?

"Poor, Gabe. He liked tater tots and apple juice. May he rest in peace." Mila's mini-eulogy was one of the saddest tributes I'd ever heard.

CHAPTER 14
NO WAY!

THE KIDS AND I ENJOYED a pleasant breakfast together Saturday morning. Mara made waffles, and I heated the Log Cabin Syrup just the way Jason likes it. Mom had gone out to breakfast with friends, but not before slipping downstairs to leave an article titled "The Cautionary Principle in Risk Management" on my refrigerator. I'm not sure what the bonnet-wearing goose and the scarf-wearing pig magnets thought about this new trend in topics. I ripped it off, almost tossed it, then thought "why not?" and set it aside to read later.

I hadn't seen Mom leave, but just knowing she was out there somewhere sharing food and laughs with friends made me a bit jealous. It had been a while since I'd had friends to do things with, whether to go out for breakfast, or to a movie, attend a concert, whatever. Since we'd moved to the area, I'd been too busy getting through day-to-day living to make new friends. I kept in touch with a few from my past, but that was different. I didn't have any hobbies that brought me in touch with like-minded individuals, didn't participate in activities related to the kids' school, didn't do any kind of exercise where I might meet someone, and I was absolutely opposed to any kind of online dating app. So, unless I stumbled across someone in some random way, someone who just happened to be like me, friendless and needy, I might as well get used to doing things alone.

I was starting to feel really sorry for myself, wallowing in self-inflicted misery, when my cell rang. It was Yuri. "We need to talk," he said. "Is now a good time?"

"Sure, go ahead." It was not only a good time, it was "just in time."

"I mean in person."

"Good." Oops, I didn't mean to sound so eager. "Where do you want to meet?"

"How about your place? Put the coffee on." He hung up without waiting for me to agree and without saying goodbye. Uh oh. Whatever he wants to discuss must be serious. Now I wasn't so sure that having someone to talk to was such a good thing, after all.

While I was waiting for Yuri to arrive, Mara left to go over to a friend's house to "hang out." Jason was in his room playing video games. Unless I suggested he do something more productive, I didn't anticipate he would surface for a while. I made another pot of coffee, refilled the sugar container, and tried to figure out what Yuri could possibly have on his mind. Nothing I could think of fit the urgency of his tone. I was glad he didn't make me wait long before I heard his familiar knock.

Once we were settled in the kitchen with our coffee, Yuri didn't bother with small talk. He started spooning sugar into his coffee and talking at the same time. "I've been thinking," he began, holding up a hand to prevent me from making a smart remark. "This is serious. We assume that Gabe Miller was hired by whoever wanted Gary eliminated, right?"

I nodded. "Ah, I think you've added enough sugar."

He blinked, put the spoon down, and continued. "We also assume that the person who hired Gabe was a representative of some rogue government group or agency, or some individual run amuck. Possibly the same one that hired Bondo. An entity or person we can't trace without revealing what we're up to."

I nodded again.

"As I see it, we have two choices. We can sit around and wait until Gary comes riding back on his white horse with all of the answers, which he probably won't share with us." He held up his hand again. "You don't have to defend him; I know that you promised you'd remain mum. And I respect that. But you do realize that, among other things, we are withholding evidence from both the Goldbergs and the police?"

"We don't actually have any 'evidence' to speak of. Didn't we agree that withholding a 'theory' isn't a criminal act?"

"You're splitting hairs." Yuri paused. For a moment I thought he was going to start spouting off trivia about splitting hairs. When he didn't, I knew he was deadly serious about what he was leading up to.

"I know, but even PW thinks we shouldn't pursue this line of investigation—who hired Gabe and Bondo, and, in turn, who is after Gary."

"Meanwhile, that leaves you hanging out there."

"I thought we decided they've probably given up on me as a connection to Gary."

"We also considered the possibility that they may circle back around if they don't find him and have no other leads."

"Okay, you've got my attention."

"We've considered the possibility that Gabe may have responded to some ad in one of his Soldier of Fortune magazines. Or that there's some other way he called attention to himself as a potential hit man, and they reached out to him. Either way, we have been working from the hypothesis that Gabe was hired by the person or agency that's after Gary. But what if we're wrong? What if Gary wasn't his target? What if it was a random shooting to gain attention? Maybe he really did just become unhinged after years of feeling like a powerless outsider."

"It's possible. But quite a coincidence, isn't it?"

"Yes, and maybe too much of a coincidence. But stay with me for a minute. I've been talking with my reporter friend, feeling out what she knows about the police investigation. The police are locked into the theory that our friend Gabe went a little crazy and was looking for his fifteen minutes of fame. It's case closed from their point of view."

"That's not surprising, is it?"

"Yet, the more I think about it, the more I feel as though we need to be considering both possibilities. Maybe he acted on his own, but maybe he didn't. We're trying to distance ourselves from the latter, and by doing that, we are ignoring the former."

"We can't look at the latter. That takes us back to square one. We can't suggest something without proof, something that could compromise Gary."

"What about the former?"

"I'm losing track—latter, former. Why don't we refer to Gabe acting alone or for hire?"

"Point taken. What I think we should do is look for evidence that proves whether it's one or the other. Not just assume he acted under orders from someone and ignore the other possibility."

"Remember, PW warned that we are investigating the shooter not the shooting. I think what you're suggesting crosses the line."

"Perhaps, just a little. It's a matter of interpretation. But it's something I feel strongly that we need to do."

"We?"

"I'd do it alone, but we'd have a better chance as a team."

"Is this an off the books kind of thing?"

"PW doesn't have to know unless we find something. If we do, we'll run it past her before we go any further."

I was torn between not wanting to get involved in one of Yuri's sometimes borderline schemes and my dislike of sitting around like the proverbial princess waiting for the prince to return. "So, what's your plan?"

"I thought you would never ask."

Normally I wouldn't have hesitated to leave Jason alone for a few hours in the middle of the day. But I didn't know for sure how long I would be gone, and I didn't want to violate Rule Number One so soon after agreeing to it. I hated to do it, but I called my mother to find out when she would be coming home, explaining that I needed to go with Yuri on a work assignment. Fortunately, she was already on her way.

While we waited for Mom's return, Yuri called the Millers and arranged for us to drop by. Then he paced back and forth in our living room, mumbling to himself. No-name came out of Jason's room, watched Yuri for a few minutes, then, ears down, tail between his legs, slunk down the hall and disappeared around the corner into the kitchen.

"You've upset No-name," I said.

"Sorry."

"And you're upsetting me."

"I have a feeling we're missing something," he said. "It's driving me crazy."

"Obviously."

He stopped and stared at me. "You still don't have a name for the dog?"

"The other day Jason suggested calling him Fang. Or Bruiser. Maybe it was King. I've lost track."

"Oh."

"He answers to No-name now. But Jason is still working on coming up with the perfect name."

"Bruiser isn't bad."

I groaned. "Please don't tell him that."

Mom returned, joined us in the living room and warmly greeted both of us. When she failed to point out that it was a Saturday and that I was supposed to be taking the day off, I wondered if she'd had a champagne breakfast. We didn't linger long enough to find out.

The Millers hadn't pressed about why we wanted to come by; they were apparently still more than willing to cooperate. Given their openness, we didn't anticipate any resistance to our request to take a look at Gabe's room in their house as well as at his apartment. We didn't know exactly what we were looking for, so we couldn't have told them even if they'd asked. The police had undoubtedly searched both for connections to groups or extremist ideologies to explain motive. They had also probably looked for names of possible confederates to determine whether he had acted on his own. If that kind of evidence had been there, they would have found it. We weren't sure what that left for us to discover, but it beat sitting around, waiting for something to happen.

The Millers invited us in and asked how our investigation was going. I gave them a high-level, positive overview of what we'd learned so far, without mentioning any names. They had, after all, also lost a son; they deserved some consideration. When we got around to our request, they pointed out that the police had already searched both his room in their home as well as his apartment. We reminded them that we weren't looking at their son as a criminal but were building a profile of him as a person. I told them about our conversation with the school cook the day before and how she had mentioned that Gabe liked apple juice and tater tots. After talking with her, I said, we started thinking about what we might learn by seeing where he'd lived. How it could be helpful to see belongings he cared about, what he kept close. Added to the other things we'd learned, those were the kind of details that might humanize Gabe for the Goldbergs.

It didn't take them long to make up their minds. They had already agreed to talk to us about their son, letting us see where he lived wasn't much of a stretch. Mr. Miller gave Yuri a key to Gabe's apartment and said we could drop it in their mailbox when we were through. Mrs. Miller accompanied us to his former room, explaining that they hadn't made any changes because he occasionally spent the night even after moving out. She stopped at the entrance and said, "He was a good boy in so many ways. It's hard to imagine ..." Her voice trailed off.

"We appreciate you letting us do this," I said to get past the awkward hesitation.

"Take your time," she said as she turned away, leaving us to browse on our own.

The room wasn't what I expected. Not that I'd thought much about what it would be like. But even if I had tried to guess, I never would have predicted a distinct western theme. The bedspread was covered with tiny horses running and rearing up, ridden by cowboys waving revolvers and lariats in the air. The wallpaper behind the bed depicted cowboys around a campfire at sunset. There was a replica of a wagon wheel on another wall, next to a pair of antlers. Several metal horses were lined up on the top of the dresser. The final old west touch was a black and white cowhide rug next to the bed. The entire room looked like something designed by Disney for a pre-teen boy infatuated with Buffalo Bill's Wild West. Apparently, no one had considered it important to change the décor as Gabe aged.

"It must have been like returning to his childhood each time he stayed here," Yuri said.

"I'm not sure how I feel about this." Actually, it felt kind of creepy to be in a room that seemed so Disneyesque knowing that it was where a mass shooter had spent time recently. It was difficult to reconcile the two. Even though the Wild West had been home to gun-toting men who allegedly hadn't hesitated to pull the trigger.

"It fits with his love of guns and hunting. All of these cowboys waving pistols around. The horses. The antlers on the wall."

"Think the Goldbergs will be impressed if we put this in our report?" I asked.

"Hard to know. Maybe if you tone it down a bit."

"Well, we don't want to overstay our welcome, so let's get on with it. What are we looking for again?"

"The police would have been thorough," Yuri said. "I doubt we'll find any secret hiding place or a hidden notebook or anything like that. And we can assume they've removed items of interest such as any computer or electronic devices he may have had. We need to look for something they didn't consider significant given their mindset. A name. A telephone number. A picture."

"A microchip."

"I doubt he was a spy."

"I was kidding."

We stood there a moment to study the room before getting started. Now that I was past the shock of feeling like a bit player in an old John Wayne movie, I was able to actually focus on the individual pieces of décor. To our left was a narrow table with a small television on it. Next to the table was a single shelf mounted on the wall. On it were a couple of books held in place by two halves of a horse, one-half on either side. A single bed jutted out from the side of the room. The tiny nightstand next to it was home to a goose-neck lamp and a digital clock. At the back of the room, there was a small desk with a wooden chair in front. To our right was a closet with louvered doors. A small chest of drawers next to it. Not all that much to search.

"You take the desk," Yuri said. "I'll check the closet and chest." He pulled open the closet doors as I headed for the desk.

The desk had a shallow top drawer over a space for the chair and two larger drawers on the side. I opened the top drawer and looked inside. There was a stationary box, a pad of paper and a few pens. Inside the stationary box were some pictures, mostly snapshots of kids at school. One girl appeared in several of them. Without giving it much thought, I slipped one of the pictures of her into my pocket. I knew it was wrong to take the picture, but then, it was one of several; it wouldn't be missed. And I was curious if this was the girl Mila had mentioned, the one Gabe had a crush on.

The bottom side drawer contained a clip-on fan and an empty desk caddy. The top side drawer had a stapler inside a plastic shark body, a magnetic paper clip holder, a tin of breath mints, some hand sanitizer, and a mouse pad with a picture of a pair of cowboy boots with ornate spurs.

"Nothing here that looks significant to me," I informed Yuri.

"Just a few clothes in the closet," Yuri said back. "A couple pairs of old sneakers. An empty suitcase. A few shirts and some underwear in the chest. Nothing in any of the pockets. He must have taken most of his personal belongings to his apartment."

While I examined the table with the TV and the narrow shelf next to it, Yuri checked out the bed. Out of the corner of my eye I saw him look under it. Lift up the mattress. Move the pillows aside. Pull open the drawer on the nightstand. "Nothing here," he announced, sounding disappointed. We'd agreed there might not be anything to find, but it was still a letdown not to find anything.

"Come check this out," I said. "It looks like his high school did do yearbooks." There were three annuals with the high school logo neatly lined up between the two halves of the horse bookends. "Let's see if his neighbor was right."

I pulled out the one from his senior year and thumbed through the pictures until I got to the M's. There he was, not looking directly at the camera, a slight puckered frown rather than a smile on his face. Like he hadn't wanted to have his picture taken. His mother had probably insisted. None of the pictures had majors or activities listed. Instead, there were quotations.

"No descriptors," I said. "Just quotations—wow. *You're laughing because I'm laughing. I'm laughing because I just farted.* Or, how about this one: *Remember to always be yourself–unless you suck.*"

"Pretty low bar."

"There are some serious ones too. But surprise surprise—no quotation for Gabe."

"What about Lindy, is there a picture for her?"

I quickly turned to the "M's," and sure enough, it was her. I was about to tell Yuri about the picture I'd "borrowed" when Mr. Miller appeared in the doorway.

"Anything I can help you with?"

"No, we were just looking at Gabe's yearbook." I placed it back on the shelf.

"Thank you," Yuri said. "I think that will do it."

We said goodbye to the Millers and the Old West and rode off into the sunset, well, not literally.

"Check this out," I said to Yuri as we got in the car. I handed him the picture I'd pilfered. "He had quite a few of these. I guess he did have a thing for Lindy."

"You made off with a picture?" Yuri grinned. "I've trained you well."

I snatched the picture back and started the car.

It was a short drive to Gabe's apartment. He had apparently not felt the need to get too far away from his parents. Nor had he moved into a newer apartment complex. The building his apartment was in had seen better days. It needed paint, and there was no real landscaping to speak of, just some grass out front that needed mowing.

Once inside, things did not improve. The entry hall floor hadn't been swept in a while, the walls were a dingy yellow-gray, and the table next to the mailboxes was littered with magazines and junk mail. Yuri flipped through the magazines to see if there were any Soldier of Fortunes for Gabe there. But there weren't.

Like Gabe's room at his parents' house, his apartment also surprised us. But for a different reason. The place was a mess. The police had obviously gone through it very thoroughly and hadn't bothered to clean things up. Everything in the kitchen had been taken out of cupboards. Doors and drawers stood open. A box of cereal had spilled out on the floor. The living room looked like a tornado had whipped through, leaving pillows and cushions scattered about. I hadn't asked the Millers if they'd been by recently, but my guess was that they hadn't. I would have to warn them about what to expect; I didn't want them thinking we had done this.

"No western theme here," Yuri commented. "No theme at all."

"How can you tell? The police didn't have to turn everything inside out and just leave it that way." What they had done to the place irritated me. Gabe Miller may have been a killer, but it wasn't fair to leave behind an unnecessary mess for his next of kin to clean up.

"This is about as bad as I've seen it. Maybe they were in a hurry. Or maybe someone else searched the place."

"Who?"

"The people who hired him? To make sure they couldn't be traced?"

"Seems unlikely. They probably covered their tracks in advance. My money is on the police. If we had a better reason for being here, I'd complain."

Yuri raised his eyebrows. "You mean you lied to the Millers about why we wanted to search their son's apartment?"

"Not funny."

"Don't worry. Our flimsy excuse could pass the smell test."

"But it wouldn't hold up under any real scrutiny."

"It won't come to that, so relax."

While I poked through the stuff in the living area, Yuri disappeared into another room. He was only gone a few minutes when he shouted, "Come in here."

He was in Gabe's bedroom standing next to a pegboard hanging on the wall. It was covered by the same kind of pictures I had found in the stationary box in Gabe's desk. Shots of what could have been friends. But Gabe wasn't in any of the pictures with any of his "friends." He had obviously either taken all of these shots himself or found them somewhere online. They included some close-ups. If he had taken the close-ups, it was most likely with a zoom lens.

"What do you think?" Yuri asked. We both stood in front of the pegboard and considered the myriad of pictures. Including quite a few of Lindy.

"To quote Mila, 'sad.'"

"Think he took these himself?" Yuri asked. The implication was frightening.

"He could have. But so many? Maybe he copied some from Facebook pages. Or off Instagram. A pathetic outsider documenting others having fun. Watching them play games, laughing, eating. But not with him."

"It doesn't look like the police touched any of these pictures. Everything looks intact."

"Maybe they decided they weren't related to the shooting, so why bother? All of these kids look so normal." My eyes roamed over the clustered pictures. "No Nazi flags in the background. No provocative slogans written on the walls they're posing in front of. No visible gang or prison tattoos. No T-shirts with anti-American propaganda. No jackets with extremist symbols."

"Just trendy clothes and sunshine smiles."

"Even if the police didn't attribute any significance to these pictures, given how they treated the rest of the place, I'm surprised they didn't rip this off the wall and stomp on it."

"Well, they probably didn't spend much time in here. Not much to look at. They tossed the bed. Went through the clothes in the closet. Looked in the dresser and nightstand. That's about it. Unless there was some evidence they took with them."

"It doesn't look like there were any framed pictures or anything else on the walls. I don't see any hooks or faded spots. No rug to pull back to check for loose floorboards. Pretty bare."

"Just this pegboard of people from his past," Yuri said.

I took snapshots of the pictures on the pegboard while Yuri went to check out the rest of the apartment. Lindy's life captured on camera. Lindy and her friends. I wondered why Gabe had never taken a selfie to post his own face alongside Lindy's. Maybe he was content to worship her from afar.

Then I experienced a heart-stopping moment. "No way," I said out loud. "No way." I stared for another few seconds, then yelled, "Yuri, come back in here!"

"What?" he shouted back, rushing into the room as if expecting to see me being attacked by a hoard of termites streaming out of the walls.

"Look." I pointed at a picture in the corner of the pegboard.

Yuri leaned closer and adjusted his glasses. "You've got to be kidding me."

"Coincidence?"

"No way," Yuri said, repeating my first thought when I saw the happy couple smiling for the camera—Callum Goldberg, victim, standing next to Lindy Mason, the object of Gabe's obsessive fascination.

CHAPTER 15
DON'T MOVE!

WE DIDN'T HAVE TIME to talk about our find because my phone rang. It was my mother. I was about to say that I would call her back when I realized she had me on speaker, and I could hear her talking to someone else in a very loud voice.

"Don't move," she said, sounding like she meant it. "I've called 911 to report a burglary in progress. The police are on their way."

"Mom, are you okay?" I shouted into my phone.

"Just listen, Cameron," she said. Her voice suddenly sounded far away. Like she had put the phone down.

"Let me show you our credentials," a man's voice said.

"Keep your hands where they are. Don't think I won't shoot."

"Oh my god, Yuri," I said, holding my phone off to the side. "I think my mother is pointing a gun at someone."

"Your mother? With a gun?" After only a moment's hesitation, he motioned for us to leave. I turned and headed for the door. Yuri stayed behind to lock up as I kept going, moving as fast as I could while keeping my phone pressed against my ear. Yuri had to run to catch up.

When we got in the car, I put my phone on speaker and handed it to Yuri. "Hit record," I said just in time to hear a second man speak.

"We're not burglars," he said. His voice sounded familiar.

"Truthfully, I didn't think you were. Not dressed like that."

Yuri held my phone up so we could both hear it over the roar of the engine as I practically floored the gas pedal to get out of the parking space and onto the road as fast as I dared. Then I took off toward home.

The familiar male voice spoke again, evenly, slowly, apparently trying to de-escalate the situation. "Then why don't you put the gun down. I mean, it's a nice-looking piece, but you're not going to shoot us."

"Not unless you move." My mother's voice was steely, emotionless. "The first one gets it in the foot. The second wherever I manage to aim in a hurry." Was that my mother threatening to shoot someone? Where did she get a gun? And what did he mean by "it's a nice-looking piece"?

"Okay, okay. Take it easy. I just want to show you my ID."

"You can show it to the police when they get here."

I could hear the two men talking to each other in the background. "Speak up or shut up," my mother said firmly. The two men stopped talking.

We were a good 20 minutes from my home, even at the breakneck speed I was driving. Yuri called 911 on his cell and asked if they were responding to a call from my house. He was put on hold for what seemed like forever but was probably less than a minute. Then someone came back online and assured him the police were minutes away. While he was talking to the 911 operator, there were too many voices, too many back-and-forth exchanges. I couldn't listen to both conversations at the same time and keep track of what was going on. Then I heard Mom say, very distinctly, "Don't worry, he won't attack unless I give the signal."

Who wouldn't attack? What signal? What on earth was going on? Then I heard the growling. No-name was growling at the intruders. I wondered if they were armed and whether my mom and our crazy dog could win against what appeared to be at least two men if they decided to fight back in spite of her threats. And what on earth were they doing there?

"Who are you?" I screamed into the phone. "Speak up so I can hear you."

"Cameron Chandler?" one of the men yelled back. "We've met. My name is Bondo. Call your mother off, will you? And that damn dog."

"I'm about to tell her to shoot you," I yelled back.

"Look, I can explain. We can talk this out," Bondo said.

"We'll be there any minute now. You can explain—"

Before I could finish my sentence, I heard someone yell, "Police. We're coming in."

After that there were so many voices and so much commotion it was impossible to make out what was happening. No-name was barking, my mother was shouting, Bondo was trying to be heard above the fray, and the police were giving orders that everyone seemed to be ignoring. Then everything quieted down and a male voice came on the line and asked who I was. I explained it was my house they were in and that my mother was the woman with the gun. I added that one of the men claimed to be named Bondo, but that was bogus. He and whoever he was with had no right to be there, no matter who they claimed to be.

"Stay on the line," he ordered, his voice trailing off.

"Wait," I shouted.

He came back and repeated: "Stay on the line."

"I need to know if my mother is okay."

He didn't reply, but moments later my mother picked up the phone and said, "Everything's fine, Cameron." She sounded relaxed, and a bit self-satisfied. As if just minutes ago she hadn't been threatening to shoot someone but had been busy in the kitchen making coffee for our guests.

"Yuri and I are about ten minutes away," I said. "Don't let them turn Bondo and his buddy loose, got that? No matter who they claim to be."

"I don't intend to."

"Is it just the two of them?"

"Yes, two unwelcome intruders."

"Are the kids alright?"

"They both went to visit friends. Thank heavens. See you soon." Silence.

"She hung up," I said to Yuri. "I can't believe she hung up on me."

"We're almost there. Don't worry. It sounds like your mom has everything under control."

"Yuri, my mother was threatening to shoot Bondo and another man. That's not what I would call having things under control. And you heard him, No-name was going berserk."

When we arrived, there were two police cars out front, lights flashing. We parked in the alley and raced to the front door. It was standing open, a uniformed officer off to the side talking on his phone. He motioned for us to stop, but I rushed past him into the main room, Yuri right behind me. For a moment I thought the whole thing had been a hoax. Everyone was standing around talking in normal voices. If they'd had drinks in their hands, I would have sworn I was late to a party being thrown in my own home.

Mother glanced in my direction briefly and waved at me. She was talking to an officer who was taking notes about what she was saying. With her perfect hair, flowered apron, white blouse and tan slacks, she looked like she had stepped out of a set for a television cooking show.

I rushed over to the officer talking to Bondo and another man I didn't recognize. "You *are* arresting these two, aren't you?" Their conversation looked a little too friendly to me. Bondo was clearly slathering on the charm, and the officer was nodding and smiling in response. "Why aren't these two in handcuffs?" I demanded.

"Well, it seems they are with the FBI," the officer said, almost apologetically.

"That may be what they told you, but I can assure you they aren't. You'd better check on that." Bondo rolled his eyes as if to let the officers know I didn't have a clue what I was talking about. "This guy here . . ." I pointed at Bondo. ". . . he hired my agency to do some work for him, and we did our due diligence and ran a background check." I wanted to emphasize that Penny-wise was a savvy agency that followed best practices when taking on a client. "You can check with my boss if you want more detail."

Bondo looked chagrinned but quickly recovered and started explaining that I was misinformed when Yuri stopped him.

"She's right, officer," he said. "I'm her colleague, and I can attest to the fact that this man who calls himself Bondo failed a background check."

"Come on," Bondo said. "You obviously don't understand what it means to work undercover."

Before he could mansplain to me about what it meant to be a fake undercover FBI agent, I cut him off. "Even if he was who he claims to be, Officer, they have no right to break into my home. Did he show you a warrant?"

The officer hesitated, then shook his head no. I turned to glare at Bondo. "What are you doing here, anyway? And what gives you the right to threaten a woman in her own home?"

"We didn't threaten anyone. *She* threatened us."

"I was listening on the phone, so you don't have to tell me what happened. I heard it with my own ears. You entered our home without permission, so I'm going to ask you again: what are you doing here?"

Bondo looked to the officer for support, but the officer was apparently torn as to which side to take and was willing to let us continue arguing while he made up his mind.

"We have reason to believe you are in contact with a criminal we are trying to locate," Bondo said in an authoritative if condescending manner.

"Criminal? I don't know any criminals."

"Does the name Gary Miles mean anything to you?"

"Yes, of course. He helped me out on a case a while back. But he isn't a criminal. And we don't keep in touch."

"You haven't seen him or talked with him recently?"

"No. I haven't. And even if I had, that doesn't explain why you've broken into my house. It seems to me like you're the criminals in this situation."

"Who do you report to?" Yuri suddenly asked. "How can we get in touch with your superior to verify what you are telling us and this officer?"

The officer's head was swiveling back and forth as we talked, like someone following a tennis match to see if the other person could return the volley.

"That's confidential," Bondo said.

That statement was the clincher. The officer finally made up his mind. "Then I'm afraid I'm going to have to take you to the station to get this sorted out."

"That won't be necessary," Bondo said. "I can put you in touch with someone who can clarify the situation. But I don't owe *them* any explanations." He was really smooth and smug. No wonder No-name had growled at him.

"I think you do," I countered. "It's *my* house you've broken into, *my* family you've been harassing."

"I have no idea what you're talking about."

I turned to the officer. "I want to press charges. They broke into my home. They frightened my mother. And what if my kids had been home? What would they have done then?"

Bondo said, "*She* scared me actually. And we knew your kids were out."

"So, you've been stalking me? Watching my house, waiting for the perfect time to break in?"

Mom had been talking to the other officer but came over when she heard us talking about her. "I'm just sorry you didn't give me a reason to shoot you."

"Hey, now," the officer said. "Let's all calm down."

"Are you going to arrest them or not?" I asked. I took out my phone and snapped pictures of the two men. Then one of the officer in charge.

"You can't do that," Bondo said.

"I just did. And I'm sending them to my boss. Along with the recording I made of the entire exchange, beginning with when my mother first called me." I made a point of sending a text. "Done. And you didn't think I could do it."

"You're going to regret this."

"Are you threatening *me* now?" I must have sounded mad enough to go after the man physically because Yuri put his hand on my arm, and the officer sent me a warning look.

"The point is," Yuri said, "you're wasting your time. I don't know who you are or why you think Cameron has kept in touch with that guy from the island, but you're wrong about it. Flat wrong. What can she say or do to make you go away and leave her and her family alone?"

"We tracked him to Seattle," Bondo's friend said.

"So? Seattle's a big place. It also has several airports. Did you consider that?" Now Yuri was getting wound up.

Bondo and his friend exchanged looks. The friend said, "This is a very dangerous guy we're talking about. If you're covering for him, it could get you in a lot of trouble."

"Why would I cover for someone I met one time? What part of that don't you get?" I knew my voice was too loud, but I had thoroughly immersed myself in the role of innocent bystander.

The two police officers apparently were tired of the bickering and declared they were going to take the two men downtown and charge them.

"I think it should be for home invasion. And impersonation of a federal officer."

The two officers exchanged looks.

"Check their credentials—then you might be able to determine the correct charge," Yuri advised.

Bondo looked like he wanted to say something but didn't. He probably thought he had a better chance of persuading the officers to see it from their point of view once Yuri and I were out of the picture. After that, the two went quietly, undoubtedly grateful to get away from us. All of us, especially No-name and my mother.

After they were gone, Yuri said: "I'm going to call PW and see if she wants to follow up while they're still in custody. I wouldn't be surprised if they let them go pretty quickly." He went into the kitchen to make the call, leaving me alone with my mother.

"Well," Mom said, "you certainly convinced *me* that you haven't heard from Gary." The implicit message was that I was becoming an accomplished liar. Another black mark against the PI business. But she had her own behaviors to answer for.

"What's with the pink gun?" I nodded at the pistol she was holding.

"It's a Glock 43, lightweight and concealable but with considerable firepower. Very reliable. Made for smaller hands."

"Mom, you sound like a gun commercial. My question is why do you have a gun in the first place? Any gun, let alone one that is half hot pink."

"Don't worry. It's legal. I showed the officer my registration."

"But why?" I couldn't reconcile the mother I had known all my life with the woman holding the pink and black pistol.

"I got it when you became a detective. It made me feel safer."

Her explanation was like a gut punch. "I'm sorry" was all I could think of to say. It hadn't occurred to me that my mother felt personally unsafe because of my profession. And, in spite of that, she had granted me permission to stay with it. I hoped getting a visit from Bondo and his friend hadn't nullified our truce.

Yuri came back and joined us, grinning at my mother. "You put on quite the show," he said. "Sorry we only got the audio version. I particularly liked the bit about shooting one in the foot but the other wherever you could manage."

"I'm sorry," I said again. "I thought they had given up on me as a potential link to Gary."

"It's alright, Cameron. People like that shouldn't be allowed to harass civilians for any reason." Mom was apparently feeling generous. Probably because she'd had the opportunity to play a kickass woman role in her own production.

"Love the gun," Yuri said. "Can I look at it?"

Mom handed him the gun and he checked it out.

"Please don't say 'lightweight with considerable firepower,'" I pleaded.

He seemed to miss my sarcasm as he continued to inspect my mother's gun. "Well balanced, good grip, and it *is* lightweight."

I groaned and glared at him.

Yuri handed the gun back to my mother. "What I don't understand is why they broke in while you were here."

"Probably because I left my car at the repair shop to get some work done. A friend dropped me off in the alley because my new shoes were hurting my feet. I didn't want to walk any farther than necessary."

"So, when they saw the kids leave, they thought they had some time," Yuri said. "I bet there was a third guy, a lookout. If there was, he or she must have been out front and probably took off when the police arrived."

"They weren't making any attempt to be quiet," Mom said. "When I heard them, I got my gun and sneaked down the stairs. You should have seen their faces when I ordered them to turn towards me with their hands in the air."

Yuri laughed and I felt myself involuntarily smiling at the image.

"Did they say anything we should know before you called me?" I asked.

"No, I figured it had something to do with Duffy, so I didn't bother asking them much. I knew they would just lie."

"We don't know for sure that they aren't working for the FBI," I said. "Bondo is a consultant who does a lot of work for the government." I'd told Yuri about the truce and my Mom's two rules for me going forward, so he wasn't surprised when, to honor Rule Number Two about keeping her informed, I told her about Bondo's government connection. Although he probably would have told her anyway, figuring she had earned the right to know by capturing them.

"A somewhat well-run operation," Mom said. "But with a few significant screw-ups. Sounds like government to me. If not working for the FBI, maybe Homeland Security? Or the CIA? I've always thought the CIA has a tendency to go overboard from time to time."

"MI-6 with American accents," Yuri said. They both laughed.

By kidding around about Bondo's employer, it felt like they weren't taking what happened seriously enough. They were treating it like it was a bad movie plot. "There's nothing funny about this situation. There is no legitimacy behind their investigation. Gary is NOT a criminal."

Yuri looked down at his feet. Mom shook her head to let me know she was both sorry for making fun of the situation and yet pitied me for my naiveté. "I know you think you did the right thing, Cameron, but you don't really know this man. He may have done something illegal. You have to face that."

"And," Yuri said, "we all need to acknowledge that whoever these men are, they are determined and possibly ruthless. There has to be a reason for their actions."

I wished I could share the reason, but somehow, even if I could, I didn't think either my mother or Yuri would be appeased. They might even label what Gary had done and what he might be doing at this very moment as criminal.

CHAPTER 16
WHAT IF?

AFTER MOM WENT UPSTAIRS, taking her pink and black gun with her, Yuri and I called PW. She answered on the second ring, and we put her on speaker. "I know Yuri gave you an overview of what happened here tonight, but we wanted to fill you in on some details from something we discovered earlier. It muddies the waters a bit."

"First," PW said, "let me tell you what our lawyer said about the breaking and entry charge. You won't like this, but I think it's for the best. Since we don't really want to dig deeper into the question of who Bondo and his colleague work for, he thinks you should let it go."

"But they broke into my home. While my mother was here."

"Yes, and from what Yuri told me, your mother did a good job of defending herself. Not that I'm suggesting she should've had to do that. At the same time, it sounds like you did an excellent job of denying any connection with Gary. If what we want is for them to leave you and your family alone, then tonight's incident may have done the trick."

"Won't the police discover Bondo and his sidekick aren't FBI?" I asked.

"I would certainly hope so. But they might be intimidated by the same firewall that we encountered. Or perhaps Bondo has a better cover for a law enforcement inquiry. Most likely, he has someone in government who will vouch for them. In any case, it doesn't serve our interests to prosecute them for a misdemeanor such as criminal trespass, and it would be very difficult to make something more serious stick. And, I might add, if they are determined to go after you, Bondo would just be replaced by someone else. That may have already happened."

I understood her reasoning, and I was sure Gary would want us to stay out of his business, but I still resisted. "Can we ask for an apology? Or an explanation?"

"They already told you they were looking for Gary," Yuri said.

"And I don't think our Mr. Bondo is a man who apologizes for much of anything," PW added.

There was no choice but to acquiesce. "What do I tell my mother?"

"Tell her that they must have had some official affiliation because they were released without being charged. She may still feel they had no right to enter your home like that—and I wholeheartedly agree. But she will certainly understand why we don't want to poke the monster that is trying to find Gary."

"Okay. I think I can convince her that this is the best option under the circumstances. But it makes me really angry. Bondo is so … so …"

"Arrogant? Smarmy? Deceitful? Rude? Overbearing? Am I coming close?" PW asked.

"All of the above."

"If you let every man you meet who fits these labels get to you, you will spend a lot of time angry." She sounded half-serious, like she had been there.

"You've made your point. I'll let it go." Hearing the truth doesn't always help when you're angry, but intellectually I knew it was time to move on.

"She doesn't really mean that," Yuri said to PW. "She'll be venting for at least a month."

"And you will lend a sympathetic ear, like the good team player that you are," PW's tone was playful, but it was clearly a strong recommendation.

"I believe that was a directive from the boss," I said. "Just so you know, I *do* intend to vent for a full month."

"If that's settled," PW said, "I believe you called to tell me something."

"Yes, it's a bit complicated though. Maybe Yuri should give you the background." I didn't add "since it was his idea," but he knew what I meant. PW probably would too after she heard what we had to say. He was usually the instigator.

"In going back over our assignment for the Goldbergs and what the police appear to have concluded, we thought it would be a good idea to at least consider the possibility that the police, and not us, were on the right track." I heard the "we" but didn't correct him. After all, it had become a "we" once I'd agreed to his plan.

"The reason we assumed Gabe was after Gary was that we knew from Cameron that Gary was on the run. And because of that assumption, we also concluded that he had been tailed to the mall by either Gabe or someone giving Gabe orders. But what if we were wrong about that? What if we are dealing with two separate events? With that in mind, we decided to take a look around Gabe's room at his parents' house as well as at his apartment. Just in case the police missed something."

"We were still focusing on the shooter and not the shooting," I said quickly. "As it turned out, it did give us some insight into Gabe's life. Including some observations that we can use for the Goldberg report."

"The really good news though is that we found something the police overlooked." Yuri paused, long enough for a silent drumroll. "Cameron found a box full of pictures in Gabe's room. A lot of them were of a girl, Lindy Mason. Turns out he had a huge crush on her in high school, an obsessive crush." Another pause for a silent drumroll. "Then, when we searched his apartment, we discovered an entire pegboard covered with pictures. Many of them of this same girl. And one of them showed the girl with another boy, Callum Goldberg, the only victim from the shooting."

PW always listened without interrupting, saving her questions until the person speaking finished saying what they had to say. She believed you got a more honest report if you didn't ask something that might funnel or influence the speaker's train of thought. Usually, her face was a mask of neutrality when listening to an update, but I wondered whether this evening, given the enormity of Yuri's pronouncement, whether she was reacting or not. I regretted we weren't delivering our update in person.

"If I understand you correctly, based on that picture, you've changed your theory about the shooter's target." It wasn't a question. "That would explain a few anomalies, but—"

Yuri leapt in. "Like Yogi Berra said, 'That's too coincidental to be a coincidence.' On the other hand, it's only a coincidence if we give it that label. Was it a coincidence that Gary happened to be in the mall when another target was shot at? Or was it a coincidence that the shooter killed the boyfriend of the girl he was fixated on by accident while aiming at Gary? At this point it seems entirely possible that we may be looking at two totally unrelated events that happened to overlap in time and place."

I couldn't believe Yuri had just quoted Yogi Berra to PW to defend our latest theory, but it did seem appropriate. "Gary was surprised they had tracked him to the mall," I said. "Maybe they hadn't. At least not right away. Maybe they only went there after the fact, after somehow making a connection between me and Gary. Although they had to know it wasn't a strong connection. That would explain why they didn't reveal their hand at first. Why approach me directly if I didn't know anything for sure? Although launching an elaborate ploy like hiring us to find Gary's dog seems like overkill."

"Not really," Yuri said. "By doing it that way, they avoided calling attention to themselves; it can't be good for business to get caught harassing the wrong person."

"Well, they certainly blew their cover when they broke into my house."

"I can't help but feel that their employers will not be happy with them about that," PW said. "And I do think you may be onto something. Unfortunately, it lands you in that gray area between profiling the shooter and investigating the shooting. Still, I think it's a line of inquiry you need to pursue. We may have been slow to put this together because we didn't want to pry into Gary's business, but given what you've learned, I don't see how we can simply walk away. Talk to this young woman and see what she has to say."

"We'll get on it right away," Yuri said.

"And remember," PW cautioned, "... even if you're right, it doesn't change the fact that Bondo and whoever hired him are determined to find Gary, and not to present him with a medal. They remain a threat. The good news is that, if you're correct, we don't have any conflict of interest. To be honest, that would ease my mind a great deal."

Mine too. And it would also be good news for Gary. He may not have been responsible for getting an innocent bystander killed.

"And check with Jenny about the dog," PW added. "Whoever these men are who are looking for Gary, they are thorough. We don't want to put Jenny in the crosshairs on this one."

We were about to hang up when PW thought of something else. "One last thing. You didn't happen to keep any of those pictures, did you?"

"Well, I may have removed one from the box in Gabe's desk."

"*May* have?"

"Did," I reluctantly corrected.

"I would advise that you put it back. If you are interviewed, you wouldn't want to admit to being in possession of illegally obtained evidence."

"We didn't take the one of Lindy and Callum," Yuri pointed out. "But Cameron took pictures of the pegboard."

"Good. If you're right about all of this, your visit to his apartment will become part of the official record."

As soon as we hung up, I called Jenny and was pleased to get through to her on a Saturday evening. She knew it wasn't a social call, so I got right to the point and asked if she had seen any strangers around her farm.

"I'm way ahead of you on this one. I started thinking about the possibility of these guys checking on all of us Penny-wise employees. So, much to the disappointment of my daughter, I moved him to a friend's farm. We're still referring to him as Duffy by the way. I've told her to lie if anyone comes to the farm and asks about him. I think she was pleased to have permission to lie, no matter what it's about. I've cautioned her not to overdo it though. Actually, teaching her how to lie effectively was a bit uncomfortable. As for Bandit, I know it's hard on him being moved around so much, but it seemed like a good idea."

"Thank you—definitely a good idea. I just hope he stays put."

"I think he will. I know this sounds strange to say, but I think he's aware that something unusual is happening. And I believe he has faith that his owner will one day return. What's your best guess?"

"If he can, he will."

"That sounds ominous. But if he doesn't return, I'll take Bandit back. My daughter really likes him."

I felt a catch in my throat. "I'm still hoping he will return" was all I could manage.

Yuri was giving me a strange look, part sympathy, part judgmental concern. I knew he didn't want me to get involved with Gary, and I agreed that it wasn't a smart thing to do. But I had enjoyed the fantasy and wanted to hold onto it for as long as possible. Like the vision of the perfect day: alone on a sandy beach with the sun overhead and a cool drink in your hand or skiing down a slope of fresh snow with ease and grace, or bumping into the love of your life in a coffee shop, or ... The reality was that I was engaging in an awful lot of wishful thinking about a man who would never fit into my life.

CHAPTER 17
OBSESSION

"WANT TO SEE IF we can find a number for Lindy Mason now or wait until morning?" Yuri asked.

"Now. I won't be able to concentrate on anything else anyway. Let's hope she hasn't married and changed her name."

An hour later we had numbers for three Lindy Masons in the Seattle area. It always surprised me how many names were duplicated, even uncommon ones. Of course, there was the possibility that "our" Lindy wasn't any of these. She could have moved out of state or changed her name. But we were hoping to get lucky. We'd been lucky once; it could happen again.

Call number one answered, but she was not the right Lindy Mason and didn't know the other two in the area. In fact, she was surprised there were two other people with the same name as hers living nearby. Obviously, none of them was defaulting on any loans because that was one of the common ways people discovered their namesakes. At Penny-wise we'd handled several such cases since I'd been there, helping someone prove they weren't the offending party.

The second number had been disconnected. So much for an up-to-date resource.

The third went to voicemail. I left a message with a very brief explanation of who I was and asked her to call me. I didn't threaten to call again if I didn't hear from her, but I fully intended to do so. I would call her again. And again, if necessary. If that didn't work, we would have to track her down in person. One way or the other, we intended to get in touch with the girl in Gabe's pictures.

There was no way to know if or when Lindy would call, but I offered to make us some sandwiches while we waited. Yuri never turns down food. I had just set out all of the ingredients for building our own sandwiches when Mom came down to see how we were doing, and to ask about our call with PW. She was so desperate for information she agreed to have a sandwich with us. Without mayo or onions, of course.

"What do you do next?" Mom asked.

"I go out and buy myself a gun with pink flowers on it," Yuri kidded. "Or maybe a pearl-handled pistol."

"The sales guy talked me into it," Mom said. "The grip is sized for a woman's hand."

"And fashion tastes."

"I don't deny that I like the fact that it doesn't look like something a gangster would carry."

"Depends on the gangster's gender, doesn't it?" I said, but Mom ignored my dig.

"Did you take any lessons?" Yuri asked on a more serious note. "I'd be happy to do a practice session with you."

"Yuri!" I said, a tad too loud. I was about to add, don't encourage her, when my mother responded.

"I went to a shooting range to try it out."

"You WHAT?" It was one surprise after another this evening.

"Well, it wouldn't do me any good to have a gun if I didn't know how to use it, now, would it?"

Yuri was laughing at our exchange. "Like mother, like daughter," he said.

Now my mother was smiling, too. But I failed to see the humor in the comparison.

"Do Mara and Jason know about your gun?"

"No, I haven't told them. And I keep it locked up. I purchased a special gun safe for the purpose. Lately, however, since we've been having these, ah, visits, I've been carrying it in my purse during the day. Until now, I thought we were safe at night."

"I would suggest you show it to Mara and Jason," Yuri said. "Talk to them about gun safety. It can't hurt."

"I didn't want to alarm them," Mom said.

"Emphasize it's a precaution, not a solution."

"Let's not mention what happened tonight though, okay?" I said. Then I told her about PW's recommendation to not prosecute Bondo and friend. Like me, my mother didn't like the idea. But in the end, she agreed. I thought about extending a month's venting rights to her but thought better of it at the last minute.

"As long as you think Bondo and his buddy won't return to do whatever it was they intended to do," she said.

"We don't think they will, but you need to stay vigilant," Yuri said. "Just don't overdo it."

I was about to say "I'm sorry" again when Yuri suggested we take our food into the other room and watch a movie to help us unwind. It took us a while to a agree on a movie, but we finally picked a rom-com to watch. There were a few steamy scenes that made me feel uncomfortable watching with my mother sitting next to me and my work colleague nearby. I'm not sure if I was embarrassed for her or for me. Mother-daughter relationships are complicated. No-name joined us for few minutes, couldn't get into the movie and left. In the end, Mom was teary-eyed, I was critical of the writers for their implausible plot, and Yuri declared falling in love at first sight to be unrealistic but entertaining. Even given the mixed reviews, it had done the trick, momentarily distracting us from worries about pink pistols, fake FBI men, and debates over the probability of coincidences being nothing more than coincidences.

Yuri said he was going to drop off the keys to Gabe's apartment on his way home and reminded me that I was supposed to warn the Millers about the mess the police had left behind. Then we called it a night.

Sunday morning Mom made breakfast for the family. There was a vegetable frittata and homemade scones with honey. Mara pointed out that the label on the honey declared it to be local and organic. I wasn't sure how you could control where bees roamed; it seemed to me they could easily sneak into a neighbor's field and suck the nectar of flowers treated with chemicals. However, I chose not to bring up the issue because Mara seemed pleased that it was labeled organic, and the flavor was delicious. Mom had only put mushrooms in part of the frittata, but Jason managed to find one in his portion, removed it with the precision of a surgeon and placed it on the edge of his plate. Mara opened her mouth to give her brother a hard time, but I shot her a look to let it go. She rolled her eyes but kept her mouth shut. After all, she had just ordered an expensive new cell phone and had almost decided on the jacket she wanted to replace the one stolen. She could afford to be generous with her brother.

No-name was going back and forth between Mara and Jason as if expecting to get a taste of something. "I certainly hope no one has been giving No-name people food, especially while we're eating. We don't want to train him to beg."

Mom jumped up. "He was such a good boy yesterday." She went over to a cupboard and came back with a small dog bone treat. "Here," she said to Jason. "You give it to him."

"Not at the—" I started to say. But it was too late. Then I noticed that the mushroom was no longer gracing the edge of Jason's plate. At some point I would have to have a talk with Jason about why people food wasn't good for dogs, but it wasn't a battle I felt up to taking on at the moment.

My phone rang while I was helping Mom clean up. It was Lindy number three. As soon as I'd ascertained that I had the right person on the other end, I asked if a colleague and I could come by to talk to her about Gabe Miller.

"I have nothing to say about him."

"Let me explain," I said quickly, before she could hang up. "The Goldbergs are our clients. They are understandably devastated. You would be doing this for them."

She was silent a moment. "I don't think there's anything I can tell you. I didn't know Gabe Miller. But I guess I could meet you in about an hour. Just for a few minutes though."

We agreed to meet at a coffee shop near where she lived. I called Yuri and suggested he meet me there. Mom had heard my end of both conversations and waved off further help with the breakfast dishes. "Go get some answers," she said. "All I ask is that at some point you fill me in on what's going on."

"Yes," I said. "Rule Number Two. And, depending on what Lindy has to tell us, you may find this piece of the investigation quite interesting." I surprised her with a quick hug before hurrying off.

The coffee shop we'd agreed on resembled three-quarters of the coffee shops in the greater Seattle area. There was the line of customers wending their way through low wood display cases with stacks of sweet and savory snacks. Next came the larger, glass-enclosed cases filled with more substantial offerings, including pastries, quiches, sandwiches and cold drinks. At the end of all these temptations was the main reason most people were there: the caffeine of your choice. It was, after all, referred to as a coffee shop.

As I entered, I noted the unusually short line of people waiting to order. At the same time, I saw an attractive young woman sitting at a table with two empty chairs. I was instinctively drawn to the short line, but at that moment, the woman looked in my direction. I had to forego the urge to get a cuppa before joining her.

In just two years Lindy had lost her girlish high school look. Her hair was cut in a professional bob, her complexion was flawless, and her outfit was stylish casual rather than trendy, wanna-be grown up. As I sat down, Yuri appeared and quickly joined us, glancing, as I had, at the short line on his way over.

"Can I get everyone something to drink? he asked.

"I don't have much time," Lindy said. She already had a drink in front of her. Yuri noted that and looked at me. I shook my head and said, "No thanks." Yuri sat down, reluctantly, I thought.

I gave Lindy a card and explained a little more about what we hoped to do for the Goldbergs. Then I asked if she'd been dating Callum at the time of the shooting.

"No, we broke up a couple of months ago."

"Sorry. I know that can be tough."

Her eyes narrowed. "Especially if he cheats on you with your former best friend."

"Ouch. That sucks," Yuri offered.

"I was devastated," Lindy said. "Really devastated."

"I'm so sorry." I seemed to be saying that a lot lately.

"I can never forgive him, but I'm sorry he died."

"Do you know if Gabe Miller knew about your breakup?"

She looked genuinely surprised by my question. "Why would he?"

"You haven't been in touch?"

"I was never 'in touch' with Gabe Miller. Never. As I told you on the phone, I didn't know him."

"But you knew he had a crush on you."

She blinked. "In high school. Sort of. A couple of my friends may have mentioned it. But I never paid any attention."

"What did you think of him back then?"

"To be honest, I didn't think of him at all. He wasn't friends with anyone I knew. He didn't do sports or go to any of the parties I went to. He was … a nobody. I'm sorry if that sounds snobbish."

Yuri said, "We think he still had a thing for you. Even after high school. You don't remember seeing him around, do you?"

"You mean like was he stalking me or something?"

"I'm just asking if you've run into him or seen him recently."

She gave it some thought. "It's possible," she said. "Even after I saw his picture on TV after the shooting, I couldn't quite place him. But I have this recollection of seeing someone who looked kinda like him near the food court where I sometimes eat lunch."

"Do you eat with friends?"

"Yes, of course."

"And have you talked with them about your breakup with Callum?"

"I don't see why that's relevant—"

"We're trying to establish whether Gabe knew about the breakup."

"What if he did?" Suddenly she seemed to see where our somewhat clumsy questioning was heading.

"You don't think—I mean, why would he—I've never even talked to him!"

"I'm sorry if this upsets you," I said. "It's not uncommon for someone to be unaware of an individual's fixation with them."

"And we don't know whether he was actually stalking you or trolling you online," Yuri said. "But he did have some pictures of you that he had taken. Or that he had found online. One was of you and Callum." He paused to let that sink in. "He knew the two of you were a couple."

"Would Callum have told you if Gabe had threatened him?" I asked.

"I don't know."

"Is there someone else he may have confided in?"

"You think it wasn't a random shot that killed Callum? You think Gabe was *trying* to kill him?" As her face paled, a splotch of crimson flush appeared on her neck.

"We're just considering the possibility. We could be way off base. That's why we wanted to talk with you and anyone else who might have noticed Gabe following you around."

"If someone had noticed Gabe hanging around, I'm sure they would have said something to me. And if Callum talked to someone about Gabe, don't you think they would have come forward by now? I haven't heard anyone even hint at what you're suggesting."

"There's a lot we don't understand about Gabe's reason for doing what he did. But we do know he was obsessed with you. And it isn't uncommon for a stalker to stay out of sight. Although that could have changed at some point. He might have eventually approached you."

"I can't believe it. I mean, I didn't encourage him in any way."

"Unfortunately, he didn't need encouragement. It was something that started in high school and apparently continued afterwards."

Lindy took a piece of paper out of her purse "I'll give you the name of Callum's best friend. Maybe he knows something that will help you." She wrote down his name and number from memory.

"You keep in touch with his best friend?" I asked.

She blushed beneath the perfectly applied makeup. "At first I was just trying to get back at Callum. He was dating my best friend, my *former* best friend, behind my back, so why not date *his* best friend?"

"Did that upset him?"

"Yes, we had one very nasty exchange … in the food court." She hesitated. "It never occurred to me that … that someone like Gabe might have overheard our fight."

"How upset did you get?"

"He yelled at me. And I broke down and cried, like a stupid schoolgirl. I was just so upset. I mean, I didn't actually think he was the love of my life, but I hated the fact that he had cheated on me, and with my best friend."

She'd referred to her best friend so many times I had the sense that she felt almost more betrayed by her than by her boyfriend. Relationships were complicated.

As we prepared to leave, I encouraged her to call me if she thought of anything, or even if she just wanted to talk.

"Will you be telling the police about this? I mean, is this going to become public?"

"I honestly don't know." She looked stricken. "But none of this is your fault—you didn't encourage him. Whatever happened, this is on him, not you."

"Thank you," she said. She might thank me now, but if it made the news, my guess is she would curse me instead.

We went to my car and Yuri called Callum's friend. When he answered, Yuri put him on speaker. At this point we only had two questions for him: Had Callum mentioned seeing Gabe hanging around or did he know whether Callum had talked to Gabe recently. If the friend had said "yes" to either question, we would have asked for a meeting. But he couldn't remember who Gabe was and was positive Callum hadn't mentioned him. Another dead end.

The picture of Lindy and Callum together posted on the pegboard in Gabe's apartment was suggestive, but not conclusive. Nor could we prove that Gabe had overheard the fight between Callum and Lindy or that he had learned about their bitter breakup in some other way. The bottom line was that the police had seen the same pictures we had and had not followed up. Although I could think of a number of reasons for that. Maybe two different sets of officers had searched the Millers' home and Gabe's apartment. Maybe they had noted what they found but no one had compared lists and made the connection. Maybe no one had recognized Callum in spite of his face appearing on TV and in newspapers. Maybe they were so convinced it was a random mass shooting that they didn't feel it was necessary to look further. Lack of coordination and psychological tunnel vision. One or the other, or a combination of both.

We stayed in my car, going over and over what we knew and making note of gaps in our understanding. The evidence favoring Callum as Gabe's intended victim was all circumstantial. If we took our theory to the police, they were unlikely to pursue it. They had already closed the case. It was over. Another unsettling mass shooting with more questions than answers, but the shooter was dead. End of story.

CHAPTER 18
EPIPHANY

I'D PUT OFF CALLING the Millers about the mess in Gabe's apartment, but I finally forced myself to do it. When I got their voicemail, relief flooded my system. I was leaving a message when Mrs. Miller broke in.

"Hello? Hello?"

"Mrs. Miller," I said. "This is Cameron Chandler with Penny-wise. Sorry to call you on a Sunday evening, but there's something you need to know." I took a deep breath and spit it out. "The police left quite a mess at Gabe's apartment, a really big mess—things overturned, drawers tossed, food on the floor. I don't like being the one to tell you, but I wanted you to be prepared."

"We haven't been able to face going there," she said.

"I can understand. I'm so sorry that this is one more thing you have to cope with."

"You are very kind. Not everyone has been."

I could imagine how people reacted to the parents of a mass shooter. I told her once again that I was sorry and said to feel free to call if I could be of any help. It was a hollow gesture; there was nothing anyone could do to ease their pain. Only time might help.

The kids were in bed and I was just about to turn in when Mom came home. She'd been to the symphony with friends, followed by a late dinner. She was humming a familiar piece of music when she came in, reaching a dramatic finale that made me instantly feel like I should be standing in front of an orchestra with a baton in my hand.

"Bravo," I called to her from the living room.

When she realized I was still up she asked if I would like a cup of hot chocolate. In the past I would have been worried that was code for "we need to talk," but now that we had our truce and ground rules in place, I knew she just wanted an update on our meeting with Lindy Mason.

"You look nice," I said. She had on a black, calf-length dress with long sleeves and a high neckline. An imposing ruby pendant necklace stood out against the black backdrop.

She touched the necklace. "Do you remember this? Your father gave it to me for an anniversary one year. I've always suspected someone else picked it out for him, but I wanted to think he did it himself. Wives can be foolish about such things, can't they?"

"I don't remember it, but it's lovely."

She headed for my kettle, and I jumped up to do the honors. "Here, you sit down, I'll fix the hot chocolate."

Mom stepped aside and moved over to the cupboard. "Want a couple of mini marshmallows in it?" She and Mara often worked together in our kitchen, so she knew where everything was, probably including my "secret" supplies of what she would consider junk food: store-bought cookies, salted crackers, a jar of Tootsie Roll Minis, and, from time to time, flavored potato chips. Even so, I was surprised she was asking if I wanted a sugar rush to go with the caffeine in the chocolate at this late hour. But why not?

"Sure."

"I keep thinking about the mall shooting," she said, holding the bag of marshmallows while I prepared the hot chocolate. "I know there are things you can't tell me about the cases you're working on, but something doesn't feel right."

"I need to tell you about the new theory Yuri and I have."

I poured the hot chocolate into two mugs and Mom scattered tiny marshmallows on top. I love the smell of hot chocolate. And the tiny marshmallows instantly took me back to my childhood. Before my mother became a health-conscious cook. I breathed in the familiar aroma. The first sip was never as good as the first sniff.

"You always liked to smell your hot chocolate," Mom said.

"Really?" I didn't remember that.

"Mara does that, too."

I was tempted to say "I know that," but I had to admit to myself that it wasn't something I'd noticed. Did that make me a bad mother, I wondered? "I do love the sweet chocolatey scent," I said instead.

"So, what's the new theory?"

I began by warning her that we didn't actually have any real proof, no more than speculation and circumstantial evidence. Then I plunged into the narration, first giving her a verbal tour of Gabe's room in his parents' house, a Western motif time capsule. I described the sad photo in his senior year annual. And I told her about the box of pictures I'd found in his desk, most of them of the same girl, Lindy Mason.

"Lindy is the girl the school cook told you he had a crush on, right?" Mom asked.

"Right." I moved on to a description of Gabe's apartment and the pegboard filled with pictures.

"Pathetic," Mom said.

I ended by telling her about our conversation with Lindy, how she'd been unaware of Gabe's obsession with her, and how she'd had a heated argument with Callum in the food court where she could have been overheard by Gabe.

"If you're right, and Gabe wanted to kill Callum but didn't want anyone to know that's what he was doing, then the mall was the perfect location and a mass shooting the perfect cover. He could get revenge for the way Callum treated Lindy and leave her entirely in the clear. A thoughtful killer."

"I hadn't thought of it like that, but that makes sense. Well, not really, but given his twisted way of thinking it does."

"There's one thing we've left out though—he would have wanted Lindy to know what he had done for her."

"You're right again. But if that's the case, why didn't he leave a note or an online message? If he had, that kind of thing would surely have leaked to the press by now."

"Maybe it's out there somewhere no one has looked yet." Mom sipped her hot chocolate, carefully wiping a tiny line of marshmallow off with a napkin.

"If he did leave her a private message, wouldn't he have left it somewhere obvious, somewhere she would be sure to find it? She didn't even seem to know he was stalking her and claimed they had never talked. It felt like she was telling the truth. If she was, then there was no message."

"What about a public message? An 'in case I die' sort of thing?"

"I'm sure the police searched every nook and cranny of his room and his apartment. There's no reason for them to keep quiet about finding a note like that."

Mom stirred her hot chocolate with a spoon, swirling the three mini marshmallows in her cup around and around. She'd dumped quite a few in mine but limited herself to three. I wouldn't have been happy with only three.

We sat there in companionable silence for a minute or so. We hadn't done that for a while. It was a nice feeling. Mom broke the silence after taking a long sip of hot chocolate. Now there were only two mini marshmallows in her cup.

"If he deliberately killed Callum, you have to ask yourself who he would want to tell about it. The only person I can think of is Lindy. I mean, if he had a bigger message, some complaint against a group or the government or even the mall, he would have left a note or an online statement that would be easily found by the police. But if this was a personal act of revenge on her behalf, then she would have been the only person he cared about telling."

"And he must have at least considered the possibility that he wouldn't make it out alive," I said.

"He probably hoped he could get away with it, but from what I've read in the papers, not many mass shooters do."

"Unless all of my instincts are dead, I could swear Lindy had no idea that he was watching her. Even when they were in high school. And she seemed sincerely shocked by the idea that he might have witnessed her fight with Callum in the food court."

"Maybe he sent the message, but she didn't get it," Mom said.

The realization of what might have happened came crashing down on me. It was more than an *aha* moment. It felt almost physical, like suddenly walking under a waterfall, feeling the individual drops pummeling your skin. "Mom, you're a genius." I pushed my chair back from the table and went over and gave her a big hug, a real hug, not just a hug lite. She didn't quite resist, but it was a bit like hugging an inanimate object. We needed to work on that.

"What did I say?" she asked.

"It's about protecting those you love. Being willing to take action and not tell anyone. Gabe thought he was protecting Lindy. But he wasn't the only one who would want to protect her, was he?"

Mom suddenly caught my *aha*. "Of course—her family. You're suggesting a family member intercepted the message. But how?"

"Did I mention Lindy lives in a basement apartment in her parents' house? I have no doubt there is only one mailbox."

CHAPTER 19
I'LL NEVER TELL

MONDAY MORNING. I could hardly wait to talk to Yuri about my epiphany. There seemed to be more traffic than usual, and several times I found myself yelling at the car ahead to get a move on. Each stoplight was an irritant. Each pedestrian too slow for words. And although the parking lot at the mall was practically empty, I managed to get behind a car that crawled into the one-lane entrance, delaying a sprint to my final destination.

I didn't even stop for coffee at any of the kiosks I passed, denying the alluring aroma of coffee beans and fresh pastries, a smell-o-rama I suspected sellers of using to attract customers. Once inside I hurried past Blaine with a perfunctory "Good morning." Norm and Adele were in the pit. But no Yuri.

I mumbled a few greetings, poured a cup of coffee, and tried to concentrate on organizing the report for the Goldbergs. Leaving out our latest theory and my epiphany.

When Yuri finally arrived, I gave him just enough time to grab a cup of coffee before ushering him into the closet. "I almost called you last night," I said. "I even considered calling you when I got up this morning. But I wanted to see your face when I tell you what my mother and I came up with." I was talking fast, speeding toward the checkered flag at the end of the race.

Yuri sat up straight, hooked by my enthusiasm. I dumped my Mom-inspired epiphany on him and waited. When he didn't respond with the same level of excitement I was feeling, I felt deflated, and somewhat peeved.

"Why would one or both of her parents have withheld a message from Gabe?" Yuri asked. "Explain that to me again."

"Well, they certainly wouldn't have shared it with the police. That would have dragged their daughter into an ugly news cycle of exploitation and speculation. The police might even have wondered whether Lindy knew in advance about his plan. You never know how things are going to look to officials or what lines of inquiry they feel duty-bound to pursue."

"Okay, I get that. And I know we agreed that she seemed authentically oblivious to the idea that Gabe was stalking her. But what if we're wrong? What if she *did* know about Gabe's obsession with her? Maybe, in the heat of the moment, after her fight with Callum in the food court, she decided to use his fixation to her advantage. She could have enlisted his help in getting revenge on Callum for what he'd done to her. I'm not saying she asked Gabe to kill him. At the most, she probably thought he would rough him up a bit. It may have been an instance of fantasy revenge gone terribly awry."

"That makes sense—if I hadn't seen her reaction when we brought up Gabe's obsession with her. She seemed truly shocked and turned off by it. Do you really believe she was lying about everything?"

"No, not really, but the urge for self-protection can be powerful. You never know what someone might do or say to avoid getting caught. One way or the other though, I still don't get why a parent would intercept a note like that."

"I hate to pull the parent card, but I can not only understand why they wouldn't want their child dragged into a front-page news story about a shooting in a mall, but also why they wouldn't want them burdened with the knowledge that they were indirectly responsible for someone's death. I'd definitely keep a secret like that to protect one of my children."

"Okay, mama bear, put that way, I buy it. What's next?"

"We need to get PW up to speed."

"Let's do it."

PW listened while we explained that we'd found no additional evidence to demonstrate Gabe's obsession with Lindy. All we had was what we'd described to her before, the school cook's observations and the pictures we'd found. And although he may have had opportunity to find out about how upset Lindy was over the breakup with Callum and why, we couldn't even prove he knew they had broken up. *If* he had known about the details of the break-up, however, there was the possibility that he'd decided to prove his manhood and devotion to Lindy by killing Callum, punishing him for his infidelity. The fact that Callum probably embodied everything Gabe hadn't been in high school, in our opinion, could have been added incentive.

"The question is whether one or both of Lindy's parents would have intercepted a message from Gabe about the shooting," Yuri said.

"That seems entirely plausible to me," PW said. "People try to protect loved ones, not always giving serious consideration to the consequences of their actions."

"This may be sexist, but I think it's more likely to have been Lindy's mother who found the note and kept it from her," I said.

"It seems to me that either parent is a candidate for that kind of protective act." PW caressed the lone cigarette in her antique ashtray, thoughtfully, as if stroking a pet. "But I don't think it would be wise to confront them together. If only one of them is involved, they are less likely to admit it in front of their spouse."

"No matter which one did it," Yuri said, "do we have any reason to think they will confess to destroying a note from Gabe? I mean, what's in it for them to tell the truth at this point?"

"I agree. But I still want to make a try."

"Are you trying to solve a crime?" PW asked me. "Or do you simply seek closure for yourself?"

"Maybe a little of both," I admitted.

"Sometimes it's best if the truth remains buried," PW observed.

"But doesn't Gary need to know if he wasn't Gabe's target?" Yuri asked. I was surprised to hear him mention following up on the lead in order to help Gary.

"It's been a while. He may already know who is responsible," PW said.

"That's true. But he isn't here to share that information with us." I didn't add that he might never return to share that information, but Yuri and PW had to be thinking along the same lines. "In the meantime, another benefit of confirming this possibility is that I won't feel as guilty about what happened. I know I didn't ask Gary to bring Bandit to me, but he came because of me. If Gary was the target, then I'm indirectly responsible for Callum's death."

"I won't lecture you on what you should or shouldn't feel. And I can't see any harm in pursuing this. Here's what I want you to do." Once PW makes a decision, she seems to see a clear means to an end. In this instance, the means was me and the end was to get a confession from Lindy's mother. "It's more likely that she will talk to another sympathetic mother than to two investigators," PW concluded. "And I would drop by rather than making an appointment. Don't give her time to prepare a defense."

Yuri and I went back to the pit to finish our coffee and strategize. Yuri was still struggling not only with the thought of a parent destroying a piece of evidence, but if so, which parent might be the more likely to have done it.

"If it was the father instead of the mother, and he didn't tell his wife, you will be revealing his deception with your questions," Yuri said. "Keep that in mind when you broach the subject. It could even have been the mother and father acting together. If that's the case, she may be reluctant to say anything that would incriminate the two of them."

In the end, we decided I couldn't anticipate what questions might get her to talk. We didn't know enough about her or her relationship with her daughter and husband to make any good guesses. I would have to rely on instinct and my assessment of her in the moment.

A half hour later I was on my way to drop in on Mrs. Mason. I was almost hoping she wouldn't be at home. Or that someone would be there with her and I would have to come back another time. I didn't relish confronting her. If she had intercepted a message to her daughter, she had done so out of love and concern. And I was aiming to shatter the wall she had erected around her daughter's vulnerability.

When she answered the door, I had to take a deep breath and gusty myself up while she stood there expectantly, waiting for me to explain who I was and why I was standing on her porch. She was an attractive woman, an older version of her daughter. She was wearing navy-blue sweats and a matching long-sleeved T-shirt. My first impression was that she didn't seem pleased to be interrupted in whatever she'd been doing, but she was neither rude nor dismissive.

I handed her a card and said I would like to talk to her about her daughter's ex-boyfriend. She only hesitated a moment before agreeing to chat. I couldn't help wondering if she guessed why I was there, if she had anticipated that eventually someone would show up and ask awkward questions. Maybe it would be a relief to get her secret off her chest.

She invited me to take a seat on an uncomfortable beige leather chair with a sloping back that made it difficult to sit upright. I perched on the edge to avoid sliding into an inclined position. Mrs. Mason sat down across from me in a wood rocking chair and began rocking back and forth. Was it to hide signs of nervousness or was it an unconscious need to stay in motion?

"I'll get right to the point," I said, acting on PW's suggestion that I not give her time to think about a defense. Of course, if she was guilty, she'd already had plenty of time to consider what she would say if someone questioned her about Callum's death. "I was at the mall the day of the shooting. In fact, I saw Callum get shot. At the time I didn't know it was fatal. But that's one of the reasons I'm here. I have a theory about what happened that day."

I paused to take in her initial reaction. She had stopped rocking and was sitting perfectly still. But she didn't say anything.

"Callum's parents hired Penny-wise Investigations to do a profile on Gabe Miller. While looking into Gabe's life, we discovered that he was obsessed with your daughter." I paused again to let the fact that I knew about Gabe sink in. "He was stalking her. And he was there when your daughter and Callum fought about their break-up. He overheard your daughter accusing Callum of betraying her with her best friend. He saw her crying. He knew how very upset she was." I leaned forward and looked directly into her eyes.

"I know what you did. And I'm not saying you were wrong to do it. In your shoes, I think I would have done the same thing for my own daughter." Mrs. Mason hesitated a second too long before responding.

"I have no idea what you're talking about."

"I think you do. And it's up to you if you decide to keep your secret. You think it wouldn't benefit anyone to know that Gabe killed Callum because he thought it would impress your daughter. Or because he wanted to seek revenge on her behalf. That's why you haven't said anything, isn't it?"

"I really have no idea what you're talking about."

"The letter Gabe wrote to Lindy. You opened it, didn't you?"

She remained silent, but she looked uncertain. Her right eye twitched and she reached up to stop it.

"When you read his letter, you realized that it would be headline material. That it would make the front page in all the newspapers. That it would be the subject of interviews and speculation on local TV programs. That it might even attract national attention. It was that kind of story.

"More importantly, you knew that it would make Lindy feel responsible for Callum's death. Even though she wasn't aware of Gabe's unhealthy feelings for her. I know that because my colleague and I talked with Lindy. At this point, however, she has a pretty good idea that Gabe could have overheard the argument she had with Callum. She may even think that Gabe deliberately killed him. But she doesn't know for sure.

"If you don't admit to destroying his letter—I'm assuming you've destroyed it; I would have done so—then she can at least live in doubt, perhaps eventually convincing herself it was a coincidence, that Gabe was a twisted person who just happened to shoot her ex-boyfriend."

Without a word, Mrs. Mason stood up and went over to the window and looked out. Finally, she turned back to me and asked, "If she were your daughter, would you want her to know what you'd done?"

"No, but that's a pretty big secret to bear alone. Have you told your husband?"

She looked out the window again, whether seeking comfort at the familiar site, or giving herself time to think, I couldn't tell.

"I wouldn't be here," I said, "except I know someone who thinks that bullet was meant for him. I'd like to be able to tell him it wasn't."

"Why would he think that?"

"Because someone is very displeased with something he did. And he almost got shot that day. He's in hiding, afraid for his life. If he wasn't Gabe's target, that would make a big difference to him."

"Do you plan to go to the police?" she asked.

"There's no evidence."

"And I'd say you made it all up."

"I don't want to see your daughter suffer. I just want to know the truth."

"The truth is that Gabe was crazy," she said. "He said he'd been admiring her from afar and that he hoped one day she could thank him in person for eliminating someone who had hurt her. Then he went on and on about how attractive she was and how much he wanted to … be with her. It was disgusting.

"At the end of the letter he said that he was aware that he might not survive and asked that, if he didn't, would she put flowers on his grave. He acted like he was doing her a favor and that she owed him one in return."

"Passions run high at that age," I said. "Gabe carried around what he considered his love for your daughter for years. He probably believed he was doing something she would have wanted. From his perspective he was willing to sacrifice himself for her happiness. I'm not defending his actions. Nor am I dismissing them as the act of a madman. I don't know if it helps you to think of it that way or not."

"I don't know what to think. But I can see how, in his warped way, he thought he was in love with my daughter."

"Secrets are hard to keep," I said, getting back to the point of my visit. "And in this case, you destroyed evidence related to a serious crime. If you intend to keep this to yourself, then you better resolve never to tell anyone. Ever."

"I can't tell anyone about something that never happened."

I almost smiled. A mother's protective instincts are incredibly strong. She would deny it if I went to the police. And if I leaked it to the press, it might make a splash for a day or two, but the story would quickly fade, to be replaced by something more scandalous. Besides, I didn't see how exposing what had happened would benefit anyone. And I could think of a number of ways in which people would be hurt by knowing the truth.

I had what I wanted. It was fine with me if she kept her secret. I hoped Yuri and PW agreed.

CHAPTER 20
SECRETS

I WAS SURPRISED when PW suggested a lunch meeting with Yuri and me. In the whole time I'd been there, we had never done that before. She was always supportive, but she kept a professional distance. And although she asked after our families and knew a lot about each employee, we knew very little about her. Several Penny-wise investigators, Yuri included, were fascinated by her secrecy and always on the lookout for clues to unravel her mysterious life and past.

As for me, I joined in when they had a new scheme for unlocking her secrets, but only to engage as part of the group. I was fine with her wanting her privacy. Although if I accidently stumbled across a clue as to where she lived or discovered a way to learn more about her private life, I would be tempted to pursue it on my own. If I learned something enticing, I could always decide afterwards whether to share it with the others. It would depend on the nature of the secret.

Most of the restaurants in the mall were busy and noisy, but there was one Thai place where the high-backed booths and ornate, drop ceiling panel created a sense of privacy and seemed to dampen the sound of voices between booths. As soon as we'd ordered, PW asked for a report on my conversation with Lindy's mom. I didn't hold anything back. Even though I was uncertain how PW and Yuri would feel about me encouraging her to keep what she knew a secret.

"I admit that I've been agonizing over this," I said. "Trying to decide if there is anyone who is hurt by our lack of transparency. And who would be hurt if we put our speculations out there. It seems to me that knowing the connection between Gabe, Lindy, and Callum hurts more people than it serves. Even the police would probably prefer to close the case as is. Am I wrong about this?"

"It's problematic," PW said. "On the one hand, we have a legal obligation to turn over evidence of a crime to the authorities. On the other hand, we still don't have any actual evidence. Just theories. And, as she told you, she would deny knowing anything about a letter."

"There are the pictures that Gabe either took or collected. The one of Callum and Lindy is still on the pegboard in his apartment."

"I advised you to return the one you took," PW said. "I stand by that advice." She looked at me for confirmation.

I nodded agreement even though I wasn't sure how she expected me to "return" the picture without calling attention to the fact that I had taken it without permission. I felt certain no one would know it had ever been there and that if Yuri had taken it, it would simply disappear at this point. I was going to take my cue from Yuri.

Yuri said, "The pictures may be evidence, but, like we've discussed before, the police have already seen them and either chose to ignore them or didn't understand their significance. Either way, I'm not sure they would appreciate our speculations."

PW nodded. "Since they were in plain sight, we wouldn't be calling attention to anything new."

"I'm okay with not mentioning anything about the pictures, but there's one other thing that bothers me," I said. "The public thinks Gabe intended to shoot as many people as he could and was taken out before he could complete his mission. Would it be better for the collective psyche if they knew it was a personal rather than a random shooting?"

"I've thought about that, too," Yuri said. "We already have mass shootings from time to time. And sometimes people also die because they are in the wrong place during a domestic dispute or a robbery, that sort of thing. In this instance, two people were shot, but only one died. How much safer would the public feel knowing that this was someone seeking personal revenge?"

"I see your point, but I admit to being uncomfortable about making that call. It's our responsibility as PIs to tell the truth based on fact and observation."

"We need to put all of this into perspective," PW said. "I, too, am concerned with our ethical responsibilities, but things aren't always as black and white as depicted in professional codes of conduct. Think of what has to happen in order for the 'truth' to be revealed in this instance. The police have to listen to and follow up on your theory. Then they have to find actual evidence to support your assertions. Mrs. Mason has to either confess or be discredited. And, Cameron, you might have to testify about your original concern over Gary's role in all of it.

"Next, consider the impact to the Goldbergs, our clients. Their son's reputation would be tainted by his alleged betrayal of his girlfriend. And don't forget how Lindy will be seen by a scandal-driven public. Finally, you may feel as though you are taking the responsibility for making this decision, but you only have control over one small piece of it. I feel comfortable stepping back and letting the police run with their own theories and observations."

"What should we include in our report to the Goldbergs?" Yuri asked.

"Limit your report to what they asked for. Only include what you can back up." The message was clear. Mrs. Mason's secret was going to remain hers to keep or to reveal.

The server brought our lunch specials and for a moment we fell silent.

"Everyone has secrets," PW said, pausing for effect. "Even me. My advice is to learn to distinguish between necessary secrets and transparency. Buddha said, 'Three things cannot long stay hidden: the sun, the moon, and the truth.' But I've found that 'truth' is seldom absolute."

"The more you know, the more you know you don't know," Yuri said.

"That's often attributed to Aristotle," I pointed out, "but that isn't actually what he said."

PW ended our quibble about quotation attribution before it got under way by changing the subject. "When you talk with Gary, you can tell him what you've learned. I believe he is a man who knows how to keep a secret."

With that, we turned our full attention to our meal. PW asked after my mother and children. And Yuri regaled us with some trivia about prairie dogs.

"Did you know that research has found that prairie dog communication is pretty specific? They can tell another prairie dog that a tall human wearing blue is headed toward their burrows."

If PW hadn't been there, I would have asked about different colors, but I held my tongue. PW smiled but didn't encourage him, and he eventually lost interest in prairie dogs.

After lunch I said I had a personal errand to run and excused myself. "I'll be back in time to help you finish up the Goldberg report," I told Yuri. If PW hadn't been there, he would have asked where I was going. I had counted on that.

My errand *was* personal, in a way. It was related to the case, but it had more to do with preserving Gary's cover than fulfilling any obligation to a client. Once outside the mall, I called the number I had looked up the day before for the Lee family. The remaining loose end was to find out whether Timothy Lee was going to continue playing the hero, or whether he was going to own up to the truth.

Annette Lee, Timothy's mother, answered the phone, her voice hesitant at first. Not recognizing my number, she might have thought it was a robocall. I quickly explained that I had been hired by the Goldbergs to put together a profile of Gabe Miller. I mentioned that I knew that her son and the victim had played basketball on rival teams and knew each other from that experience. And that her son and the shooter were from the same school. From there I made a leap to asking if she would be willing to talk to me.

"I'm not sure what I can tell you," she said.

"I assume you attended your son's games, and I'm hoping to get a feel for the rivalry between the two schools.

Gabe may not have participated in sports, but he may have attended some of the games. Understanding the larger picture will help me fill in some gaps in his profile." It was flimsy, but I hoped it would get me in the door. "The Goldbergs main goal is to better understand Gabe as a person and why he ended up as a mass shooter. But another part of the story is the fact that Callum was within a few feet of your son when he died. They knew each other, both loved basketball, and both were shot on that tragic day."

"Well ..."

"I won't take up much of your time."

For a moment I thought she was going to refuse my request, but she didn't. She said she was home, and I was welcome to drop by.

The Lee home was in a row of older homes, each with its own unique features. Theirs was on a corner. Its chalet-style architecture—wood siding, steep roof and ornate trim—reminded me of structures you would see in ski resorts and Swiss villages. It seemed a little out of place but was nicely kept up. Along the sidewalk was a row of carefully sculpted bushes. Two large planters with colorful arrangements guarded the entrance to the front porch.

Annette Lee answered the door wearing a salmon-colored shirt covered with flour. Her hands were also white. "Sorry," she said, "I can't shake hands. Please, come into the kitchen with me. I'm baking bread."

I followed her into a sunny kitchen with large windows that looked out over a wooded ravine bordering a narrow city park. It was only a few blocks to the lake. "Beautiful," I said. "What a fantastic location."

"Yes, we love the neighborhood." She pointed a white hand at a Cuisinart Coffee Maker and suggested I help myself to a cup of coffee. "There are mugs in that cupboard next to the sink." The coffee smelled great. I got a mug and poured myself a cup.

"This is really good," I said after the first sip.

"It's my weakness, organic coffee beans. I grind my own each morning."

"And you're baking bread, I'm impressed."

"Timothy is a bit on the thin side, so I try to tempt him with carbs that he likes."

"How's he handling the fame of being a hero?" I asked. It was a good segue into the conversation I was hoping to have with her.

"Oh, at first I think he was embarrassed. He was a bit fuzzy about events at the time. But now, well, I think it was just the kind of ego boost he needed. Don't misunderstand me, what happened was tragic, I didn't mean it that way."

"You have to look for silver linings," I said.

"He's always been shy."

"Teenagers are a work in process," I said. "They're all struggling to figure out who they are. My two kids are just entering that stage now." We chatted for a moment about my kids, two mothers bonding. Then I asked about her impressions of Callum.

"He was a good basketball player. But he was one of those kids who … Oh, I'm sorry, I was about to say something I probably shouldn't—"

"It's okay, I know that some high school athletes can be pretty full of themselves."

"Boys like Callum don't seem to understand that the world doesn't care how many basketball games they won in high school. Or how many cheerleaders they made out with in the back seat of some car." She was kneading the bread, a rhythmic pounding that looked like it was a satisfying and calming activity. Maybe I should take up bread making to reduce stress. The kids would like the by-product.

"I take it you didn't care for him."

"I can't say that I did. It seemed to me that he was a bit rough on the court. But Timothy admired him because he was one of the popular boys."

"What's Timothy up to now?"

"He's taking classes at the community college. That's why I'm baking bread. He stops by for dinner before his Monday and Wednesday classes. I suppose he's taking advantage of his fawning mother, but I like having him come by."

"I understand the gun wasn't his."

She stopped pounding the dough and looked at me with eyebrows raised.

"I don't mean to pry. It's just that I was there right after he collapsed. I've wondered how he was doing. It was a scary thing."

She started kneading the dough again. "No, the gun wasn't his." Then she picked up the dough and slapped it down on the board. "Look, there's something we've kept under wraps—it hasn't been in any of the coverage about the shooting." She stopped kneading and looked at me as if trying to decide how much to reveal. "He's suffering from a form of dissociative amnesia. It's referred to as psychogenic or situation-specific amnesia. It's like a post-traumatic stress disorder."

"You're saying he doesn't actually remember where the gun came from?"

"When he initially said he didn't remember owning a gun, some reporter *suggested* very strongly that he must have found it. He went along with that, and now, well, now he realizes that his memory of the event is faulty. It's hard to take back his original statement when he doesn't have any idea where he got the gun." She started rolling the bread back and forth again, then paused to look directly at me. "You won't tell anyone that, will you? I mean, as soon as he remembers, he'll tell the truth."

"No, I won't say anything."

She turned her attention back to her dough. "In some ways I'm relieved that he doesn't remember what happened."

"I understand. Suppressing a traumatic event has its advantages." I had reached the crucial question, the reason I had come by in the first place: "Do they anticipate that the memories will return some day?"

"They say it could be weeks, months, years, maybe never. It's hard to tell. But as I said, I'd be fine if he never recovers that five minutes of memory."

We chatted a bit more about Timothy's life since leaving high school. I finished my coffee, said I was glad to hear that Timothy was okay, and that I would let myself out so she could finish her bread making.

Now I had my own secret to keep. The only person I intended to tell was Gary. He needed to know that the person he planted his gun on might one day—or never—reveal what had happened. The longer it took, the less likely Gary would be implicated. I agreed with Timothy's mother that in some ways it would be nice if her son didn't recover his memory. Both for him and for Gary. I was also glad that something good had come out of Gary's act of deception. I hoped that if and when Timothy regained his memory, he had gained confidence in himself for other reasons.

Mark Twain was right when he said that if you tell the truth you don't have to remember anything. Once you start keeping secrets, you need an excel spreadsheet for your brain so you can remember which lie you told and to whom you told it.

CHAPTER 21
GOOD NEWS

THE DAYS BETWEEN Monday and the weekend were the slowest ever recorded, at least in my mind. I kept hoping to hear something from Gary, but the phone he gave me refused to ring. I was starting to wonder if my concern about keeping his secret was moot. Maybe I needed instead to start planning for Bandit's long-term care.

Then, shortly after breakfast, Jason came back into the kitchen where I was lingering over a third cup of coffee and announced:

"Good news, they caught that Arman Kazemi guy."

"Who?"

"Arman Kazemi, you know, the Iranian terrorist."

"Iranian terrorist?"

"Don't you follow what's happening in the world?" he asked in his superior pre-teen to mother voice.

"I get all of the news I need from you." I smiled at my precocious son and was starting mentally to drift away when it hit me what he had said. "Who was that again?"

"Arman Kazemi." Jason repeated the name slowly with the best articulation I've ever heard from him. If I hadn't known he was being patronizing, I might have praised him for it. "He was on everyone's list as one of the world's most wanted terrorists."

"Who caught him?" I asked, almost afraid to hear the answer.

"The US has been trying to catch him for years. About a year ago there was a failed attempt—you may remember that."

I didn't, but I nodded to keep him talking.

"Then, just like that, he's handed over to the UN Counter-Terrorism Committee. The report I heard on TV was a little sketchy on details. I'm thinking it must have been some elite Israeli unit. They're good at that sort of thing. Could even have been a covert US team. If it had been an authorized capture, our government would be bragging about it."

"So, no one has claimed responsibility."

"Not yet." He paused. "But it's a big deal."

If I was right about what I was thinking, this was indeed an even bigger deal than Jason could possibly imagine. Gary might be calling any minute—*if* he and his friends had been the ones responsible for delivering Kazemi to the UN. Unless he didn't survive the operation. That was always a possibility. But someone he was working with must have. Unless this particular terrorist wasn't the one Gary and his team had been after. I should have demanded more details so I could follow what was happening in the news. If I didn't hear from Gary, what was I going to do? Give it a week or two more and then try to track down one of the people on the list he'd made me memorize? We should have had a better contingency plan.

I went from being lethargic to hyped by the news Jason had shared. I put Gary's phone in my pocket and carried it around with me in case he called. Then I started cleaning. That's not my usual response to stress, but I didn't want to leave the house in case he called and I needed privacy to talk. The kitchen seemed like a good place to start. The refrigerator needed cleaning, but I didn't want to take everything out and then have to leave it to take his call, so I scrubbed the stove instead. I had just started in on wiping down the cabinets for fingerprints when Mara came to get something to drink from the fridge.

"What's going on?" she asked.

"Saturday morning cleaning spree."

"You never clean anything on Saturday morning."

"I've been known to."

"You usually only clean something when it gets so bad you can't stand it anymore. Or when Grandma makes a comment."

"Well, that may be true lately, but I used to clean on a regular basis. Don't you remember?"

"Before you went back to work full time, you mean?"

"And we keep things picked up, don't we?"

"I'm not complaining," Mara said, suddenly appearing to realize that our conversation could have repercussions for her. "I was just curious what was going on." She got a flavored water out of the fridge and made a quick exit.

Now that I thought about it, I had let things slide of late. That probably didn't set a good example for my kids. My mother's occasional articles on cleaning products hadn't moved me to action. But maybe it would be good to get back into a cleaning routine.

I had finished scrubbing down everything in the bathroom and was reconsidering whether to take on the refrigerator when the phone in my pocket rang. I grabbed it and stared a moment before answering. I almost couldn't believe it was finally happening. "Hello?"

"Hey, how's it going?" Gary said, his tone chatty, as if we talked on the phone all the time.

"Ah, okay. And how's it going with you?" Why did I sound so formal instead of expressing the relief and joy I was feeling? On the other hand, why was he being so casual, didn't he realize what he had put me through?

"Fine. And how's Bandit?"

Fine? That was all he was going to say about what he'd been up to? *Fine!* "Bandit's fine," I said with a hint of sarcasm.

"Can I speak to him?" I knew he just wanted Bandit to hear his voice, but he made it seem like I could simply turn the telephone over to his dog so they could catch up on things.

"Sorry. He isn't here. I had to move him to Jenny's farm. And, well, it's a long story. Will I be able to explain in person soon?" I was still talking like a British maid asking if he would like his tea served in the drawing room.

"But Bandit is okay."

"I understand from Jenny that he loves farm life. Although I'm sure if he were here that he would love to hear from you." Now I sounded like Siri. Had the cleaning chemicals affected my vocal cords?

"It will be good to see you," he said.

I wanted to say that it would be good to see him too … for a number of reasons. Instead, I said, "I understand it was a successful business trip."

"You understand correctly. All present and accounted for."

"I'm … I'm relieved."

"Are you up for a visit?"

"When will you be back?"

"Next Saturday. I have a few things to attend to first."

I wanted to say more and to know more, but his careful choice of words suggested he was concerned that we might be overheard. How or by whom wasn't clear. But if he was keeping things vague, then I would follow his lead. "Will you need a ride from the airport?"

"Thanks, but I'll rent a car. Well, have to run."

"Okay."

"And Cameron. I can't tell you how grateful I am for your help."

I was about to add something personal in response, but the line disconnected.

CHAPTER 22
A HAPPY ENDING?

NOW THAT I KNEW Gary was alive and about to return, three things happened. First, I lost the urge to continue my cleaning spree. Cleaning was never more than a momentary respite anyway. The dust would return. The fingerprints on the refrigerator would magically reappear. The spiderwebs respun by ambitious spiders. And No-name would continue to hunt down the crumbs that oftentimes lingered in the nooks and crannies on the kitchen floor.

Second, I started thinking about seeing Gary again. It had been a long time since I'd dated anyone. Not that Gary was the kind of guy you went out on dates with. And I wasn't in a position to have a casual fling with anyone. I wasn't even certain I would want that if I could manage it. Thinking about a relationship with Gary was like trying to see through a thick fog; I could sense there might be something there, but I wasn't sure what. Besides, I couldn't imagine him wanting a relationship with the real me, the mother with two kids and a mostly stable lifestyle. What had happened on the island was a one-time thing, the culmination of an adrenaline-filled night of danger and foolhardy acts of daring.

And finally, I started to relax. If Gary's trip had been successful and he was openly returning home, he must be confident that there was no longer anyone out to kill him. And if that was the case, there wouldn't be anyone coming after me or members of my family to get information as to his whereabouts. Mom could keep her pink gun in its safe. I could start parking in the alley again. And Yuri could end his late-night vigils to my neighborhood to see if there were any dangerous people lurking about.

On Sunday, the sun promised summer was on its way. I took the kids and No-name to a nearby park for a short hike. Trees were budding. Birds flitted around low-lying bushes and zipped from one tree to another. We saw several squirrels and perhaps a raccoon. The raccoon may have been a dog; we only caught a glimpse. But No-name barked up a storm as he raced to the end of his retractable leash. He apparently had no idea that he was no match for any wild critter. Or maybe he felt safe because he was tethered to us—the leash more reassurance than restraint.

Later, Mara and I put together a nice vegetarian meal for Sunday dinner that met both my mother's and Jason's meal preferences. We all enjoyed the food and had a pleasant conversation. Mara had baked some shortbread bar cookies. I waited until she set out her dessert before making my announcement.

"Good news," I said. I immediately had everyone's attention. Well, almost. Jason looked away long enough to snatch a cookie, stuff most of it in his mouth and start chewing. I had already given Mom a head's up since I had some explaining to do to prepare Jason for what I was about to tell everyone. "First of all, Jason, Duffy's name is actually Bandit."

"I knew it!" he said. "Well, I didn't know his name was Bandit, but I knew it couldn't be Duffy. He didn't look like a Duffy."

"We were trying to throw off anyone who might have been looking for him," I continued. "It seemed best to give him an alias rather than putting it on you to keep the names straight."

"That makes sense," Jason said. Then he seemed to notice that Mara hadn't reacted to my confession that Duffy was really Bandit. "Did *you* know?" he asked her.

"Not at first," she said. I silently sent her a 'thank you.'

"Mara guessed whose dog it was at one point," I said.

"How'd you do that?" Jason sounded really upset that he hadn't been in on the secret. I couldn't blame him. When you find out someone has been trying to protect you from a danger you didn't know existed, the impulse is to feel like you didn't need protecting. I've been there.

Mom heard the whine in Jason's voice and decided it was time to take control of the conversation. "Jason, you remember the time your mother was rescued by a man and his dog on an island in the San Juans?"

"Sure. Oh, the dog's name was Bandit, wasn't it?"

"And when that man asked your mother to keep his dog safe from some people who were after him for reasons we don't know, she said yes. Because she felt she owed him that. But she tried to keep us out of it."

"Unfortunately, I wasn't all that successful," I admitted. "That's why we all had to lie about Bandit ever being here."

"Why didn't you just tell us?" It was a fair question. One that I still couldn't completely answer.

"At first I didn't think having Bandit here would be a

problem. Then one thing happened. Then another. Things just kept getting more complicated."

Jason suddenly looked smug. "That's why you shouldn't lie. It's too hard to keep your facts straight."

"It's not how I would have chosen to make that point, but you're right."

"So, what's the good news, Mom? Is Gary coming to pick up Bandit?" Mara asked.

"Yes."

"Can we say goodbye?" Jason asked.

"That would be nice," Mara agreed.

"I'll see what I can arrange."

Mom stayed behind to help me clean up. "You got off the hook for that one pretty easily."

"Thanks for helping. For a moment I thought it was going to go downhill fast."

"Kids are resilient. Jason may be a bit ticked that Mara figured it out when he didn't, but he still doesn't have all the facts. You'll have to decide whether to tell him about the incident with Mara's phone."

"That's a tough call. I don't want to encourage either of them to take risks like that in the future."

"Let's let it ride for a while. There may come a time when it feels right to tell him. And to talk to them about risk-taking."

Her words echoed in my mind as I thought about why I hadn't told Yuri yet that I had heard from Gary. Was I waiting for the "right time" because I had a good idea about the lecture on Gary that would follow my news? There wasn't anything Yuri could tell me about him that I didn't already know. But hearing it from him would force me to face my doubts head-on. To make it even worse, I still couldn't tell Yuri about what Gary had done, either initially to get himself in trouble or what he and his friends had done to correct the situation. Not that I knew all of the details myself. And probably never would.

Monday morning was the "right time" whether I wanted it to be or not. I needed to tell Yuri, PW, Jenny, and Grant about Gary's "return." In that order. I also needed to let Adele know that Bondo and his cohorts were no longer a concern for us. Yes, it was time to move on.

I arrived a few minutes early at the mall and stopped at my favorite coffee kiosk to buy Yuri a cup of Costa Rican special blend doctored just the way he liked it. "What's the occasion?" he asked when I handed him the drink and suggested we step into the closet. He had a box of donuts on his desk and grabbed them to take with us. Once seated, I made a show of picking out a chocolate covered cake donut before telling him the news. He surprised me with his response.

"That's great. Caitlan will be disappointed, but I bet Bandit will be happy to get back to the island."

"That's it? That's all you're going to say?"

"I'm glad it's over. Things can get back to normal." He took a bite of a jelly donut, a tiny blob popped out and landed on the table. I reached over and wiped it up with a Kleenex from my pocket. "Things *will* get back to normal, won't they?" he added.

"Yes. They will," I assured him.

Yuri went with me to see PW. She was wearing a light-colored tweed pants suit with strands of hot pink adding pop to an otherwise drab British tradition. Her hot pink silk blouse was an eye catcher. The beige hat on her clothes rack had a matching hot pink band.

"It's over," I said. "Gary will be back to pick up Bandit on Saturday."

"Good. It's time to put this entire incident behind us." PW paused to see if there was any more information forthcoming. When I didn't offer any, she didn't press. Like Grant, she seemed satisfied only knowing part of the story. I appreciated having a boss and colleagues who didn't mind living with a little ambiguity.

Jenny wasn't in the office, so I called her to let her know that it was safe for her to pick up Bandit and that Gary and I would come by next Saturday. She suggested I bring Mara and Jason and that we make it a day of celebration. That sounded like a great idea to me. The kids would be pleased.

"By the way," I said. "I've been meaning to mention something about our Mr. Bondo, our Mr. *James* Bondo . . ." I paused briefly for effect. "His real name is Drake Dick of DD Consultants."

"Nooo. You're not serious?! And you didn't tell me?"

"I was saving it up for a special occasion. Now you can prepare your one-liners for our Saturday celebration."

"Don't think I won't!"

Next, I talked to Grant and Adele together, letting them know that there was no one trying to pressure me for information any longer and that all of the loose ends were neatly tucked into place. Both looked relieved. Neither asked for details, although I was certain Grant would guess that the dog we'd been harboring was going home.

Mid-morning Yuri suggested we have lunch later. There was something about the way he suggested it that made me think he wasn't going to be trying out his latest trivia topic on me. He had shown restraint earlier, but maybe he'd simply needed time to assemble his arguments.

We ate in the Food Court. He got a hamburger and French fries, and I got a tuna salad on sourdough. We found a table away from most of the crowd near a phony pillar that seemed to have been randomly placed. If it actually was for structural support, we were in trouble. My sandwich came with a dill pickle. He took a bite out of the pickle before I could stop him, so I grabbed a couple of his fries. It all felt like we were back to normal.

About half-way through our meal, he said, "What I'm about to say, I'm telling you for your own good." No conversation that starts like that ends well. And ours wouldn't have if Yuri hadn't paused, reached across the table, taken my hands into his and followed his opening statement with, "Let me start over. I want you to use me as a sounding board because I care about you. If you don't want to talk about Gary, then we'll talk about something else, and I won't bring him up again."

"Prairie dogs?" I asked.

"You want to talk about prairie dogs? I can do that. Did you know that their historical range has shrunk by more than 95 percent? There used to be hundreds of millions of them. Today they are down to 10-20 million."

"That's still a lot of prairie dogs."

"Yes."

"And I could use a sounding board."

"Really?"

"Really. But I think I know what you will say. He's not what you would call someone you take home to mother—

anyone's mother—but especially not mine. He's not someone to enter into any kind of long-term relationship. He does questionable work for hire. And I'm a single mom who requires stability. I get it."

Yuri looked relieved. "On the other hand, it wouldn't hurt you to get back into the dating world."

"Not you, too! If you start leaving articles on dating on my refrigerator, we are done as friends. Done. Got that?"

"How about I pull the sign-you-up for an online matchmaking service? After a few bumps and missteps that usually results in a happy ending. At least on the Hallmark Channel."

"Don't you dare. I've got enough to keep me busy right now. And I'm not ready for a second try at marriage. One time may have been enough for me. And besides, if you start in on my love life, I'm going to reciprocate. With a vengeance."

I meant everything I said during my lunch conversation with Yuri, but when Gary showed up on my doorstep that Saturday just as we were finishing breakfast, I really wanted to hug him. And not in a we're-just-friends way. No-name had come to answer the door with me. He dropped the remains of his toy pangolin at Gary's feet and sniffed his legs, ears back, ready to defend my honor if called upon. Gary knelt down and ruffled the fur on his head. "Hello, you miserable excuse for a dog. What's this beast you have with you?" From that angle I had a bird's-eye view of the thinning hair on the top of his head. I noted that he had started to regrow his beard. No-name seemed to enjoy the attention but retrieved his pangolin and made himself scarce as soon as Gary released him.

Before I got a chance to say anything to Gary in private, Mara and Jason joined us. I introduced him to my two kids as Gary, Bandit's owner. Jason held back, eyeing him warily. "You know someone was trying real hard to find you, don't you?"

"Yes, I do. And I appreciate you looking out for Bandit."

"We had to call him Duffy. And we couldn't keep him here," Mara said. "The people looking for you were a bit scary."

Since I hadn't had a chance to fill Gary in on what my kids had done to get the bad guys off his trail, he must have been surprised by their reaction, but he took it in stride. "Sorry, I didn't mean to cause anyone any trouble. But thank you for having my back."

Jason looked slightly mollified, but I could tell Mara wasn't sure what she thought of this casually dressed man with a few days' growth of beard. She probably had an image in her mind as to what a dog loving male being chased by bad guys should look like. I'm not sure what that was, maybe a bumbling Hugh Grant type.

"I'll fill you in later on what Mara and Jason did to throw the men looking for you off your scent. They were pretty amazing, actually. Even if they are my kids." Jason gave me his *Aw, mom* look and Mara turned slightly pink.

Mom had obviously heard us and made quite an entrance in light blue matching slacks and jacket. Her dark blue shoes were the same color as her purse. Not a hair was out of place.

"On your way out?" I asked.

"I'm meeting friends for brunch." Saturday brunch out was becoming a regular event for her.

I introduced her to Gary. She checked him out carefully, as if she might be called upon to describe him to a sketch artist sometime in the future. I could tell she was assessing not only the man but his clothes. He was wearing jeans and a worn leather jacket over a plain white T-shirt. He could have been auditioning for a 1970s Steve McQueen movie.

Gary made an effort to be pleasant and almost succeeded in acting as though his visit was nothing unusual. But there were too many strikes against him for my mother to be more than barely civil. Even my kids remained leery of this man who had indirectly disrupted their lives. If only I'd been able to tell Jason about what I suspected was Gary's connection to Arman Kazemi, he would have fallen all over him. Even my mother might have been impressed, although that wouldn't have made her like him any better.

The kids ran off to grab what they needed to go with us to the farm. They were excited about getting to see Bandit again and about going horseback riding. I called Jenny to give her a heads-up as to when we might arrive. She said Bandit was going to be thrilled to see Gary and that she was looking forward to meeting him. I explained that we were coming separately because Gary needed to leave from there to return to the island. We left in a flurry of last-minute "do you have this" checks with my kids, the kind of thing that made me feel like a soccer mom stereotype. I caught a glimpse of Gary grinning at the commotion before he got in his car and took off.

Gary was already at Jenny's farm when we arrived. I saw him and Jenny together in the distance, laughing, Bandit beside them, actually wagging his tail. Like your average dog, happy to be alive. Not at all like the trained attack dog Gary had warned me about when we first met.

As soon as we released No-name, he charged over to the trio, and dropped down and rolled on his back when he reached Bandit. Bandit smelled him and started to turn away. Then he caught sight of us and trotted in our direction. I was slightly hurt that he went to Mara first. "Hey, Duffy, I like your new look," she said. "I mean, 'Bandit.'" Bandit's blond streaks somehow made him look more sophisticated, like he could pass for a city dog.

"Bandit," I said. "Remember me?" He turned to me and nuzzled my leg. I knelt and gave him a good rubbing. By then Gary and Jenny had joined us.

"You didn't warn me about his new 'do,'" Gary said.

Jenny laughed and touched Gary's arm, like an old friend. "I've been telling him about Bandit's adventures. How he had to go undercover. And I've asked him what he's been up to, but he keeps changing the subject." They smiled at each other. I could practically see the sparks flying between them. It hit me that I should have realized they would be attracted to each other. And even though I had decided he and I would never work out, I felt a pang of jealousy. A sharp sense of loss for something I'd never had.

Jenny's daughter, Caitlan, suddenly came out from the barn and waved. Mara and Jason took off in her direction, with No-name tagging along.

"Caitlan has everything set up for the three of them to go riding," Jenny explained. "She borrowed one of the neighbor's horses for herself and Mara so Jason can ride her new horse, the one she got to replace the pony that she outgrew."

"Will they be okay?" The question popped out before I realized how it sounded—the worried, risk-avoidant mom. "I mean, I know they'll be fine. It's just …" Just what? I asked myself. It's just that I was an over-protective city mom whereas Jenny was a go-with-the-flow, mellow, outdoorsy mother.

"Don't worry. Now come on inside. I've got coffee and scones waiting. Cameron, you and I can grill this tall, silent man, see if we can pry a few secrets out of him."

"We'll catch up with you," I said. "I have a few things to tell him in private, okay?" Bandit had started after Jenny but turned back when he saw Gary wasn't following. He took a few steps toward us, then apparently changed his mind and hurried after Jenny. Did he know that Gary wouldn't leave him a second time? Or had he bonded that strongly with Jenny? Was I really the type of person who would be envious about a dog's attentions?

Gary and I took a stroll around the farm while I gave him the Cliff Notes version of the shooter's motivation and what the situation was with the young man he had transformed into a hero. "So," I concluded, "you weren't the target. But you helped a young man improve his self-image."

"And you haven't told the authorities any of this?"

"Only PW, Yuri, and I know about the shooter's real target. And they don't know I talked to the alleged hero's mother. But given what they do know, they agreed that it doesn't serve anyone's interests to put theories out there that may or may not be provable. Theories that no one necessarily wants to know and, if confirmed, might cause more harm than good."

"All of this is good news from my point of view," he said.

"I know. Now, before we go inside, is there anything you can tell me that you don't want to share with Jenny?" I couldn't help hoping there was something, some tiny scrap of information that suggested we had a close if limited relationship.

"I understand Arman Kazemi showing up at the UN made the news. Did you catch that?"

"Yes, Jason was exited. He told me about it the instant it was reported."

"The whole operation went smoothly. He's in good hands and will have to answer for what he's done."

"Can he identify you?"

"No worries there."

"And are you certain there's no one still out there trying to eliminate you and your colleagues?"

"We managed to handle that."

"That's all I get? You 'handled' it?"

He laughed. "You are a determined woman, you know that? But in this instance, you're better off not knowing the details. And I would appreciate it if you would make it a point to forget the names I asked you to memorize."

"I can't even remember my license plate number, so I'm sure I can manage it."

Gary stopped walking and turned to face me. "I want you to know that I'm truly sorry my situation caused you and your family so many problems at this end." I waited for him to say more. Instead, he started walking again.

"You don't know the half of it," I said. "Wait until I tell you what my mother and kids did to protect Bandit. I admit, they surprised me, especially my mother. Jenny's already heard these stories, but she won't mind hearing them a second time. Let's go get our coffee."

"And homemade scones. Impressive."

"She's the best," I agreed.

Jenny and I filled Gary in on our phony client and his request that we search for his dog who just happened to be a remarkable doppelganger for Bandit. Jenny made wisecracks about Bondo's alleged name and his real name. We all laughed about the "wallet photo" Bondo had provided. Gary was very impressed with how Mara had tricked the bad guys into stealing her cell phone and how Jason and Mara had convinced them that Duffy aka Bandit had never been there. And he laughed out loud at the image of my mother with her pink handgun holding two alleged FBI agents at bay.

"I guess I shouldn't be surprised at the boldness of the Chandler women," Gary said. "You were amazing dealing with the survivalists, Cameron." I appreciated his praise but seeing him with Jenny had reaffirmed my decision. The magic had faded, and it was too late to rekindle the dying flame.

"Well, I wouldn't have made it without you and Bandit."

Bandit had been lying on the floor at Gary's feet. At the sound of his name, he got up and put his head on Gary's knee. "It's good to have you back, buddy," Gary said, rubbing the dog's ears.

"And it's good that you made it back safely," I said. There was a moment of silence in which Gary's eyes acknowledged my comment. Then Jenny pushed her chair back and got up.

"More coffee, anyone?" she asked.

The next few hours flew by. I went out to check on the kids, leaving Jenny and Gary behind. No-name was wandering around on his own, eyeing the free-range chickens, and avoiding coming anywhere near the pygmy goats. I wondered if he had already experienced the wrath of a goat's hooves or if instinct kept him at bay.

To my surprise, Bandit showed up and padded along beside me for a while. Maybe sensing my need for comfort. "Thanks, Bandit," I said. "You take good care of him, okay?"

I could see the kids in the distance, heading back. Suddenly No-name barked as a rooster darted at him. He immediately raced over and tried to get between my legs, glancing back to make sure the rooster hadn't followed him. "Hey, you're too big for that," I said. "You'll make me bowlegged." He moved to the side but stayed close.

When No-name saw the kids in the distance, he set his fear of roosters aside and dashed off to meet them. I pictured him begging them to take him back to civilization.

When the time came to leave, it took a while for everyone to say their goodbyes. Gary hugged me and repeated how grateful he was to have someone he could count on in a pinch. When I asked if he was headed back to the island, all he said was, "Soon."

Jenny walked me to the car as the kids and dogs raced ahead. "You don't mind, do you?" she asked. "I mean, Yuri said that you don't have a thing with Gary. But I wouldn't want to step on your toes."

"No problem with my toes," I assured her. "It's obvious that you two have hit it off. I'm happy for you both."

"Well, be happy for us in the moment, okay? Neither of us is looking for a 'forever' thing." She squeezed my arm and said to drive carefully. The kids and dog piled into the car, and we left the farm and a few fond memories behind.

EPILOGUE

THE FALLOUT FROM Bondo's break-in into my home ended up producing a tiny crack in the wall of secrecy around our mysterious boss. It started with a trip I made to the police station to follow up on a trespassing complaint made by a new client. While I was there, I ran into the officer who had hauled Bondo and his colleague away that night. He recognized me and stopped to chat.

"They were quite the pair, weren't they?" he said. Then he grinned. "But your mother took them down a peg or two."

"Yes, with her pink gun. They must have loved that."

"They did complain about her a bit." He didn't elaborate, but I had a pretty good idea about what they might have said, none of it flattering, and probably more than a little ageist and sexist. A salve to their own bruised egos.

"I know they claimed to be FBI. Did you check on their credentials?" I'd wondered about that at the time. It seemed safe to ask now, after the fact.

"Didn't get a chance. Your boss talked to my superior and that was that."

"I thought it was just a matter of our lawyer's advice about not pressing charges," I said.

"I think there was more to it. Your boss apparently has some clout. We didn't even record the complaint."

"Is that unusual?" I asked. This was a bit of information I hadn't anticipated.

"It happens. But not often."

Afterwards, I told Yuri about the conversation I'd had with the police officer. We agreed that what he'd told me didn't quite synch with PW's description of what had taken place. What we couldn't get our minds wrapped around is why she would go out on a limb to get the two phony FBI agents released. Yuri thought it might have been to keep my connection with Gary hidden. But by simply not pressing charges, the result would have been the same.

After a few days, we gave up trying to solve the puzzle of why PW had misled us. Then, out of the blue, she asked us out to lunch a second time. Once ensconced in the same private booth as the last time we'd had lunch, we chatted about a variety of insignificant things, sharing our family style meal as if having a friendly lunch together was something we did all the time.

As soon as the dishes were removed and we were sitting back with a fresh pot of tea, PW said, "I owe you an explanation."

Yuri reached up to adjust his glasses, something he does when he's uncomfortable. They ended up askew, but he didn't seem to notice. I tried to act natural, suddenly wishing I knew what my "tell" was so I could control my response to what she was about to say. I hadn't a clue what was coming.

"I assume you know that I stepped in after Bondo and his colleague were arrested."

Yuri and I both hesitated, then nodded to affirm that we knew. Given the timing, I assumed she'd learned about my conversation with the police officer. I suppose I shouldn't have been surprised, but I was. How did she do it?

She smiled. "But you didn't ask me about it ... why?"

Yuri and I looked at each other. He indicated I should answer. "I can't speak for Yuri," I said pointedly. "But I thought it might have something to do with people you know in the intelligence community. Lines of communication and support you want to preserve. And I didn't want to ask something you might feel was none of my business."

PW smiled. "I appreciate that. Yuri?"

"You're pretty close-mouthed about the details of your life," Yuri said. He was being bolder than I would have expected. "It crossed my mind that they might have known something about you that you didn't want to reveal."

"You thought they were blackmailing me?" This time her smile threatened to break out into laughter.

"Something like that."

"Yuri, you have a vivid imagination. It's what makes you such a good detective." She looked at each of us in turn. "I don't want you to hesitate to ask me if you have questions about something, anything. If I don't want to share that information with you, I will tell you." She paused before continuing. "I admit to having a few secrets. And I like keeping my work and my private life separate." She paused again. "I should have told you right after it happened. But things hadn't been completely sorted out yet. To be honest, there's still some question about who in the chain of command ordered the hit on Gary. That is to say, Gary may know, but I don't think it's common knowledge in the intelligence community.

"What I can tell you is that there's been a shakeup in a group that is in the homeland security chain of command. If anyone knows why, they aren't sharing it with any of my contacts. I wasn't sure where Bondo and his friend fit in, but initially I felt that an investigation into their backgrounds could impact whatever Gary was trying to do. My main concern was making it clear that they needed to stay away from you, Cameron, and your family. In the end, we came to an agreement about that." She took a sip of tea, a physical act that seemed to suggest that what she was about to say was very important.

"You have guessed all along that I have some history with a number of government agencies. Those connections need to remain private in order to be of use to me, and to us. As we've talked about before, there are some secrets that need to be safeguarded. I admit to having secrets of that nature."

She finished off her tea, looked at us and asked, "Are we good?"

"Absolutely," I said.

"Good, yes," Yuri agreed.

Yuri and I didn't get a chance to talk in private until he walked me to my car after work. He seemed more thoughtful than usual. "Remember when Will got a picture of PW in that restaurant having dinner with an attractive Russian man?" he asked.

I nodded.

"And that Russian cigarette in the Faberge ashtray on her desk, the one embossed with a double-headed Imperial eagle?"

I nodded again, not sure where he was going with his line of thought.

"Well, you don't suppose she's a Russian sleeper, do you?"

"Don't be ridiculous." I swatted his arm. Then I realized he was teasing me. "More like counter-intelligence."

"I wonder if we'll ever find out anything about her past—"

"She's trying her best to keep her private life private. We should probably respect that." Even as the words were coming out of my mouth, I was thinking about the four names Gary had given me when he first asked me to keep Bandit for him. I'd promised to let them fade from my memory bank. But they were still there, indelibly imprinted on my brain cells. I wondered if I could look up his government contact without being caught and whether that might lead to one of PW's secret connections.

Yuri then vocalized what I was thinking: "What can I say—my lips may be sealed, but my mind can't let it go."

ACKNOWLEDGMENTS

WHEN I STARTED WRITING this series, malls were still expanding in size and were consistently filled with shoppers. Today, many have closed, downsized, or have been converted to other uses. This will pose some challenges as I continue to write my series, but I believe there will always be a market for discount detective services.

Many thanks to the incredible women of Amphorae: Kristina Makansi, Laura Robinson, and Lisa Miller, and to my agent, Donna Eastman, for helping me bring the Discount Detective series to life.

Most of all, I want to thank you for reading this book. The Discount Detective series is fun to write, and I hope you find them fun to read. If you do, please take a few minutes to write a short review. Reviews are every author's best friend.

Visit my website at www.charlottestuart.com.

Or contact me on twitter and Facebook:

https://twitter.com/quirkymysteries

https://www.facebook.com/charlotte.stuart.mysterywriter

ABOUT THE AUTHOR

IN A WORLD FILLED with uncertainty and too little chocolate, Charlotte Stuart has always anchored herself in writing. As an academic with a Ph.D. in communications, she wrote serious articles on obscure topics with titles that included phrases such as "summational anecdote" and "a rhetorical perspective." As a commercial fisher in Alaska, she turned to writing humorous articles on boating and fishing. Long days on the ocean fighting seasickness required a little humor. Then, as a management consultant, she got serious again. Although even when giving presentations on serious issues she tried for a playful spin. Stress—Clutter and Cortisol or Leadership—Super Glue, Duct Tape and Velcro.

Her current passions include pro bono consulting for small nonprofits and writing lighthearted mysteries. A curious mix of problem solving: pragmatic and fantasy. Charlotte lives and writes on Vashon Island in Washington State's Puget Sound and spends time each day entertained by herons, seals, and eagles and hoping the deer and raccoons don't raid her vegetable garden.